UNDENIABLE #2

MADELINE SHEEHAN

Unbeautifully

ISBN-13: 978-1489521538
ISBN-10: 1489521534

Edited by
Pam Berehulke, Bulletproof Editing

Cover Design by
Jena Gregoire, Pure Textuality PR

Interior Design by
Champagne Formats

Dedicated to Undeniable love.

Note to Readers

UnBeautifully begins where *Undeniable's* epilogue ended. The story then backtracks to the years that passed between the last chapter and epilogue in *Undeniable,* and then continues until the present. Enjoy!

PROLOGUE

No sooner met but they looked,
no sooner looked but they loved,
no sooner loved but they sighed,
no sooner sighed but they
asked one another the reason,
no sooner knew the reason
but they sought the remedy . . .
—William Shakespeare

I DON'T BELIEVE IN FATE. I FIRMLY BELIEVE THAT LIFE IS what you make of it, that life will react to your actions, and that your final destination has nothing to do with destiny but instead everything to do with the choices you make along the way.

With one exception.

Love.

There are no rules when it comes to love.

Love is not a reaction or an action; it is not a destiny or a choice.

Love is a feeling, a real, raw, and unscripted emotion so sensationally pure, unable to dull even under the strain of a world against it, strong enough to heal the broken and warm even the coldest of hearts.

Innate.

Unavoidable.

Undeniable.

And sometimes, love is unconventional and it breaks all the rules and blurs all the lines and basks in its glory, shining as bright as the sun, unapologetically glowing even under the narrowed stares of society and its screaming, self-righteous morals, berating and judging that which it doesn't understand.

The first time I fell in love, it was with a pair of blue eyes and a wide, dimpled grin.

"Your old man loves ya, Danny girl," he whispered. "You never, ever forget that, yeah?"

I never did. And I never thought I could ever love any man as much as I loved my father. But as we grow, we change, we begin to make our own decisions and thus become independent and self-sufficient, and start turning away from our parents and turning to others. We begin experiencing life outside of the bubble we grew up in and form friendships, strong bonds, and unbreakable ties.

And we fall in love . . . a second time.

The second time I fell in love it was with a badly scarred face, the stuff of nightmares, the sort of disfigurement that mothers steer their children away from. Ugly, jagged slashes marred the skin from the top of his skull, down over his right eye, an eye that had been dug out of his face with a serrated blade. The scars continued across his cheek, over his lips, and down his neck, ending at the top of his shoulder. His chest was a hundred times worse, scar tissue as far as the eye could see.

"Baby," he said gruffly. "Man like me got no business with a girl like you. You're nothin' but fuckin' beauty and I'm a whole lot of fuckin' ugly who's already halfway to hell."

But he was wrong.

Everything has beauty. Even the ugly. Especially the ugly.

Because without ugly, there would be no beauty.

Because without beauty, we would not survive our pain, our sorrow, and our suffering.

And in the world I lived in, the world he lived in, a secret world within the world, a world of constant crime and cruelty, a cold world full of despair and death, there was almost nothing but suffering.

"You may not be beautiful the way you were before," I whispered, cupping his ruined cheek. "But you're still beautiful. To me."

Ours was the furthest thing from a picture-perfect romance; it was more of a car crash, a metal-bending, blood-splattered disaster that left no survivors, only bad memories and heartache.

But it was ours.

And because it was ours . . . I wouldn't change a thing.

CHAPTER 1

SLIPPING ON A PAIR OF SUNGLASSES, I STEPPED OUT OF the clubhouse into the bright midday Montana sun and surveyed the backyard where my family, both related by blood and not, were enjoying a Saturday afternoon cookout. If the sun was shining and the weather decent, this was how the Miles City, Montana, chapter of the Hell's Horsemen Motorcycle Club, or MC, unwound.

The voices of Willie Nelson, Waylon Jennings, Johnny Cash, and Kris Kristofferson were belting the lyrics of "Highwayman" through the speakers, the sizzling scents of cooking meat floated tantalizingly along the warm breeze, and children were running back and forth playing with inflatable beach balls and water guns.

My father, Deuce, the Horsemen's president, stood off to the side of the party, drinking beer with his father-in-law,

Damon "Preacher" Fox, president of the notorious Silver Demons Motorcycle Club run out of New York City. Across the yard, my stepmother Eva, her friends Kami and Dorothy, and a few bikers and their old ladies were deep in conversation.

I headed for my father.

"Hey, darlin'," he said, swinging a thick, heavy arm across my shoulders and pulling me into a hug, crushing my face against his leather cut, the vest worn from age and use.

The scent of bike fumes, sweat-stained leather, and cigarette smoke filled my nostrils and I inhaled deeply. I loved that smell. It was the smell of my childhood, the smell of safety and home.

My very first memory was of being three years old, metal and Harley Davidson wings gleaming in the sunlight, the thick, acrid smell of exhaust fumes, clouds of cigarette smoke, stale sweat stained yellow on white T-shirts, the bitter sting of alcohol filling my nostrils, worn and cracked leather soft against my cheek, grease-stained hands lifting me up into the air, accompanied by loud, raucous laughter.

I smiled up at my father. "Love you, Daddy."

Grinning, he planted a big, wet kiss on my forehead.

Even at fifty-three, my father was a great-looking guy. He was tall and broad, thickly muscled, with a pair of sparkling ice blue eyes identical to my own. His graying hair was long and blond, usually pulled back, and a short beard framed his face. But it was his grin that got him into trouble. My father grinned and women swooned.

Honestly, I didn't have a clue how Eva put up with all the female attention he got around the club. Whenever I asked, she'd always shrug and say, "It's typical."

Eva and I were both biker brats, but whereas Preacher raised her inside his clubhouse alongside his boys, I was raised at home. I frequented the clubhouse on occasion but hadn't become an integral part of "the life" until my father brought Eva home with him, pregnant with my little sister, Ivy, about five years back. And everything changed.

Because of Eva, I'd been able to start spending more time at the club, finally getting a chance to know the men I'd known all my life but had never gotten the chance to really, truly know until now. I'd formed relationships with all of them—Tap, Bucket, ZZ, Marsh, Hawk, Mick, Freebird, Cox, Blue, Chip, Worm, Dimebag, Dirty, and Jase. And also Danny D. and Danny L. who, because they had the same first name as me, I ended up calling them DoubleD and DL, which they loved, and eventually the names stuck.

They were all so different, young and old, their appearances varying as much as their ages, but they all had one thing in common.

Brotherhood.

It was everything to them; they would take a bullet for one another as soon as take their next breath. And my father, their president, in return for their loyalty took care of them and their families. It was a never-ending cycle of allegiance and respect and . . . love.

Even so, I knew this life wasn't all sunshine and roses. Being the daughter of a hardened criminal, I knew sunshine and roses for what they really were. Few and far between. Especially in my family.

When I was seven my father attended a parent/teacher conference with my mother. It was his first and his last. My second grade teacher had made the mistake of informing my parents I was falling behind in class and would probably need to repeat second grade. Needless to say, my father took this as a slam against me and a personal insult to his parenting. Mr. Steinberg never did return to teaching after he'd recovered from his injuries.

When I was twelve my brother took on four boys who were picking on me and in turn got his ass kicked. As he limped away, he spit out a tooth and grinned at me. "They'll think twice next time, little sister," he said, slinging his arm over my shoulders. "No one's gonna mess with a girl who's got a brother crazy enough to take on four guys at once."

And I thought . . . that's what love is.

To some, the idea of violence being interpreted as love is ludicrous, but to me, it was my reality. *It is my reality.*

"Hiya, Danny girl," Preacher said, holding out his arms.

My father let me go, and I wrapped my arms around Preacher's middle and squeezed.

"Lookin' gorgeous as always, sweetheart," he said in his gruff, raspy voice. He gave me a quick kiss on the cheek and released me.

Grabbing a beer from a cooler, I crossed the lawn headed for Eva. Talking with Kami, Eva paused to shoot me a quick smile. Eva and Kami were polar opposites in every way. Married with two kids with Cox, my father's super sexy tattooed and pierced road chief, Kami was blue-eyed and blonde, tall and runway-model thin, whereas Eva had smoky gray eyes, long dark hair, and curves. But they were kindred spirits, had been friends for thirty years now, and I often found myself jealous of what they shared, their ability to tell each other anything and everything, to be there for each other no matter what.

I'd never had that. With anyone.

And I wanted it. Desperately.

But I've wanted a lot of things over the years that I'd never gotten, and eventually I learned to accept the fact that some things would forever be out of my reach.

I stepped up beside Dorothy, placed my palm on her swollen belly, and gave her a light rub. Blowing out a breath, she shoved her red hair out of her eyes and covered my hand with hers.

"Only a few more weeks, Danny." She sighed. "I can't wait for this baby to come out. I'm too old to be pregnant."

I gave her a sympathetic smile.

At thirty-six, Dorothy wasn't old, but she was an old soul. She'd gotten pregnant at fifteen, married at eighteen, and had lived for too long in a bad marriage with a man who wanted nothing to do with her. In her early twenties she met Jase, one of my father's lifers, and started coming to the club to be with him when he wasn't at home with his wife, Chrissy, and their three kids.

Dorothy Kelley wasn't like the rest of the club whores that flocked to the MC. She truly loved Jase and Jase adored her. Just not enough to leave his wife. Now she was a permanent fixture at the club. She was paid to cook, clean, and do the laundry, and she'd since left her husband and lived in an apartment Jase paid for in town. Her daughter, Tegen, two years younger than me, was away at college in San Francisco. Now Dorothy spent practically all of her time at the club. She and I had grown close over the past four years, and although I disapproved of the love triangle she was involved in, I loved her with all my heart.

A familiar arm slid around my middle and pulled me close.

"Hey, baby," ZZ whispered, slipping his fingertips in the waistband of my jeans. With his other hand, he grabbed my beer and took a long swallow.

I turned into his big, hard body and slipped my arms around his waist. "Hey, you," I whispered back, kissing his sternum.

ZZ was another lifer, thirty years old, big and strong, long brown hair, matching brown eyes, squared handsome features, and a perpetual five o'clock shadow. And he was a sweetheart. As far as boyfriends went, I'd hit the jackpot. Kind and thoughtful, educated and well-read, faithful in a club constantly filled with whores, ZZ was everything a girl could hope for in a man.

"Evie." Kami laughed. "Big, sexy, and scary is staring again."

We all turned to find my father watching Eva the way he always watched Eva. Intense. Wholly possessive. Sexual to the nth degree.

Grossed out, I turned away.

"Watch this," Eva whispered, and bent over to pick up Kami's one-year-old son, Diesel. Her jeans pulled down, her shirt pulled up, and deuce, tattooed above her ass in large scrolling script, was front and center in my father's line of sight.

I didn't have to look to know my father was ten seconds away from stalking across the lawn and throwing her over his shoulder. That he was a caveman, when it came to Eva, was putting it mildly. As happy as I was that they were happy, the ick factor at watching my father always groping my stepmother was off the charts.

But all that said, my father and Eva had come a long way. A few years back, right before my eighteenth birthday, Eva's now deceased husband, Frankie "Crazy" Deluva, had brutalized her in front of my father. The whole ordeal had ended with Eva forced to kill her husband, all of which had left her relationship with my father terribly damaged. It had been a hard road back, and seeing them like this, happy and still very much in love, was truly a blessing.

"You're terrible," Adriana told Eva, laughing.

Adriana's husband, Mick, my father's VP and best friend, pulled her close and kissed her cheek.

"Babe," he growled. "I'm thinkin' you need to start bein' more terrible."

Adriana giggled.

"Be right back, babe," ZZ whispered, kissing my lips as he squeezed my backside. Grabbing Mick, he flashed me a shit-eating grin and took off across the lawn just as a blaze of pink and pigtails came streaking by.

"Get back here, you crazy little shit!" Cage bellowed, running after Ivy. "And give me my keys!"

Laughing like a maniac, Ivy kept running. Cage ran faster, shooting past her, and Ivy tried to go left, but Cage was quicker and grabbed her.

"Gotcha!" he said as she shrieked and giggled until he set her down.

"Ivy Olivia West!" Eva yelled. "Give your brother his keys!"

"Here," Ivy muttered, slapping the keys into his outstretched hand.

Cage's hand closed around hers and he pulled her

forward into a bear hug. "Love you, you crazy little shit," he growled. "Couldn't have asked for a better sister. 'Cause, ya know, Danny's kinda bitchy."

Rolling my eyes, I flipped them off and in return received two grins identical to my own.

I shook my head. Ivy was learning all of her life lessons from our arrogant, womanizing, prankster of a brother. The arrogance I couldn't fault him for. He was a great-looking guy, a younger, less harsh version of our father. Tall and muscular with long blond hair and dark chocolate eyes, the girls loved him. And he loved them back. However, the womanizing and constant pranks I could fault him for, and Ivy was following in his footsteps. She knew just the right thing to say to get her way, putting on the perfect pouty face and batting her wide blue eyes . . . ugh. And Eva, always keeping her in pigtails and Chucks, making both my father's and brother's hearts melt every time they laid eyes on her. Blech. Blargh. Blah. I had no doubt when she was older, she would be giving our elderly father several dozen heart attacks.

"She is such a little monster," Eva said, smiling fondly at Ivy.

"An adorable monster," Kami added.

"Ha," Eva scoffed. "You only think she's adorable because you don't h—"

Done with the conversation, I shoved my hands in my pockets and walked off, weaving my way through the groups of bikers, women, and children who were talking, laughing, dancing. It was serene. Picture-perfect.

Well, almost picture-perfect.

"Danny!"

Cringing, I spun around, ready to hurry in the opposite direction but wasn't fast enough. My longtime friend Anabeth snatched my bicep and yanked me sideways. I stumbled to a stop and faced her. Like me, Anabeth was blonde, blue-eyed, and pretty. We were both in shape but whereas Anabeth was thin, I was more muscular. Ten years of gymnastics and four years of cheerleading will do that to you. I kept my hair long, highlighted, and styled, and Anabeth had hers short, cut into a smooth bob with razor-straight bangs. Currently she was wearing a deep blue mini dress and chunky blue espadrilles. In her ears were giant blue hoops, much like the fifty-plus she had on each of her arms. A few years ago I would have complimented her outfit, would have been wearing something similar myself, most likely pink. But that wasn't the case anymore. Anabeth and I were worlds apart. Actually, everyone and I were worlds apart . . .

I'd lost something inside of me, something important, something special that had made me who I'd been, and slowly the color had seeped out of my world.

Anabeth gave my dark-washed jeans and black V-neck tee a once-over. Her gaze landed on my feet and she narrowed her eyes. "Are you wearing green . . . Converse sneakers?"

Sighing, I looked down at my feet. I was. Chucks were all Eva wore aside from a few pairs of flip-flops, so in turn, Chucks were all Ivy and I got when Eva went shoe shopping. Combined, I would say the three of us had about a hundred pairs in a wide variety of colors.

"I kinda like them," I said and shrugged.

"I dig 'em," Freebird said. Freebird was an old biker

who'd left his brain back in nineteen sixty-five. He had his old lady with him today, Apple Dumplin', who, like him, had long gray hair and more wrinkles then a crinkled-up piece of paper.

"Wat up, Danny girl?" Tap said, holding out his fist. I fist-bumped him and smiled.

Tap was in his late forties, not overly tall but made up for what he lacked in height in muscle. Built like a boxer, his muscles along with his long black hair and goatee were intimidating unless you knew him. He was one of the Horsemen's most even-tempered boys.

"Hannah says her hellos. She's hopin' you're comin' to visit Atlanta again soon."

Hannah was Tap's daughter. When Tap's wife, Tara, had left him, she'd taken Hannah and moved to Atlanta. Hannah was older than me, but we were both the daughters of Horsemen and had always known each other.

"I called her last week," I said, smiling. "She told me the good news."

He grinned. "Can't believe my baby's havin' a baby."

"Here ya go, babe," Ripper said, shoving in between Tap and Apple, offering a bottle of beer to Anabeth.

"Thanks," Anabeth said, smiling up at him.

Ripper stared down at Anabeth, his lips curving into a grin, his expression smug, knowing.

My stomach lurched and I quickly turned away, wanting to make a hasty exit before he noticed I was standing there. Ripper and I were . . . There just weren't words for what Ripper and I were.

I was three years old when my father met Erik "Ripper" Jacobs at a bike rally while on a run through San Antonio.

Ripper was only seventeen at the time, having just lost both his parents to a drunk driving accident back home in Los Angeles. He had skipped town two days after the funeral on a stolen motorcycle, just three weeks before his high school graduation.

The boys liked him immediately, and when the Hell's Horsemen returned to Montana, he was with them.

After only three months of doing grunt work around the club, he was unanimously voted and patched in as a brother. A year later, my father promoted him to sergeant at arms and coined him "Ripper" after "Jack the Ripper," for being as talented with a blade as he was.

Being so young and new to the club and the life, moving up in the ranks so quickly was virtually unheard of. But Ripper was special and everyone knew it. He always had a smile on his face, a joke on the tip of his tongue. He was good with people, could talk nearly anyone into anything just by flashing a grin.

"Hey there, Ripper!" Apple said happily. "Danny was just tellin' us that she talked to Hannah last week. Tell us what else she said, Danny girl."

I stopped retreating and turned slowly back around. Ripper's deep blue gaze found mine.

He had his glass eye in today, a very realistic copy of the one that had been painfully taken from him, along with his fun-loving personality, by the same man who'd almost ruined my father's relationship with Eva. Frankie.

But Ripper didn't care about how he looked, unless . . .

I glanced back at Anabeth.

Unless he was trying to impress someone.

I pushed my sunglasses up over my head. "Ripper," I

said, greeting him evenly.

We stared at each other.

Whore, I thought bitterly.

His expression went cold. *Don't start, Danny,* his face said.

My fists clenched. I hated our silent conversations, but since neither of us could be civil to each other, silent was the only form of communication we had. And even silent we couldn't keep our emotions from unraveling.

"Ripper's going to take me for a ride tonight!" Anabeth said excitedly.

I glared at him. *I just bet you are.*

He glared back. *What's wrong, baby? ZZ not givin' you the kinda ride you need?*

Shut. Up.

He raised an eyebrow. *Hittin' a nerve, huh?*

Not. Anabeth, I begged him with my eyes. *Please. Not. My. Friends.*

Ripper's scar-slashed mouth twisted into a mocking smirk. *Oh, so now there are rules? You can fuck my friends but I can't fuck yours? Don't exactly seem fair, baby.*

Ripper kept his gaze on me while he slid his arm around Anabeth's shoulders and began tracing her collarbone with the tip of his finger.

"'Bout that ride, beautiful girl, where you wanna go?"

Anabeth, hearing the words "beautiful girl" in reference to her, beamed up at him.

Me, hearing the words "beautiful girl" come out of Ripper's mouth directed at anyone who wasn't me, had my insides roiling.

Seeing this, Ripper looked triumphant. *What's wrong,*

Danny? You look upset. Was it somethin' I said?

I covered my mouth with my hand and tried to stay calm. Looking anywhere but at Ripper, I caught eyes with Kajika, a young Native American woman from a nearby Indian reservation who Cox and Kami had employed as their nanny.

She was beautiful, with long black hair and unforgettable, exaggerated features. Her eyes, nearly black and framed with thick, lush lashes, were all too knowing for my comfort.

Smiling kindly at me, she only made my already combative emotions that much worse. She could see right through me, everything I tried to hide. I hated being around her. She made me doubt every decision I'd made during the past three years. With just one damn look.

"'Scuse me," ZZ said, sidling up next to me and taking my hand in his. "I need my girl."

As Ripper stiffened, his arm falling away from Anabeth, I glimpsed the pain he hid beneath the anger.

Swallowing hard, I turned away from the group and let ZZ lead me out into the center of the lawn, where he pulled me into a bear hug.

"Don't hate me," he whispered.

I glanced up at him, confused. "What? Why would I hate you?"

He grinned, then dropped to his knees.

Correction. He dropped down on one knee. Heart pounding, not breathing, I stared down at ZZ, watching as he pulled a small black box out of his leathers. He looked up at me.

"You're the most beautiful woman I have ever seen," he

said softly. "The sweetest and the kindest, too. You make me so fuckin' happy, baby, you make life so fuckin' good. So I'm askin' you if you'll marry me and let me spend the rest of my life tryin' to do the same for you."

He flipped the box open and revealed the biggest diamond ring I had ever seen.

"Oh . . . my . . . God," I whispered hoarsely, putting a shaking, sweating hand over my heart. I realized then that the yard had gone silent. Someone had shut the music off and all conversation had ceased.

I took a quick look around the yard. Everyone was grinning, smiling, and staring right at me.

This was bad. Very, very bad.

"Baby girl!" My head jerked at the sound of my father's voice.

"You say the fuckin' word and I will throw that asshole into next fuckin' week! Fact, whether you say yes or no, I'm still gonna beat the fuckin' shit outta him!"

Eva, who'd joined him, planted her palms in his stomach and playfully shoved at him. He captured her around her neck and pulled her up against him, all the while smiling at me.

ZZ must have already asked him. There was no way my father would have appreciated this being sprung on him. My father was the sort of man who had to mentally prepare himself for things like his daughter being proposed to.

Which meant . . . my father was A-OK with me marrying ZZ.

In fact, looking around at all the happy faces, everyone was A-OK with me marrying ZZ.

More than okay. Elated, really.

Everyone except one.

I zeroed in on Ripper, whose sun-kissed skin had gone an interesting shade of green.

Our gazes locked.

And for a moment . . . I thought I saw the man I loved.

Ripper stared at Danny. Stared at ZZ kneeling on the grass in front of her, asking her to marry him.

He was going to flip his shit.

These assholes all around him didn't realize it, but they were about to get sprayed with blood, bone, and brain when his head decided to explode, which was in about five motherfucking seconds.

Five . . .

Four . . .

Three . . .

Two . . .

One . . .

Fuck him.

Married.

ZZ was asking Danny to marry him.

Ah, fuck. What was happening to him? Everything inside of him suddenly felt all fucked-up and wrong. His heart started beating faster and his skin began to tingle irritably. The air around him grew thick, stuffy, making it hard to breathe. He felt light-headed, his nose stung, and his stomach clenched painfully.

Before he began shredding his own body to pieces, just to make all these damn uncomfortable and unwanted feelings go away, he grabbed Anabeth and yanked her up against him. She responded immediately and curled seductively around his body.

Feeling like ten times an asshole, he kept his gaze on Danny as he groped Anabeth's ass.

Danny's beautiful blue eyes filled with pain and her gaze dropped back to ZZ.

He stopped breathing. She was going to say yes.

Say something, his brain screamed. *STOP HER!*

FUCKING STOP HER!

But he didn't.

He never did.

Because he was a useless pussy, who would never fucking deserve her.

So he just stood there like an asshole, manhandling her friend, and watching in horrified fascination as her lips parted and—

FUCK THIS SHIT.

Fuck the club and the code, and fuck brotherhood.

He would give it all up for her. For his woman. Because she sure as shit was his, and he'd go to hell and back ten times over before he lost her forever.

He shoved Anabeth aside, his right foot moved, and . . .

"DANNY!" he bellowed. "*BABY*!"

CHAPTER 2

Three years earlier

PROM NIGHT. THE CULMINATION OF THIRTEEN YEARS OF school was ending with prom night.

All my preparing and primping, driving four towns over with Kami just to find the perfect pink dress and matching shoes, two hours at the salon getting my hair, nails, and makeup done and . . .

It all seemed so . . . anticlimactic.

But maybe that's because I was on the outside looking in.

Because I could no longer relate to the laughing, dancing, happy people inside the gymnasium.

Whereas everything inside this building, my high school, had once seemed so important, my grades, my friends, homecoming, dance committees, cheerleading, and prom . . . had once been my entire world, they weren't anymore. Hadn't been since . . .

"He made me watch him rape her!" my father roared. "Do you fuckin' get that? I was chained to a fuckin' radiator, watchin' my woman gettin' slammed by a fuckin' psychopath, and I couldn't do shit about it!"

I squeezed my eyes shut, gritting my teeth through the ugly memory.

"How'd they take him down?" Tap asked.

"They didn't," the FBI agent said. "The woman did. Nearly severed his head clean off with a dagger. She came walking out of the room holding it, half naked and covered in blood."

"She's okay, Prez," Mick said. "She's alive."

"She's alive," my father replied. "But I can tell you right fuckin' now, she sure as shit ain't okay."

My father had been right; his woman wasn't okay. Eva had seemed okay at first, she was quieter, she cried a lot, then they'd left for New York to bury Frankie. After that, she stopped talking altogether, stopped eating, showering. She spent most of her time in bed, catatonic, staring at nothing. My father wasn't any better. Most days, he would sit on the floor next to the bed, his head in his hands, not talking, not doing much of anything aside from occasionally pacing the room, during which he did a lot of redecorating the walls with his fists.

Cage and I tried to keep the house running on our own, for Ivy's sake. Not yet two years old, she didn't understand what was happening, why Mommy wouldn't get out of bed, why Daddy wasn't playing with her.

And it only got worse.

Cage couldn't do everything all of the time. My brother had jobs to do, runs to make, and there were times when he had to be at the club, if only to make sure things were running smoothly in our father's absence. I was forced to drop out of all my extracurricular activities; my gymnastics instructor, after weeks of missing practice, took me off the roster. By spring, I'd missed so much school that my grades were suffering, which led to me getting kicked off the cheerleading team. I was lucky to be graduating, and ended up resenting my innocent little sister because of it.

I hadn't even had the advantage of leaning on my real mother. When I was eight, she'd left us, moved to Forsyth, a forty-minute drive from Miles City, but where Cage and I were concerned, she might as well have been in another country. She worked ten-hour shifts waitressing at a diner, after which she spent her nights drinking with whatever skeezy boyfriend she had at the time. She called infrequently and rarely kept dates to see us.

And now . . .

Eva was out of bed. She was eating, showering, once again taking care of herself and her daughter.

My father was back on his bike, back at the club, doing what needed to be done.

But things weren't the same. When they were home together or at the club, their relationship seemed strained. They never did anything together anymore, they rarely spoke to each other unless it concerned Ivy, and eventually my father reverted to his old behavior. Not coming home for days at a time, and even when he did, he was still sleeping almost every night at the club. And Eva, she didn't seem to care what he did. She spent most of her time with Kami and Devin, and her trips home to her family in New York City became more and more frequent.

Cage had easily reverted to his old idiotic self—joking, drinking, and womanizing. He was always either at the club or out on a run. And me . . .

Because of my grades, Montana State University was no longer an option for me, not until I completed two years at Miles Community College. Which outright sucked.

My two closest friends, Anabeth and Ellie, were going to MSU. The three of us had planned for years to go off to college together, to room together since we always did everything together. Until my family fell apart and I'd been forced to take on responsibilities that took me away from my life.

A life I didn't have anymore.

I scanned the gymnasium, decorated to the theme of *A Midsummer Night's Dream*. The floor was littered with giant multicolored papier-mâché trees covered in tinsel; silver stars and moons hung from a ceiling covered corner to corner with pastel-colored balloons. It was beautiful; it was everything I'd wanted it to be when I'd still been on the planning committee. And instead of enjoying it, I was standing in the hallway watching my date bump and grind the school slut to Sir Mix-a-Lot's "Baby's Got Back."

Even worse, I didn't care.

"Danny?"

Finally. I'd called the club over an hour ago asking for a ride.

I glanced back over my shoulder and found Ripper, as usual, in head-to-toe leather. Leather pants, leather boots, a tight Metallica T-shirt, and his leather Horsemen cut. His long blond hair was pulled back in a man bun, he had a toothpick between his teeth, and a pair of aviator sunglasses hid his missing eye.

"What the fuck are you doin' out here instead of in there with all your . . ." He trailed off as he surveyed the gym. " . . . with all those stupid-looking fucks," he finished, making a disgusted face. "Never mind. I know exactly why you don't wanna be here."

"You didn't go to your prom?" I asked.

"Naw. Split Cali at seventeen. Didn't even finish high school."

I nodded. "Okay." I sighed, turning my back on what was supposed to be my last happy memory of high school. "Let's go."

"Danny girl," Ripper said quietly, not having moved an inch. "Girl's gotta dance at her prom. And you lookin' the way you're lookin', at least one dance, baby." He held out his hand. "End of an era, ya know."

I looked up at his beautiful, ruined face, wondering how he did it. How he managed to keep going after what Frankie had done to him. Frankie hadn't done anything to me, not outright anyway. I'd gotten the backlash of Frankie; his actions had caused a domino effect in which I'd been the last to fall down, with everyone else piled on top of me. I wasn't so sure I'd gotten back up yet.

I wasn't so sure any of us had.

"Okay," I said, shrugging. "But I don't really see the point."

Ripper walked me out on the dance floor during the beginning of Sarah McLachlan's "I Will Remember You."

"Terrible fuckin' music," he muttered, pulling me up

against his chest and holding tight to my waist. My four-inch heels allowed me enough extra height to put my arms around his neck and rest my cheek against his worn leather cut.

From across the room, I could see both Anabeth and Ellie gaping at me.

Whatever. I closed my eyes. I didn't care what they thought. I didn't care what anyone thought anymore.

And . . . this really wasn't so bad. We weren't actually dancing, just swaying slightly. Ripper felt tense and I got the feeling he had never danced before, but it was nice and I felt myself start to relax for the first time since everything had fallen apart.

God, how long had it been since someone had held me? Touched me? I couldn't even remember the last time someone hugged me. It felt so good, so comforting to be in Ripper's arms, holding tight to his neck, pressed up against his broad, muscular chest. I gripped him tighter, seeking a connection I didn't realize I was looking for until I felt his hands squeeze around my waist. The tension in his body began to ease and, instead of holding my waist, his hands slid up my back. I let out a shuddering breath and sank even deeper against him.

"Danny," Ripper whispered in my ear. "Three songs gone by and there's some old fuckin' bitch makin' statutory rape faces at me."

I jerked my head up and found my principal glaring at Ripper. Sighing, I pulled away from him and was nearly trampled by my friends.

"Hi, Ripper," Anabeth cooed, smiling sweetly at him. Beside her, Ellie folded her arms across her chest and rolled her eyes. The two of them couldn't be any more different. Ellie was a blue-eyed, raven-haired, curvaceous beauty with mixed Caucasian and African-American heritage, who was more concerned about grades than anything else and forever had her nose in a book, whereas Anabeth was concerned with boys, clothes, and parties. I was somewhere in between the two of them, not exactly sure what category I fit into.

"Yo," Ripper said, lifting his chin at Anabeth.

"You can dance with me too," she continued.

"Slut," Ellie muttered.

"Prude," Anabeth shot back.

"Good-bye," I told both of them, grabbing Ripper's arm. "Call you tomorrow."

"Wanna go for a ride 'fore we head home?" he asked, holding the door open for me. "I gotta make a drop-off."

"I don't actually want to go home," I said, glancing up at the stars. The thought of spending my prom night at home, in all probability all alone, was more than depressing. It was unacceptable.

Ripper straddled his bike and tossed me his helmet. "The club?"

I shook my head. Tonight was Saturday, and Saturdays at the club were a booze and woman free-for-all. The boys would be sloshed, neck-deep in cleavage, and in all likelihood, Freebird would be dancing on a pool table. Naked. Not my idea of a good time.

Ripper shook a cigarette out of his pack and pulled it out with his teeth. He lit it and took a long drag. "Throw me a bone, yeah?" he said as smoke poured from his nostrils. "I ain't a mind reader."

Hitching my dress up, I climbed on behind him and

tucked the extra material between my legs before wrapping my arms around his waist. "Surprise me," I said. "I'm up for anything."

He laughed. "Anything? You got it."

The drop-off was a straight shooter. The biannual fifty G's to the Miles City chief of police to keep the local law off their backs, and he was good to go.

Surprise her, huh? What the fuck was he supposed to surprise her with? Miles City was a whole lot of nothing. Perfect place to run a motorcycle club that was involved in a whole lot of illegal shit; not so perfect place if you were a teenage girl looking to have a good time.

Flipping through his options, Ripper decided on Riverside Park; one, because Yellowstone River ran through it, and two, because it was always deserted after dark.

He pulled off near a cluster of trees and they walked side by side toward the river. Danny, who'd already kicked off her shoes, found a decent-sized rock to sit on, allowing her to run her feet through the rushing water. He pulled up on a patch of grass beside her and leaned back on his elbows. Now what?

He glanced at Danny. Hunched over, she stared sadly at the water below her. He felt for her; he knew shit wasn't good at home because shit wasn't good at the club either. Deuce was lately either a raging psychopath who preferred punching over talking, or he was brooding silently with a bottle. And everyone knew why.

Eva motherfucking Fox.

He hated Eva. He straight up hated her. Not just because

she'd been married to the asshole who'd sliced up his face and body, and every time he looked at her all he could see was Frankie. Not just because when they'd finally found Frankie, it was because of Eva that they couldn't kill him. Not just because Frankie had killed a whole shitload of people trying to get to Eva, putting the entire club and everyone in it in danger.

No, he hated Eva for all of it. As far as he was concerned, Eva getting raped and kidnapped, being forced to kill Frankie, it had been what she'd deserved for being such a fucking moron. But he kept his feelings to himself. Had for years.

Both Deuce and Cox had fallen hard for those two New York bitches, and while they were both smoking hot, he just didn't understand the concept of being head-over-heels crazy for a woman. Not when you could just replace one bitch with another when she pissed you the fuck off, and be done with all the drama and bullshit. And Eva Fox had come with a whole lot of bullshit. Bullshit and baggage, and a fucking sick and twisted serial killer for a husband.

Everything bad in all their lives came back to that bitch. Why Deuce hadn't dumped her a long time ago, he'd never understand. So they had a kid together. Who fucking cared? The guy had two kids with that cunt Christine and he'd tossed her to the curb. Hopefully he'd be doing the same with Eva. As it was they weren't speaking, weren't spending any time together. Eva rarely came to the club anymore and Deuce was always there.

One could only hope.

Pulling his flask from the inside of his cut, he took a long swallow.

"Can I have some?"

He cut his eyes her way and grinned. "Baby, your old man would kill me."

"Doubt it," she muttered. "He doesn't seem to care about anything lately."

. . . annnnnnd, that was just another reason to hate Eva.

What the hell? It was her prom night and she was spending it on a rock with a Freddy Krueger look-alike. She deserved a little pick-me-up. He handed her the flask and pulled out a fresh roll for himself.

"You think my dad and Eva will work it out?" she asked.

He shrugged. He hoped to God not. But Danny liked Eva. Fuck, everyone liked Eva. Everyone except him.

"You never know," he muttered.

She sighed and took another swallow of tequila, following it with a slight cough and a grimace. *Way to go, Danny.*

"They love each other though . . . right?"

"I don't fuckin' know."

"Have you ever been in love?"

He snorted. "Loved my parents. Love ridin'. Love the club. Ain't never loved a woman though. Not enough to be puttin' up with the shit your old man puts up with from Eva." He shrugged and took another hit. "Ain't no woman worth a damn is gonna love a face like this anyway," he said, his voice wheezy as he held the smoke in for a beat before blowing it out.

He felt Danny's hand on his and realized she'd climbed off the rock and was sitting next to him.

"Ripper," she said softly. "There isn't anything wrong with the way you look."

"Yeah," he said sarcastically, pulling away. "I'm a fuckin' supermodel."

"Ripper, you're still beautiful," she continued. "So you've got some scars. So what?"

He stared at her; her sweetheart features, her big blue eyes, her cute little nose, and those wide pink lips. What the fuck had she just said to him? He was beautiful? Ha-ha. No, he wasn't. She was beautiful, and seeing as she thought he was beautiful, she was apparently dumb as shit too.

"Baby," he said. "Listen to me. I ain't beautiful, you are. You're so damn beautiful you got it spillin' out all over the place, blindin' you into thinkin' I'm beautiful when I ain't. Farthest thing from it."

Her lips parted and her eyes went wide and his world stopped. It just fucking stopped. Crashed into a brick wall and went utterly still.

He knew that look. He'd seen it a hundred times on a hundred different women. Women he'd been trying to talk his way into fucking and had finally found the bullshit line that had broken through. But seeing that same look on Danny . . . *Danny.*

"Thank you," she whispered, and for a moment they just stared at each other.

"Here," he muttered, handing her his roll. "Enough talking."

Because, shit, Danny wasn't pussy he should be scoping. Danny was Deuce's daughter. A bullet to the head.

Before he could stop her, she took a long drag and he ended up pounding on her back as she choked through her exhale.

"Shorter drags," he said, taking his roll back. "Like this."

An hour later he was higher than a motherfucker and Danny was . . .

"I wanna go swimming." Danny giggled, trying to stand up.

He shook his head, laughing. "Swimming drunk is never a good . . ."

He trailed off; one, because Danny was taking her clothes off, and two, because *Danny was taking her clothes off.*

He stared.

And he just kept on staring.

Stared at nothing but miles of smooth, suntanned skin and sleek, toned muscles and her tits . . . Jesus, he was certain he had never seen a pair of more perfect tits. Handfuls of high and tight flesh topped with quarter-sized brown nipples.

She was blonde. Everywhere.

His brain slid straight to his cock.

Wait, she was saying something . . .

"What?" he asked, refocusing on her face.

"I said," she slurred, "let's go swimming!" She bent over, her breasts now mere inches from his face, and held out her hand to him.

Suddenly, his half-baked brain cells in collaboration with his cock decided that, yeah, swimming was a great idea.

"Rock and fuckin' roll," he muttered, grabbing her hand.

CHAPTER 3

RIPPER'S EYES FLEW OPEN AND HE JACKKNIFED INTO A sitting position, his head whipping left and right as his hands patted down his naked body.

Naked?

Fuck.

He'd passed out at the lake.

Fuck.

He glanced beside him.

FUCK.

And all at once his memories came back, slapping him in the face, each one harder and more painful than the last.

He looked down at his flaccid cock. "Congratulations," he said. "You've just fucked yourself to death."

CHAPTER 4

I STARED AT MY REFLECTION IN THE MIRROR.

Did I look different?

No. Still blonde. Still blue-eyed. I still looked like me. But I definitely felt . . . different.

I felt sore and used and . . . delicious.

And every time I closed my eyes . . .

My head fell back as he took my breast between his teeth and sucked it inside his mouth, sucking, pulling, biting. Then his hand was between my legs and one finger was up inside me, then two, then I was gripping his head, whimpering, rocking my body back and forth over his hand.

My sex clenched in response to my thoughts and I slumped backward against the wall, feeling the overwhelming urge to touch myself.

His hips were between my thighs and I could feel him,

right where I'd wanted him, hard and ready, pushing inside of me. Grabbing his face, I kissed him, kissed him hard and deep, stroking my tongue against his, sucking and nipping his lips, pouring everything I had into it and . . .

It had been like nothing I'd ever experienced before, not that I'd experienced much, but this . . . this was something I'd never dreamed existed.

. . . we came together in a frantic rush of skin and limbs, my magnitude of need an all-consuming burn that I needed . . . needed . . . God, I just needed all of him, touching all of me.

I'd never felt like that before, the wanting, not to that magnitude—that incredible burning heat and desire. Maybe it had been the alcohol, maybe it had been Ripper. *Ripper.* I'd had sex with *Ripper.*

It was surreal, it was confusing, it was . . .

His hands were all over me, everywhere at once, making his way up and down my body. He was kneading, grabbing, and squeezing, making me cry out as he relentlessly pushed my limits of pain and pleasure, soothing my cries with sweet kisses and soft caresses and then more pain and more pleasure, and more pleasure, harder and faster, until my skin was burning, my muscles quivering, my insides clenching, and I was clawing at Ripper's body while he clawed at mine, taking me hard and fast and harder and faster, until I forgot where I was, forgot who I was, and just felt . . . all of it.

It certainly hadn't been anything like the one and only other time I'd had sex, junior year, with my one and only boyfriend that I'd had for one entire week before my father scared him off. Something he still denies doing. But during that week I'd managed to lose my virginity in the woods behind school, which had been horrible, and not just because I'd been lying on sticks and wet leaves but because he hadn't known what he was doing either and . . . ugh.

But with Ripper . . .

Holy crap.

The ride home had been awkward. In fact, everything after I'd woken up had been awkward. He wouldn't make direct eye contact with me and when he spoke, his sentences were short, his words clipped, not saying any more than he absolutely had to.

I knew he regretted it and probably wanted to forget it had ever happened, and I couldn't blame him for that. If my father ever found out, Ripper would be in serious trouble and I would probably end up locked in the basement for the rest of my life.

But even knowing all of that, I couldn't stop thinking about it.

About him.

About how he'd felt . . . inside of me.

Sated, I was lying naked in the grass; beside me, sitting up, Ripper lit a cigarette. Glancing down, he jerked his chin upward and grinned at me. "Ready for round two?"

My breath left me even as I smiled.

"Please," I whispered and his expression changed. Hardened, tightened with hunger the likes of which I'd never seen on a man before. At least, not on a man looking at me.

"Ain't like I was actually gonna give you a choice," he said, maneuvering himself between my already spread legs. His roughened hand ran up my body, pausing at my breasts to squeeze and roll, before it wrapped around my throat.

I'm not sure how long I stood there, with my hand

pressed against my belly, my eyelids fluttering, breathing shallowly, just remembering the night before when—without warning—my bedroom door flew open and I jolted upright.

Flushing with mortification, I came face-to-face with my father.

"Where's Eva?" he demanded.

I gaped at him. "Knock much? What if I'd been changing?"

He grunted. "You weren't, so who cares? Where's Eva?"

Exasperated, I threw my hands up in the air. "How should I know? I'm not her babysitter! She doesn't tell me where she's going!"

His eyes narrowed. "Did she come home last night?"

I shrugged. "I don't know."

"Why not?"

"I was at prom," I bit out.

His eyebrows shot up. "Oh."

Then his brows went back down and his eyes narrowed. "Wait, are you saying you didn't come home at all?"

Oh, so now he cared. After months and months of not giving a crap about where I was or what I was doing, he suddenly did.

I folded my arms across my chest and gave him an identical, narrow-eyed stare. "I came home pretty late," I said. "I didn't check to see if Eva was home."

"What's pretty late?" he growled.

Oh, that was it. I'd had it. He couldn't just waltz in here after nine months of being both emotionally and physically absent and suddenly start demanding details of my life.

Marching up to him, I grabbed the edge of my door.

"None of your business," I spat out angrily and slammed it closed in his face.

I expected him to burst into a tirade. I waited for it, holding my breath, but he didn't. After several moments of silence, I pressed my ear to the door and listened as his booted feet pounded the wooden floor, stomping further and further away.

With a heavy sigh, I sat down on my bed. My father, the one I knew and loved, would have gone all Incredible Hulk on me and busted down any door I slammed in his face. He would have cursed and yelled and acted like a big, blundering idiot. Then he would have apologized, hugged me, and told me he loved me. This man was not my father. He was broken and sad and I hated him.

Crap, now I was crying. I was so sick of crying.

Someone was pounding the fuck out of Ripper's door. Someone who was about to die. Lying on his belly on his bed with his head facedown in his pillow, he reached out to his right, patting around on his nightstand . . . where was it . . . keys, no . . . pack of smokes, no . . . condoms, no . . .

His fingers curled around the grip of his nine.

"Hey, asshole!" Hawk bellowed. "You gonna leave your fuckin' room sometime this century?"

"Go away!" he yelled back, his volume muffled by his face-plant in the pillow.

As the pounding continued, his thumb found the hammer.

Pulled it back.

Click.

Index finger over the trigger.

One more time, asshole . . .

"Ripper! Get your sorry ass—"

The bullet cracked across the room, in what direction he didn't know since he hadn't even bothered to lift his head.

"DID YOU JUST SHOOT AT ME?"

Ripper grinned into his pillow. Even shit-faced drunk, blinded, his hands behind his back, he could still aim.

He let another round fly. Just for the fuck of it.

"Fuck!" Hawk roared. "I swear to God, asshole, you and—"

Another bullet cracked through the air.

"Fine! I'm gone! Happy, you miserable shit?"

Happy?

Ha-ha-fucking ha.

Despite the awesome mental image of Hawk—six foot two, two hundred and thirty pounds of ripped muscle, arms heavily tattooed, and usually sporting a three-inch Mohawk—doing a bullet dance in the hallway, he was far from happy.

He hadn't been happy in . . . how long had it been since Frankie Deluva carved him up like a fucking jack-o'-lantern?

Four years? Five? Who knew? And really, who cared?

It didn't matter how many years passed, he'd still be missing his right eye, still look like he'd gone ten or twenty rounds with a mountain lion and lost, and he'd still be damn miserable because of it.

And now . . . he'd fucked Danielle West and was waiting to die. He'd been waiting to die all day long and when a man knows he's going to die but doesn't know when or how, it makes for a very unpleasant wait.

He would know. This was the second time in his life he'd waited to die.

Groaning, cursing the sun and his life and his stupid cock, Ripper pulled his pillow out from underneath himself and used it to cover his head. Holy shit, he was an idiot.

And he hadn't just fucked her, he'd been all up in that shit, mouth and hands everywhere, doing pretty much everything a man could do to a woman with the exception of a few choice activities.

He'd fucked Danielle West.

And he was going to die because of it.

He knew Danny, she was a fucking chatterbox. She was always rambling on and on about music and clothes and some asshat named Chan-a-something Tater Tots. She was going to spill to someone and then that someone would spill to someone else and then he'd be worm food.

Halfheartedly, he rolled his body over and swung his legs off the bed. As his boots hit the floor, he made a concerted effort to sit up. No go. He tried again; palming the mattress, he was able to shove himself into a standing position.

He was standing. Sweet.

Tequila – 0, Ripper – 1.

Now if only he could master the intricate art of walking.

And thus commenced his one-man stumbling circus show.

Tequila – 1, Ripper – 1.

When he finally managed to find his bathroom—which shouldn't have been as hard as it had been in his meager nine-by-ten bedroom—and locate the toilet as well, he decided he was too drunk to piss standing up. Then he, a self-proclaimed drunken, gun-wielding, biker extraordinaire, plopped his ass down on the seat, tucked his dick between his legs, and pissed like a girl.

Tequila – 1, Ripper – 1.5.

Now he had to stand up. Again.

Surprisingly, he made it to his feet but when the need for walking arose he fell forward, unable to bear his own weight, and went stumbling into the sink.

Gripping the edge of the counter, Ripper stared blurrily at his fucked-up reflection. Stared at the gaping hole where his right eye had been, the seven slashes across his right cheek, his mangled right arm, and . . .

"Why couldn't you have just let me die?" he whispered to a god that obviously didn't give two fucks about him.

He'd been ready to die.

But God hadn't granted him peace; the fucker had given him hell on earth instead. And the face of a demon to match.

Ripper gasped as Frankie swiped his blade across his chest, tearing open his skin. Again.

Naked. Hog-tied on the floor of an old warehouse, bleeding from too many wounds to count, Ripper knew he was going to die and silently, albeit a little angrily, made his peace with God.

"Not lookin' so pretty anymore, Horseman," Frankie said, laughing. "Lookin' pretty fuckin' fucked-up."

He blinked, trying to see through the blood and tears. "Fuck you," he rasped. "Fuck you."

"Sorry, fuckwad, you ain't my type. But I'll make a deal with you. You tell me what fuckin' deal Deuce worked out with Bannon's crew, how much profit he's skimmin', and I'll let

you jerk off before I slit yer fuckin' throat."

He choked back a sob. He didn't want to die and he definitely didn't want to die like this, at the hands of a madman who got off making people bleed and scream before he did them in. But there was no way in hell he would ever give up his club or his prez. No fucking way.

"Do your fuckin' worst, you cock-suckin' piece of shit," he choked out, cringing as he said it. You don't tell a man like Franklin "Crazy Frankie" Deluva to do his worst and then expect anything but his absolute worst and Frankie's worst was . . .

Ripper screamed as Frankie's blade pierced his eyeball.

Sitting on top of his bound body, stopping him from thrashing, Frankie slowly twisted his blade.

Pure.

Scalding.

Fire.

He screamed and sobbed until, thankfully, his brain chose that moment to shut the fuck down and he passed out cold.

It wasn't as if he didn't deserve what Frankie had done to him; he knew he did. When you'd taken as many lives as he had taken over the years, inflicted as much pain as he had, without giving what he'd been doing so much as a second thought . . . well then, you didn't have a right to be surprised when God decided to let karma fuck you up the ass with a pitchfork.

But that didn't mean he was happy about it.

In fact, with each passing year he was growing angrier, more and more miserable, unable to forget but desperately trying. He was drinking more, tapping into shit he shouldn't, doing whatever or whoever he felt like because

. . . really . . . who gave a fuck what he did?

Ripper didn't have any family left, didn't have a girlfriend he gave two fucks about, and if his brothers knew what had really happened with Frankie, the real reason he'd been able to get away, they'd lose all respect for him.

So, yeah, that amounted to him having a whole lot of jack-fucking-shit.

And now he could add Danny to the long list of fuckups he'd made in his life.

Danny.

Deuce's fucking daughter.

He'd fucked Deuce's fucking daughter.

He was fucked.

He was so fucking fucked.

Maybe this was how his miserable life was finally going to end: death by pussy.

Which, when he thought about it, made sense. It was because of pussy that you came screaming into this world; might as well be pussy that took you out of it.

Staring at his reflection, Ripper started laughing, because, what the fuck, this shit wasn't real. This couldn't be his life.

And then he had to look away, because what grown fucking man wanted to watch himself cry.

CHAPTER 5

DEUCE LEANED FORWARD ON HIS HANDLEBARS, scanning the park playground until he found what he was looking for. Standing beside Kami, near the sandbox Ivy was playing in, was Eva.

Cox was about twenty feet away, tossing a ball around with Devin and Mary Catherine, looking every inch the devoted father to both his daughter and the son he hadn't known he'd had up until . . . Jesus, had it been two years already?

Deuce had never been a devoted father.

He'd been a shit father.

Never home, always losing his temper, not giving a shit about what their bitch of a mother was doing, never knowing what the fuck was going on in either Cage or Danny's lives.

He'd promised himself it was going to be different with Ivy, with Eva. And it had been. Shit had been real good.

And then . . .

In his peripheral vision, Deuce saw Frankie get up on his knees and lift Eva's hips. Frankie's hand snaked around her waist and dipped between her thighs. Eva lost her battle. Her breath caught, her eyes rolled back, even as tears streamed down her face. Her legs quaking, she went face first into the pillow, crying out softly through her orgasm. Frankie followed her down, groaning loudly, his body jerking. Then Frankie turned to him. And grinned.

Deuce's chest went tight. Fuck him, he couldn't even think about it without wanting to kill someone. He'd been helpless. Him. Frankie had taken what was his, right in front of him. And laughed about it. And Eva, goddamned motherfucking Eva, had gotten off with another man's cock inside her. Raping her. In front of him.

The whole fucking shebang made him sick to his stomach.

He couldn't get past it.

He couldn't forget it.

He'd stayed by Eva's side through all her bullshit. Grieving Frankie, blaming herself, then shock had set in, followed by depression the likes of which he'd never seen before. For a while he thought she'd never shake herself out of it, and he was scared shitless because of it. Because, fuck him, he'd never loved a woman like he loved this woman, and the thought of losing her was unthinkable to him.

But he'd lost her.

She was right there. Maybe fifty feet away from him, but he'd lost her.

He'd lost her the moment she'd tried to kiss him, touch him, be with him again, and he couldn't.

He couldn't because he couldn't look at her without seeing Frankie. Without wanting to throw up. Without wanting to strangle Eva because, goddamn her, she'd fucking gotten off on it.

Kami saw him first. She nudged Eva, said something, and jerked her chin in his direction.

Eva didn't turn right away; instead she looked down at the grass and her shoulders sagged, and he felt that shit all the way to his bones. She didn't want to see him.

It was slow going as she dragged her feet toward him. She stopped a good five feet away from him but it felt like a mile, and his chest ached fiercely because of it.

He wanted to tell her that he didn't blame her, that he was going to get over this shit. He wanted to tell her a whole shitload of things, none of which he ever said because he honestly didn't know if any of them were true anymore.

He knew he loved her. But he'd never told her that either.

He should tell her; he could tell her. All he had to do was open his mouth and say three little words, and maybe shit could start moving forward instead of backpedaling into the ugly cycle the two of them always seemed to get caught up in.

It was on the tip of his tongue, he was going to tell her . . .

But then he found himself wondering why she had so much makeup on, and why her sundress was so damn short, and where the fuck she'd been spending her nights. So instead of telling her he loved her, he opened up his mouth and an angry, “Where the fuck you been?” came out instead.

“Kami’s,” she said softly.

He watched her eyes, waiting for some sort of sign that she was lying. But she kept those big gray soul-suckers trained on him, didn’t so much as blink, and he knew she was telling the truth. Which, for some ungodly reason, pissed him off even more.

“You give a fuck about Danny bein’ home all alone?” he continued, wishing the words back the moment they’d spewed out of his mouth.

“Do you?” she asked, and he internally winced.

“I got shit to do,” he shot back.

She stared at him and he stared back. Fuck, she was beautiful and he wanted her. He wanted to hold her, touch her, he wanted inside her, but the second he thought it, he saw Frankie . . . inside her . . . and his stomach cramped.

“Fuck,” he muttered, scrubbing a hand over his eyes, trying to think of something to say to her, something that didn’t result in her crying and him feeling like an asshole afterward. “Listen, D’s birthday is on Saturday. You gonna be there?”

She nodded.

“You bringin’ Ivy?”

She nodded again.

And, yeah, he was out of shit to say.

“I’m out,” he muttered, sitting up straight. “Got shit to do.”

And he left. Feeling like an asshole.

Feeling a chill that had nothing at all to do with the weather, Eva walked back to Kami with her arms wrapped around herself.

Things were bad, so very bad, and she didn't know how to fix them. She wasn't even sure that this time they could be fixed.

Which wasn't fair. She and Deuce had gone through hell and they deserved some peace. And she wanted that peace with him. All she'd ever wanted was him.

"Aw, Evie," Kami whispered after taking one look at her, probably seeing on her face how heartbroken she felt. "What are you going to do?"

For a moment she said nothing, just stared down at her daughter, the spitting image of her father with her white-blonde hair, icy blue eyes, and multi-dimpled smile. She viewed Ivy as a gift, the culmination of her and Deuce's mis-spent years, the phoenix rising from the ashes of their dev-astation, the one good that shone so brightly against all the bad, it made the bad bearable.

She shrugged. "I'm going to wait. I'm just going to wait and hope he comes back to me."

Because he had to come back.

"He's a proud man, Evie. Men like him, they don't . . ." Kami trailed off and took a deep breath. "What if he doesn't get over this, what will you do?"

Eva swallowed hard. He had to come back.

There just wasn't any other option for her. She loved him too much.

CHAPTER 6

I wasn't sure if Ripper was staring at me or glaring at me. Either way, I could feel his gaze burning holes in the back of my head, and because of it I had broken out in a cold sweat during a perfectly mild afternoon.

"You okay?" Eva asked me, touching her palm to my forehead. "You feel clammy."

I swallowed hard and nodded. "Fine," I choked out.

Fine. I was fine. It was a party and I was perfectly fine. I wasn't freaking out or anything. So I'd had a one-night stand. What was the big deal? But usually when people had one-night stands, they never saw the person again, right? But those people probably hadn't had one-night stands with a man fourteen years older than them who worked for their father, a father that would probably, no definitely freak out if he ever found out. So, what was I supposed to do? Was I supposed to act like everything between us was the same as it had been before?

Which had virtually been nothing, aside from an occasional random conversation that happened in passing.

Wat up, Danny girl?

Hey, Ripper.

That's it, that's all; no flirting, no overly long chats, and then suddenly we'd had sex and now what?

God, was I supposed to talk to him? And with Nikki here, his once-in-a-while girlfriend, hanging all over him, how could I? Suddenly, I couldn't understand what Ripper had ever seen in her. Why he'd wasted years being with a club whore. She was fake and trashy and wore horrible clothing that did nothing but exacerbate how trashy she really was. And just like that, I suddenly hated a woman I'd never given half a thought to before.

Oh God, I was so uncomfortable, feeling oddly embarrassed and exposed and wishing I were anywhere but at the club and Ripper would stop stare-glaring at me.

Stupidly, I chanced a glance, and of course he was staring at me. Or glaring. I turned away and tried to concentrate on the conversation happening around me.

"Tegen," Dorothy said, sliding an arm over her daughter's shoulders and pulling her close. "Tell everyone your news."

Dorothy's daughter was a hot mess. Almost sixteen years old and she still hadn't grown out of her middle school awkwardness. She'd inherited Dorothy's flaming red hair but hers had more of an orangey tint to it. Whereas Dorothy's was thick and long with soft waves, Tegen's was just plain frizzy and usually sticking out all over the place.

Her almond-shaped green eyes were always hidden by a pair of thick black frames, on her teeth were a full set of braces that for some reason she'd decided looked good with bright orange rubber bands. And her clothing . . .

Despite Dorothy's best efforts, Tegen refused to dress like a girl. Not that the tomboy look couldn't be sexy, it was. On women like Eva. Tegen looked like an awkward little girl swimming in ugly clothing two sizes too big for her.

"Tegen?"

Tegen didn't answer, in fact she hadn't even heard her mother. She was too busy staring across the lawn at . . .

I followed her line of sight. Cage.

I would have laughed if I didn't feel so sick to my stomach. When she wasn't sitting in a dark corner listening to Dashboard Confessional, she could be found staring at my brother.

It wasn't any secret Tegen had a serious crush on Cage; she'd never hidden it and in my opinion, her following him around like a sad little puppy dog all the time was just sad. But more so embarrassing. For me.

"Baby?" Dorothy gave her a shake.

Tegen glanced up. "What?"

"Your news," Dorothy repeated. "Tell everyone."

Tegen's cheeks turned pink. "Mom," she muttered. "Really? It's not that important."

Dorothy gaped at her. "Your story was published in a national newspaper and it's not important?"

Eva tugged on Tegen's hair and grinned. "That's so awesome, baby. I'm proud of you."

Rolling her eyes, Tegen shrugged. "It was just some stupid contest," she said and went back to not-so-secretly eyeing my brother. Dorothy and Eva continued their conversation and I went back to my cold sweat, because Ripper was still stare-glaring at me.

"Baby," Nikki cooed, running her hand up Ripper's thigh. "What is wrong with you?"

What was wrong with him? He was still waiting to die, that's what was wrong with him.

Motherfuck, he was a mess. He hadn't slept in almost a week, unless you counted passing out cold from alcohol poisoning.

Goddamn, what had she said to him?

Ripper, you're still beautiful. So you've got some scars. So what?

She'd fucked him, both literally and figuratively. He'd been done for the moment she'd called him beautiful.

Jesus, he was only human.

With twitching hands, Ripper grabbed his pack of smokes off the picnic table in front of him, shook one out and, as he brought it to his mouth, turned his gaze across the lawn.

What the fuck was her game?

She hated him. She had to. She wanted him to die.

But why would she hate him? He'd never done shit to her. He'd barely had anything to do with her.

Until now.

She hadn't told on him either.

But why would she? She'd been wholeheartedly into it, if memory served.

Ripper closed his eyes and saw Danny splashing naked

in the lake, the water only reaching her waist, her long blonde hair wet and plastered to her body, beads of water clinging to her eyelashes, lips, and breasts.

"Oh my God." She laughed. "I'm so drunk!"

Yeah, and he had a hard-on from hell that was making it hard to think about anything but grabbing her, throwing her down, and fucking the shit out of her.

"What's wrong, Mr. Grumpy?" She giggled, slinging her arms around his neck, pressing her tits up against his abdomen and her stomach into his erection. He held his breath, kept his hands fisted at his sides. He wasn't going to touch her. He was not going to touch her . . .

"Ripper?"

He glanced down and found her peeking up at him through wet eyelashes. Jesus.

"Yeah?"

"Thank you for dancing with me," she said softly, almost shyly. "And for not taking me home."

"Yeah," he said tightly. "Ain't no big deal."

Her hand slid from his neck to his chest and he closed his eyes as she traced one of the many scars there. "It was to me," she murmured.

"Danny," he growled, refusing to look at her. "You keep touchin' me like that and I ain't gonna be responsible for what I end up doin'."

Then he felt it. Her lips pressed a soft kiss on the center of his chest, over the worst of the scars and lingered there, softly kissing.

And then he heard it. Five little words that shut off his brain and spurred his body into action. "Ripper," she whispered against his ruined skin. "Make my prom night perfect."

She'd wham, bam, thank you for your services, Ripper, and they'd gone their separate ways. No need to tell anyone; no need to do it again.

Which brought up another question. Why the fuck had she done it in the first place?

Because she was drunk? To give her father a secret fuck-you?

Between Deuce and Cage constantly breathing down her neck, the girl hadn't had a whole lot of freedom to do as she pleased. So he supposed in a way it made sense that she'd ended up in bed with a brother, the only human beings with dicks that Deuce had willingly let her associate with.

But lately Deuce had been absent from the world, and Cage was usually buried in women.

If she'd just wanted a fuck, there were other brothers, younger, a lot less fucked-up looking.

Holy shit . . . had she been a virgin?

Oh God, he was going to throw up.

Why had she done this to him? What the fuck had he ever done to her?

"Hello?" Nikki snapped her fingers in front of his face. "This is a party, remember? Loosen up."

Yeah. Whatever. There was always a party. Between the club members and their families, it was always someone's birthday, a wedding, a baby being born. He froze. Birthdays. Holy fuck, how old was Danny?

Ripper scanned his memories, thinking back to the birthdays over the past year and . . .

His shoulders slumped as he sighed in relief. She was eighteen. Legal. Thank you, God. She'd turned eighteen a few weeks before he'd turned thirty-two.

Shoving Nikki's hand out of his face, he glanced back across the lawn.

And . . . she still wasn't looking at him.

He'd spent an entire week thinking about nothing but her, wondering if she'd spilled the beans, wondering if she was going to show her face at the club, wondering why he gave a shit if she showed her face at the club or not, freaking the fuck out every time he saw Deuce, thinking at any second he was going to get his balls blown off.

He stubbed out his smoke on the picnic table, grabbed his pack, and shook out another.

Was it over with?

Could he just forget the whole fucking deal and move on?

He wished someone would tell him.

That someone being Danny, who, by the way, still wasn't looking at him.

And fuck him, he was still looking at her.

He couldn't stop.

Danny was the natural version of Nikki. Naturally blonde, naturally tan, didn't have to wear a shitload of makeup.

Nine years ago, when he'd first met Nikki, he'd liked her enough to consider her his girl. She was hot as fuck, curvy as hell, and a freak in bed. Only problem was he never got to that point where he'd wanted to give up pussy on the side, and strangely enough, Nikki had been okay with it. Then when he'd come home, all fucked-up from Frankie, she hadn't even blinked. She hadn't given a fuck.

That's when Ripper knew she was just like every other club whore, only in his bed for what the club could give her. But he hadn't cared. She was just some bitch he threw a couple of bills at once in a while. She got the club and he got pussy whenever he wanted it. It worked.

He glanced over at Nikki and frowned. Her dyed blonde hair was dried out and frizzy, her makeup cakey, her eyes tired. And all those curves had expanded. The bitch looked beat-up, older than she was, and sadly still trying to rock those tiny leather skirts he used to love.

Yeah, it wasn't working anymore.

He glanced back at Danny. At that killer body, the slinky pink sundress covering it, her long blonde hair hanging down her back in soft curls and . . .

He'd been inside that.

He'd been inside that.

Fuck him. It still wasn't registering. He knew it had happened, had the memories, but couldn't fathom it. He hadn't been with a woman that beautiful since before Frankie.

Ripper couldn't even remember the last time he'd been with someone like Danny. Clean and good and . . . virtually untouched. Because she hadn't been a virgin, right? She hadn't acted like a virgin. God, he hoped like hell she hadn't been a virgin.

"Are you going to be like this all day?" Nikki asked.

He ignored her. Danny was on the move, walking toward the clubhouse, all that pink material clinging to her body, inching up her thighs. Thighs he remembered wrapped around his waist, her nails digging into his shoulders, her screaming out his name while he pounded into her.

He stared and stared and . . . she shot a glance his way and yep, he got a reaction. Her eyes went wide, her face turned red, and she quickly looked away.

So . . . what the fuck did that mean?

Was she embarrassed that she'd fucked him? A girl like her, he wouldn't blame her.

But . . . she'd begged for his cock. She'd whined and begged, grinding her pussy against his mouth, ripping his hair out of his head.

"Ripper," she'd cried out, thrashing beneath him. "Now, please, please, now . . ."

What if it hadn't been him who'd picked her up?

What if it had been Bucket or Dirty or ZZ?

Would she have fucked them instead?

Did he care?

No. Pussy was pussy. He didn't give a fuck whose pussy was giving his dick a temporary home as long as it was wet, warm, and tight.

Neither did he give a fuck who else was dipping inside that shit.

But Danny . . . And suddenly he was giving a fuck about pussy?

No. No, he did not care.

But yeah, he sort of did.

What the motherfuck was wrong with him?

Nothing was wrong with him.

He didn't give a fuck. Nikki, the club bitch standing across the lawn, the brunette in a bar bathroom a few weeks back, none of them mattered because pussy was pussy.

Ripper, make my prom night perfect.

He wasn't sure how perfect he'd made her night, but she sure as fuck made his pretty fucking spectacular.

Spectacular. When was the last time he'd used a word

like spectacular to describe sex?

The blonde slut he'd lost his virginity to? Tiffany something or other?

No. That had consisted of "holy fuck, this feels awesome" and a minute later it was over.

Ten years ago when Eva and Kami had shown up out of nowhere and he and Cox had spent three days locked in a room with that skinny rich bitch?

No. That mess could only be considered just that. A mess. A hard-core fuck fest, yeah, but still a mess considering Cox was married to the bitch now and Kami loved using Ripper to make Cox jealous when she was mad at the guy. Which was every five seconds and so goddamned annoying that he'd begun wishing the three-day fuck fest had never happened.

So, no. He'd never had spectacular sex before.

Until now.

Holy shit, what was wrong with him?

He was going insane, that's what was wrong with him.

He'd finally lost his mind.

CHAPTER 7

"YOU'RE ACTING WEIRD," ANABETH SAID, NOT bothering to look up from painting her toenails. "Weirder than usual, I mean."

Ellie glanced up from her book. "She's right. You've been acting weird since prom."

Rolling my eyes, I turned back to my vanity mirror and applied a light coating of peach lip gloss, just enough to give some shine and a boost of natural color. Then I smoothed my long blonde curls, reapplied my eyeliner, double-checked the zipper on my jeans skirt, straightened and re-straightened my pink T-shirt. Maybe my hair would look better straight today?

"Seriously, Danny, what is wrong with you? And why are you putting so much makeup on? You look like a hooker."

What was wrong with me? I was a mess. All I could think about was Ripper and what had happened at the lake.

Since Dorothy's birthday party nearly two weeks ago, I'd avoided the club like the plague. I didn't care that no one was home to hang out with me; I was terrified of running into Ripper again.

Why couldn't I stop thinking about him?

"Danny, what is wrong—"

I whirled around. "I slept with Ripper," I blurted out, then immediately slapped my hand over my mouth.

Ellie's mouth fell open, a starkly different reaction from Anabeth's grin.

"Ripper," Ellie said slowly. "As in *Ripper*, Ripper? Your dad's sergeant-whatever guy?"

I nodded.

Anabeth let out an excited shriek. "Finally!" she yelled. "I thought you were going to die a virgin!"

I glared at her. "I wasn't a virgin."

She made a face. "Shawn O'Brian does not count. That was like, what? Five minutes of horrible in the woods? So doesn't count."

"Oh God, Anabeth," Ellie muttered. "Your whole life is based around sex."

"So?" she shot back. "It's better than having sex with fictional characters!"

Ellie shot up out of my desk chair. "I do not have sex with fictional characters!"

"Oh puh-lease, I've seen the books you read, all big muscley men and virginal women and steamy sex. Why else would you read that crap if not to get off?"

Ellie was about to blow. Her eyes were bugging out of

her head, her nostrils flaring.

Ignoring her, Anabeth turned to me. "Was it good?" she asked.

I buried my face in my hands and peeked out at my friends through my fingers. "Yes."

Anabeth's smile turned sly.

Ellie turned her bug eyes on me. "Do you actually *like* him? He's so . . . old."

Like him? Um, I didn't *like him*, like him . . . did I?

Anabeth laughed. "Oh, who cares. He's only what, like, thirty?"

"Thirty-two, I think," I said, wincing as Ellie's face scrunched up in disgust.

"Ignore her," Anabeth said dismissively. "Ripper is hot. All big and bad and scarred up. And speaking of big, how big is he?"

"Scarred up?" Ellie gaped at Anabeth. "The man has half a face!"

I dropped my hands and glared at both of them.

"What? It's a legitimate question!"

"It's none of your business! And he doesn't have half a face!"

Anabeth's grin turned positively evil. "Oh. My. God. You do like him!"

"Gross," Ellie muttered. "Not only is he deformed, he's old enough to be your dad."

"That makes it even hotter," Anabeth said, nodding gravely.

"He is not old enough to be my dad!" I yelled. "My dad is like fifty!"

"Whatever," Ellie said. "That's not the point. The point is

you like an *older,* deformed man who works for your crazy dad. Do you actually see yourself dating him?"

Date him? The thought of going on a date with Ripper was absurd. He wasn't the kind of guy you went to dinner and a movie with. He was the kind of guy who dragged you out of the lake, shoved you down on the ground, growling and groping you, telling you all the dirty things he wanted to do to you . . . and then did them. No-holds-barred, invasive, mind-numbing, disturbingly awesome things. I squeezed my eyes shut, remembering . . .

"Fuck," he kept muttering, in between kisses that were growing more and more frantic. "Fuck, Danny, fuck . . . I'm gonna fuck you so hard . . . you're gonna scream, baby."

He pulled me out of the lake and we tumbled to the ground in a heap of tangled limbs, his body pressed against mine, grinding his erection into my stomach. Reflexively, I grabbed fistfuls of his hard biceps as a tidal wave of need rushed through me.

"I want that pussy, baby," he growled hoarsely, sucking and biting his way down my body. "Gimme that beautiful fuckin' pussy."

My eyes flew open. What was wrong with me? He treated me like a one-time whore, and I was fantasizing about him? Ugh.

Anabeth burst out laughing. "Who said anything about dating? Just have lots of hot, sweaty, secret sex until you're bored with him."

I turned back to my mirror, my stomach in knots, and reached for my lip gloss. "He doesn't want me," I mumbled.

Anabeth snorted. "He's just scared of your dad. All you have to do is flaunt your shit in front of him. Show him what he's missing."

And what exactly was he missing? I stared at my reflection, thinking about Nikki. He had to like her; he'd kept her around for so long. Aside from having blonde hair and blue eyes, she was everything I wasn't. She was tall; I was average height. She had hourglass figure curves and I was lean, my curves slight. She had a lot of tattoos, favored leather, red lipstick, and long nails, whereas I had no tattoos, would never be caught dead in leather, favored pastel colors, and kept my nails short and manicured.

"I don't think I'm his type."

"Oh please, you're gorgeous, you're everyone's type. Even I want you."

I thought of him glaring at me, imagined him blaming me for what had happened, and I blew out a breath. "I'm pretty sure he doesn't want me again," I whispered.

Anabeth appeared beside me.

"Do you want him again?"

I stared at her reflection.

Did I? Is that why I couldn't stop thinking about him? Or how incredible it felt to be touched by him.

"Yes," I whispered, feeling utterly ridiculous.

She grinned at me in the mirror.

"Then we'll make him want you."

"I'm not sure, but I think Prez is tryin' to punish us," Bucket said, leaning back in his patio chair, staring out across the club's backyard.

Ripper glanced across the lawn to where Danny and her two friends, the short-haired sexy blonde and curvy mulatto hottie, were sunbathing. In motherfucking bikinis. And Danny's was pink. Hot pink and more string than material. What. The. Fuck. She was doing this shit on purpose.

And Bucket was eye-fucking her. The dude was old enough to be her father but supposedly good-looking enough that the younger bitches flocked to him. As far as Ripper knew, Bucket had never fucked a bitch over twenty-five.

Something he hadn't given two fucks about until right now.

Until Danny had pranced outside basically naked and now was lying around with her tits and ass on display and Bucket was staring. Double what the fuck.

"Yes," he muttered. "He definitely is and stop fuckin' starin' or Prez is gonna have you eatin' fist."

Or he was. Yeah, he was two seconds away from knocking Bucket out.

Gritting his teeth, he looked away from Danny and tried really hard to think about something else. Anything else.

"How old are those two?" Bucket asked. "Danny's eighteen, ain't she? Her friends might be."

"Dude," Tap said. "My daughter is just a few years older. Shut the fuck up."

"It ain't your daughter I'm talkin' about," Bucket shot back.

"Don't even think about it," Eva said, taking a seat beside him, Ivy in her lap.

"What's that, Foxy?" Bucket said, grinning. "Suddenly you're a fuckin' ageist? I seem to remember your old man puttin' two slugs in Prez for takin' a dip down below."

Eva's big gray eyes narrowed. "Shut up," she shot back. "I'm only thinking of Danny. You guys acting like the pervs you are is only going to upset her."

"Pervs!" Bucket shouted, offended. "There are three hot bitches lying half naked behind my fuckin' club and I'm supposed to act like I'm fuckin' blind? Fuck that. Prez is evil. Straight up. Why the fuck isn't Danny at home?"

Because, he thought, glaring at Eva, someone's got Deuce's balls wrapped around her finger.

"Because." Eva sighed. "No one else is home, so why should she be home?"

"You could be home," he muttered. "Should be home."

Not hanging around an MC all the time; not giving teenage girls rooms at MCs, forcing him to watch them lying around in bikinis, leaving him vulnerable to accidently fucking them. Again.

Tap shot him a dirty look. "Way to be an asshole, brother," he said.

"It's fine," Eva said quietly. "But let's get one thing clear, okay, Ripper?"

"What's that, babe?" he sneered.

"I didn't know," she said evenly. "If I would have known what he'd done to you, I would have—"

"You would have what?" he yelled, jumping up and knocking his chair backward. "You would have fuckin' what, bitch? Sang him a motherfuckin' lullaby? Told him everything was gonna be A-fucking-OK? You had no fuckin' sense when it came to that man! You wouldn't have done jack-fuckin'-shit!"

Ivy burst into tears and Bucket was suddenly up in his face, pushing him backward. "Take a fuckin' walk," he hissed. "And cool the fuck off before Prez rips that fuckin' patch off you for talkin' to his old lady like that."

"She wouldn't have done shit!" he repeated, leaning around Bucket and pointing at Eva. "I saw you with him, Eva! Him givin' you bullshit, tellin' you he can't fuckin' sleep without you, him justifyin' why he put A FUCKIN' HIT ON YOU, and you cryin' like a baby, tellin' him everything's gonna be fine!"

"Get the fuck outta here!" Bucket yelled, shoving him backward.

Eva appeared beside Bucket. "I'm sorry Frankie took your fucking eye," she hissed. "He also took twenty-two years of my life from me! If anyone understands what it feels like to lose something at the hands of Frankie, it's me!"

"Fuck you," he bit out angrily. "You coulda walked away, coulda called Prez, coulda said somethin' to your old man. You had a motherfuckin' choice! I didn't have that luxury, Eva, I couldn't walk away! I couldn't fuckin' leave!"

"Neither could I," she whispered.

He stared down at her, trying to figure out what the fuck she meant by that.

"Heads up," Bucket muttered, moving aside as Deuce stepped out onto the back patio, eying them warily.

"What the fuck is goin' on?" Deuce growled.

"Nothing," Eva said evenly, her eyes still on him. "Ripper and I were just having a small argument over which one of Danny's friends looked better in their bikini."

Deuce's eyes shot to the lawn and went saucer-wide, his nostrils flaring. "Danielle Elizabeth fuckin' West!" he roared and pushed past them, headed for his daughter. "What the fuck are you not wearin'?"

Eva gave him a small, sad smile. "Two birds, one stone," she said softly and turned away. After retrieving Ivy from Tap, she disappeared inside the clubhouse.

"Dude," Tap said, getting to his feet. "You are a first class asshole."

"Second that," Bucket said, glaring at him. "Foxy doesn't deserve your hate, brother. Frankie does."

Ignoring them, feeling like an asshole, a justified asshole, Ripper stormed across the patio and into the club. He should have never opened his mouth. He'd gone this long keeping his true feelings about Eva to himself, but his nerves were shot from this shit with Danny. He felt strung out half the time and the other half . . .

He wanted her. She was too damn beautiful. And he'd owned that shit. There wasn't a part of that body he hadn't touched, hadn't had his mouth on.

He wanted more.

Ah, fuck, what was he doing?

He was supposed to be flushing her out, not fantasizing about her. Fantasizing about her was only going to lead to fucking her again, and fucking her again would lead to fucking her again and again and again.

Fuck, he wished she would go away. Go home, go hang out somewhere else, go live with her mom, go to college in France.

Ripper had his key in his door when the sound of giggling brought him up short. Turning his head, he found Danny with her two friends, and Deuce herding the three of them down the hall. Her friends were staring at him, the blonde giggling, the mulatto scowling, and Danny was bright fucking red, looking anywhere but at him.

Fuck. She'd told them. She'd fucking opened her big fat mouth and told her dumbass friends.

He was so busy staring at her he didn't even notice that Deuce had stopped beside him until he was being smacked across the back of his head.

"What the fuck you lookin' at?" Deuce demanded and smacked him again.

"Nothin'," he muttered. Turning his key, he pushed open his door and shut it quickly behind him. Sliding down the door, he hit the floor and buried his face in his hands. What the fuck was wrong with him? Why couldn't he stop thinking about her?

He hadn't given a fuck about anything in so long he'd forgotten what it felt like. Forgotten how horrible it was to feel anything at all.

The last time he'd given a fuck was . . .

Ripper came back to consciousness on fire. Everywhere. He coughed and gagged as hot, wet, fire poured down over his face and chest. Sputtering and screaming, he tried to jerk away but his bonds allowed him no movement.

"Wake up, sleepin' beauty." Frankie laughed and Ripper heard the sharp slide of a zipper, then felt the air shift as Frankie knelt down beside him. Spitting out a mouthful of hot piss, he gasped for air.

"Gonna try this shit one last time, Horseman. You don't give me what I want, you're goin' to ground."

His body shaking from shock, his skin burning, unable to see what was going to be the final death blow, Ripper stayed silent, praying it would be over soon.

Cursing, Frankie tugged on the rope binding his ankles to his wrists and started sawing through it. No longer bound in the fetal position, Ripper fell sideways, sprawled on his back. Grabbing hold of his balls, Frankie squeezed and twisted.

"Talk, you fuckin' shithead," he growled.

Breathe. He just had to keep breathing through it. He just had to breathe, in and out, until Frankie finally ended it.

"TALK!" Frankie roared and twisted further.

Pain hurtled up his groin and exploded into his stomach. He couldn't talk now, even if he'd wanted to.

Breathe.

Just fucking breathe.

BREATHE, DAMN IT. BREATHE.

"Yo, Frankie!" a loud voice bellowed.

Frankie released him and his trembling body went lax. Gagging, he turned his head and released a stomach full of spit, piss, and bile.

"What?" Frankie growled.

"Eva's blowin' up my fuckin' phone, brother."

Ripper heard Frankie jump to his feet, heard his heavy booted steps crossing the floor, heard a door creak open, then slam shut.

It took a moment to realize that he was alone.

Alone . . .

He had two choices. He could keep lying there, naked and bleeding out on the ground and wait to die, or he could try.

He couldn't let it end like this.

He couldn't die a high school dropout, a criminal who'd never done shit with his life, with no woman or kids to care if he'd gone.

He had to try.

Dry heaving, tears streaming down his cheeks, he struggled to roll to his side. Sucking air in through his teeth and breathing out hard, labored breaths, he folded his body in half.

Breathe.

Just fucking breathe.

Gritting his teeth through the blinding pain, he reached down his body with his bound wrists . . .

His fingertips brushed against the rope on his ankles.

With a heave and a shout of pain, with every ounce of energy he had, he stretched his body just a little more and grabbed hold of the knot.

Yeah. The last time he'd given a fuck about anything was when he'd thought he was going to die at the hands of a crazy motherfucker. After that, he'd become consumed with what hadn't happened, so much so, he'd started wishing it had.

Until now.

Until he'd accidentally fucked a little blonde bitch with the face of an angel and a body built to drive a man crazy. Danny was every man's wet dream; an honest-to-God good, sweet, girl who was drop-dead gorgeous and fucked like a whore.

If she were anybody else, anybody else's daughter, he'd have spent a week straight up inside of her, fucking her half to death, splitting her down the middle, taking what he wanted. And fuck him, he wanted.

He wanted.

But she wasn't anyone else's daughter. She was Deuce's daughter, and every bit as lethal to him as Frankie had been.

Pulling on a pair of sweatpants, I glared at Anabeth. "That

was a terrible plan."

She waved me off. "Oh, please, he was staring at you the entire time. If your dad hadn't gone ballistic, Danny, I guarantee you'd be bent over his motorcycle right now."

Right. Instead I'd gotten yelled at by my father *in front of everyone* and was now even more embarrassed then I had been. Actually, I was pretty sure this was the most embarrassed I'd ever been in my entire life.

"Oh. My. God." Ellie shut my bedroom door behind her and leaned back against it.

"What's wrong with you?" Anabeth asked.

"Some guy whose name is Dirty, and may I just say kudos to his parents for aptly naming him, just asked me to blow him. Ordered me, actually."

"Did you?" Anabeth asked.

"You did not just ask me that!"

"Yes, Miss Prude, I did."

"Um, ew. He really is dirty."

Anabeth snorted. "Are you actually upset? So he hit on you, so what?"

Ellie crossed her arms over her chest. "I'm not sure that '*Bitch, get the fuck on your knees and suck me*' should be considered being hit on. I believe I was demeaned to the least common denominator possible."

"You liked it," Anabeth scoffed.

"You know what I liked?" Ellie yelled, her eyes bugging out. "I liked it when Cage told me I'm a better fuck than you!"

My mouth fell open, Anabeth let out a banshee-worthy screech, and Ellie ducked as a pillow went flying across the room.

"You slut!" Anabeth screamed.

"Me?" Ellie screamed. "You've slept with half the town!"

"You're both sluts!" I yelled. "And traitors!"

"Oh please, Danny, you can't get mad. Your brother is the hottest piece of ass in this Podunk town."

"No! He's a whore and a jackass and I'm convinced he might be somewhat brain-dead, but he is most definitely not hot!"

"Sorry, Danny," Ellie said dryly. "He really is."

I gaped at both of them. "Do you realize what you've done? You've ruined our friendship! You cannot be friends with someone while you're sleeping with their brother!"

Anabeth waved me off and went back to painting her toenails. "Please, Danny. You know Cage never fucks anyone twice."

"No, I did not know that, and do you know why I didn't know that? *Because he is my brother*!"

"Well, now you know," Ellie said, turning back to her book. "So, calm down."

I dropped to the floor with a loud thump and buried my face in my hands. "Oh my God," I muttered. "I hate my life."

"This is why you don't have a boyfriend," Anabeth said pointedly. "You're so dramatic."

Clutching a fresh bottle of tequila, Ripper poked his head into the hallway, looked right, then left. The coast clear of Deuce or Danny, he wandered around the empty club before deciding on the kitchen, where he found Dorothy bent over the sink, washing dishes, and Hawk seated at the head of the long wooden table, nursing a beer.

Hawk lifted his chin. "Wat up."

"Nothin'," he muttered, sliding into the chair beside him.

Dorothy glanced over her shoulder and frowned. "You want some coffee?"

He glared at her. "Do I fuckin' look like I want coffee?" he said, waving his bottle in the air.

With an exaggerated eye roll tossed his way, she went back to the dishes.

Whatever. She could think he was a drunk. He didn't give a fuck.

"I'm fuckin' bored," Dirty announced as he walked into the kitchen. "Anyone else goin' crazy?"

Holding up two fingers, Ripper nodded. "Yeah."

Grabbing the chair across from him, Dirty turned it around and straddled it. "I've gone a month without pussy. I got cum backed up straight to my fuckin' brain."

Dorothy turned toward Dirty, looking repulsed. "Why?" she asked. "Why must you be so disgusting?"

Dirty ignored her. "I need this shit sucked or fucked before my head explodes."

Hawk started laughing and Dirty shot him a look.

"Naw, dude, for real. This shit keeps up, my dick is gonna shrivel up and die."

Not Ripper. He was having the opposite problem. His dick was going to explode. Between what had gone down at the lake still wreaking havoc on his thoughts, playing on fucking repeat, and now that bikini bullshit yesterday. Goddamn Danny.

"Maybe you should shower?" Dorothy suggested.

"Women like that sort of thing."

Dirty grinned at her. "What's wrong, D? You don't like me in my natural state?"

Dirty's "natural state" was a nasty fucking mess. The dude's long brown hair was as greasy as fuck, his hands and clothes were stained black from motor oil, his fingernails were long and yellowed, caked with dirt, and he always stunk like week-old garbage. The only club bitches that went to bed with him had either drunk themselves into unconsciousness or gotten roofied by Dirty himself.

"Let's ride," Dirty said. "Get the fuck outta Miles and hit up Billings, grab some pussy to go."

Maybe that's what he needed. Fresh meat to flush Danny out of his system.

"I'm down," Hawk muttered and no sooner than the words had left the guy's mouth, a ceramic bowl came hurtling through the air. They all ducked; the thing hit the wall and shattered on impact. As shards of ceramic went flying in all directions, Hawk jumped up, causing his chair to tip backward.

"Woman," Hawk growled, glaring at Dorothy. "I'm well past sick of your bullshit."

Confused, Ripper glanced between the two of them.

Dorothy's dishcloth hit the counter with a wet slap and she matched Hawk's glare with one of her own.

Which would have been funny if he wasn't so confused, seeing as Dorothy was all of five foot nothing, a tiny slip of a woman, and he was positive he'd seen Hawk eat steaks bigger than her.

"You've got no right to be sick of my bullshit!"

Hawk's mouth flattened and his fists clenched. "The

fuck I don't," he growled low.

"You don't!" she cried.

"Bitch, you throwin' dishes at my fuckin' head, actin' straight up jealous, is tellin' me I got a fuckin' right."

Dorothy's now wide, horrified eyes shot to Dirty, then him, then back to Hawk.

"What is wrong with you?" she yelled. "You've already done enough damage and now you're making it worse!"

Eyebrows raised, Ripper got the feeling he was missing something.

Hawk kicked at his fallen chair and took a menacing step toward her. "Damage!" he roared. "Is that what you call it? 'Cause I'm—"

The swinging kitchen doors burst open and Cage ran in, holding a purple backpack over his head.

"Asshole!" Tegen shrieked, running after him. "Give it back!"

"Language!" Dorothy chastised.

Still holding her backpack over his head, Cage grinned down at her. "Aw, Teacup, what's the matter?"

"Don't call me that!" she yelled, jumping up and down like a jackrabbit on crack, trying to reach her bag when it was obvious that unless she grew about six inches in the next five seconds, there was no way in hell she was going to even come close. "I'm not a little kid anymore!"

"No?" He laughed. "You finally grow outta that trainin' bra?"

"Cage!" Dorothy snapped. "Inappropriate!"

Tegen's pale, freckled face turned bright red with rage and just as Ripper thought she was about to blow, Cage faked left and then went right, darting around Tegen and back into the hallway.

Letting out a frustrated scream, Tegen went shrieking after him.

"Dammit," Dorothy muttered, following them. Just before she left, she shot a glaring look in Hawk's direction that promised all sorts of pain in the genital region.

"In case you forgot," Dirty said. "That's Jase's woman."

"No," Hawk growled, "she's Jase's whore. He's never gonna leave Chrissy."

Dirty shook his head. "Brother, don't go there. Not with Jase, not over D. He ain't gonna give her up."

Hawk's hard brown eyes bored into Dirty. "Dude," he muttered, smiling grimly, "you're a couple years too late with that bullshit."

Surprised, Dirty glanced at Ripper and he shrugged in return. He hadn't seen that shit coming either, but the truth of the matter was that Dorothy wasn't Jase's old lady, she was club ass, always had been. So if Hawk wanted to go toe-to-toe with Jase over the little redheaded bitch, he didn't give a fuck.

"So, I'm guessin' that means no pussy to go," Dirty said dryly.

"Yeah," Hawk muttered. "Not really feelin' it."

Dirty turned to him. "Ripper?"

He looked down at his bottle. If he were being honest, he really didn't want any pussy. Except the one he wasn't supposed to want. The one in the pink bikini with the firm little ass and perfect tits and tight, sweet pussy.

Internally, he groaned. He had to stop this shit.

Then, as if the entire motherfucking universe was against him and setting out to make his life as miserable as possible, Danny chose that very moment to walk into the kitchen. She took one look at him, turned bright red, and walked right back out.

Sighing, he glanced up at Dirty.

"Naw, dude," he muttered. "I got a hot date with a dead worm."

CHAPTER 8

DEUCE PULLED UP TO THE HOUSE ON HIS BIKE AND CUT his engine. His truck was here, meaning Eva was here, something he'd been hoping to avoid. He hadn't seen her since she'd shown up at the club with Ivy, and that had been weeks ago.

Sighing, he climbed off the bike and headed for the door. He didn't have much of a choice. He had to make a run to Manhattan; Preacher wanted proof that business was going bad on the west coast, that his boys out there were double dipping off his profits. Audio proof that ZZ had recorded on a disposable cell phone he'd been keeping in his bedroom safe.

Upon entering the house, he found the downstairs dark and the house quiet. Relief filled him. Maybe she wasn't home. Maybe Kami had picked her up, maybe—

At the top of the stairs, he found Eva laying Ivy down in her crib. Leaning over the railing, softly stroking her hair, she kissed their daughter good night and whispered, "I love you."

Watching them, his woman and his daughter, Deuce's chest started to ache. He missed them both. He missed all of it. Coming home to his family, watching his kids interact with each other, the laughter, the bickering, even the yelling, just taking it all in and enjoying everything he hadn't had growing up. Then later, after Ivy was asleep, Danny in her room on her phone and Cage gone for the night, he would take Eva upstairs, strip her naked, and fuck the hell out of her.

"You're home."

His eyes flew open.

"So are you," he said, hating that his words came out sounding like an accusation.

"For some reason Danny hasn't been going to the club at all lately," she said softly, nodding toward Danny's closed bedroom door. "And like you said, she shouldn't be home all alone."

Guilt swamped him. He'd said that and yet he'd done nothing about it.

"Are you leaving?"

He glanced back at Eva.

"Yeah," he muttered. "Demon delivery."

"Is everything okay?"

"Yeah."

She waited a moment, expecting him to offer up more information, and when he didn't, she nodded and turned away. He followed her down the hallway and into their room, watching as she bent down to pull open her bottom dresser drawer. She emerged with a pair of ratty sweatpants and an old T-shirt, both his, tossed them on the bed, and started undressing.

He kept watching until she was naked, taking it all in. The flower tattoos down her arm, the natural slope of her heavy breasts, the hills and valleys of a body he'd never tired of, the slight bow of her stomach, the ring through her belly button, the tattooed stars encircling it, her perfect, heart-shaped ass.

Everything hit him at once: the little girl he'd met in the family visiting room at Rikers, singing Janis, wearing Chucks, stealing what was left of his broken-down, battered heart. And when she was older, listening to her ramble on about Halloween costumes, thinking no kid as sweet as she was should be living in this life, and wanting better for her. After that the memories changed, as had his feelings for her. Fondness and adoration turned to lust and he'd taken that first kiss, that first taste and touch. Two years later, lust turned to need and he took that pussy first too. Four years passed, and he claimed not just her body but her. Because need had turned to love.

He had her now, he owned her—her body, her baby, her future—it was all his and knowing that, having that, had made every chance meeting over the years, every fuck, every fight, every letdown . . .

It had made it worth it.

Deuce was rock hard by the time she'd finished dressing. Hard and aching for her.

She took one look at him and knew, she always knew. Those damn beautiful eyes traveled down his body, flaring with heat when she came to his hips. Those juicy lips parted, sucking in a sharp breath, a sound he knew very well. A sound that made him crazy.

"I miss you," she whispered.

"Babe," he said quietly. "Yeah."

She took a small step forward, then stopped. "Can . . . can I touch you?"

He didn't like this version of Eva, this timid, unsure woman who was nothing like the quirky, outgoing kid she'd been, or the teenager who didn't give a fuck about what other people thought, or the young woman who'd refused to take shit from him or anyone else.

But now, that kid, that teenager, that young woman . . . they were gone.

He couldn't fault Frankie for this, or the life. This shit was his fault. True, the life had taken its toll on her and Frankie had beat her down, pounded on her something fierce, but she'd persevered through it all.

It had been him, by refusing to let it go, refusing to love her the way a man should, who'd thrown the killing blow.

Deuce could fix it, he knew he could. He could bring the woman he loved back to life. He held that precious power in his hands.

He wanted to fix it.

"Come here, darlin'," he said hoarsely. All of a second passed before Eva was in his arms and he was carrying her across the room and dropping her on their bed and her hands were in his hair and her mouth . . .

"This is my fuckin' mouth," he growled, kissing her roughly. He tore at her clothes, stripping her violently, grabbing her breasts, telling her over and over again that every part of her was his. Had always been his.

Fuck, he needed her, he needed to be inside of her again. He freed himself and pushed against her; she was ready for him, wet and whimpering, needing him just as badly.

It had been so long since he'd been inside of her, since he'd been able to take what was his, it had been since . . .

Her breath caught, her eyes rolled back even as tears streamed down her face. Her legs quaking, she went face first into the pillow, crying out softly through her orgasm. Frankie followed her down, groaning loudly, his body jerking.

He fought against the memory, fought it with everything he had. Eva was his. She was motherfucking his. Frankie was dead, gone, he couldn't take her away from him anymore. She was his. She was his . . .

Then Frankie turned to him. And grinned.

He hadn't fucked her since before Frankie. Frankie had been the last man inside his woman. Grinning. That's all he could see, was that fucking asshole grinning.

"FUCK!" he roared, pushing off the bed and turning away.

"Wait," she cried, reaching for him. "Baby, wa—"

Anger and pain had him slapping her hands off him. "Shut up," he growled, yanking his jeans up. "Just shut the fuck up."

"Deuce—"

"No!" he bellowed. "You liked it, you fuckin' liked it! You got off on bein' raped!"

Her fists came down on the mattress. "I loved him!" she screamed.

Rage bubbled up inside him. "You loved him? You loved a man who did nothin' but hurt you? How long had he been hurtin' you, Eva? You fuckin' tell me how long."

She looked up at him with tears in her eyes. "It doesn't matter," she whispered. "He's gone now."

He stared down at her. "Gone?" he asked hoarsely. "He ain't fuckin' gone. He's still standin' right between us, laughin' his fuckin' ass off."

In a flash she was off the bed and shoving at him. "Only because you're letting him!" she screamed. "You're not letting me fix it!"

Deuce grabbed her wrists and held her still. "Shoulda never been nothin' to fix," he growled. "Ten fuckin' years ago you showed up here wantin' me and, bitch, you knew I wanted you, you knew you didn't ever have to go back to that shit! It didn't have to go down this way, Eva, 'cause you fuckin' had me, you always fuckin' had me!"

He shook her hard. "You tell me why I should fuckin' care 'bout you tryin' to fix anything, when you spent your whole fuckin' life tryin' to fix him and not us? Was it because you loved him more? Did you love that motherfucker *more than me*?"

"He needed me," she whispered.

With a hard shove he pushed her off him. "BITCH," he roared. "SO THE FUCK DID I!"

Storming across the room, he punched in the code on his wall safe, grabbed what he needed, and got the fuck out of there, doing his best to ignore Danny glaring at him from her bedroom doorway and Eva's soft sobbing coming from his own bedroom. He practically ran down the stairs and burst out the front door because, fuck him, he couldn't deal with this shit, he didn't know how to deal with this shit.

He suddenly wanted out. He wanted out of the club, out

of this mess with Eva, out of being a father, out of all of it because if he were gone, in the long run they would all be better off. His boys, Eva, his kids . . . they didn't need some angry, fucked-up asshole in their lives. They needed stability, someone who was going to be there for them no matter what.

Someone who could put aside their own problems and put the people he loved first.

And that someone wasn't him.

It had never been him.

He'd been kidding himself all these years thinking shit was going to get better. He'd had only brief moments of "better." Teases of happiness, fucking with him, dangling what he wanted in front of him, but leaving it just out of reach.

It was just like his old man had always said . . . he was a fuckup.

CHAPTER 9

RIPPER, TAP, AND COX CUT THEIR ENGINES A SMALL WAYS away from an old abandoned group of condos on the edge of town. Warily they eyed the dark, decrepit scene before them.

"You trust this bitch?" Tap asked Cox.

Cox laughed coldly. "I don't trust any bitch, least of all this one, but she contacted us when she coulda just snagged our shit from Marcus and split."

Fucking Marcus. One of their main distributors. They got a shipment in, then they cut, bagged, and tagged it and sent it packing with several different runners. Only Marcus had fucked up. Got himself ganked.

By a fucking woman.

Looking off in the distance, Cox squinted. "There she be."

Ripper followed Cox's finger to an attractive young black woman with an afro the size of a house and an ass to match, who was sauntering their way.

"You've got to be kiddin' me," he growled, looking her over.

Skintight leather jacket. Skintight jeans. And thigh-high leather boots with what he was guessing were six-inch heels.

"Holy shit," Tap breathed. "Holy fuckin' shit . . . *look at that ass*."

Cox laughed. "Calls herself Mama Vi."

Mama Vi? Shit. Why the fuck did that sound so familiar to him?

"Boys." She greeted them, flashing a white smile, stark against her bright red lips and deep chocolate skin.

"Diana fuckin' Ross," he shot back, staring in horror at her hair. "Where the fuck is our shit?"

Tsk-tsking him, she grinned. "Gotta proposition for ya first," she drawled.

"I'm listenin'," Tap said, staring the bitch up and down with a dumbass smile on his face.

"Ain't you a sweet-lookin' little white boy," she cooed, stepping forward and placing her hand on Tap's chest. Ripper caught sight of her nails, three inches long, curved like claws, and also bright red.

Sweet-looking little white boy? Tap?

Grabbing Mama Vi's wrist, Tap slammed her hand down over his cock. "Ain't nothin' little 'bout me," he growled.

Her grin grew.

"Ta think, Big Jay had said bikers weren't nothin' but sheep-fuckin', honkey-tonkin' rednecks."

Ripper's heart skipped a beat.

Big Jay.

Shit. *Shit, shit, shit.*

Cox growled. "I look like a fuckin' redneck to you?"

Stepping away from Tap, she glanced over at Cox. "No, boo," she said silkily. "You lookin' like a mighty fine piece of *pandillero* meat to Mama Vi."

"*Gracias, niña,*" Cox said, dipping his head.

"*El placer es mío.*" She giggled.

Ripper glanced between a love-struck Tap, and Cox, who seemed to be having some sort of an identity crisis. "What the fuck is wrong with you assholes?" he demanded. "Did you not just hear what the bitch fuckin' said? Big Jay! She works for motherfuckin' Big Jay! She ain't no bitch of his, either. She's his crazy-ass little sister, Vivian Jones. Gotta rep a mile fuckin' long, most of it for killin' white boys who fuck her brother over."

Both his brothers turned to him, confused.

"Who?"

"What?"

Mama Vi's deep, silky laughter echoed throughout the empty parking lot. "You homegrown, white boy, ain'tcha?"

"Yeah," he growled. "Born and fuckin' raised and still workin' the Cali territories. Now start fuckin' talkin'. What's a boss from LA like Big fuckin' Jay doin' messin' with my club?"

"Word's out," she said. "Preacher done dropped science on the Horsemen. You boys hit the big time and you gotta start payin' the piper."

Preacher. Another thing he could lay at Eva's feet. If it weren't for Deuce's alliance with the Demons, this shit wouldn't be happening.

"I'm guessin' we ain't gettin' our shit back?" Cox growled.

"Not this time," she said. "You been chin-checked. Think of it as a good faith payment."

"Fuck that!" Cox shouted. "We don't gotta to listen to some fuckin' hood rat—"

"No," Ripper interrupted before Cox got himself killed. "We're not interested."

"You sure about that?" Mama Vi asked sweetly, her dark eyes on him. Appraising. Assessing. Scaring the ever-loving shit out of him. The stories he'd heard about her . . . Her skills and finely honed specialties were right up there with Frankie's sick and twisted bullshit.

"I'm sure," he said, already knowing Deuce wouldn't play ball with street gangs, no matter how high up the food chain they were. Most of them were unorganized, their distribution messy, full of snitches and junkies, making it too easy for the law to get the drop on them.

"You're makin' a mistake."

Tap's jaw clenched. "You threatenin' us?"

Mama Vi smiled nastily. "I am. You don't play it our way, Deuce is gonna have a war on his hands."

Fuck. Deuce was going to be pissed. First, because he was in New York and not able to deal with this bitch himself, and second, for threatening the club. No one threatened the club and got away with it. Deuce was going to want blood. And speaking of wanting blood . . .

"You want a war, bitch, you fuckin' got one. Now, where's our boy?" he asked.

"White boy, *you are makin' a mistake*."

He pulled his piece mere moments before she pulled

hers. Half a second later both Cox and Tap had their guns trained on her, but he wasn't under the false impression that any of them were safe. The bitch had deadly reflexes and was more than likely armed with an entire arsenal.

"Bitch," he growled. "First, you're gonna learn right the fuck now that no one is gonna threaten my prez, my club, or any of my brothers and get away with it. Second, I ain't white, I'm motherfuckin' tan. Third, you tell me where our fuckin' boy is or I'm puttin' a bullet in your big black ass."

For several heart-pounding moments, no one moved until Mama Vi tucked her gun back inside her jacket.

"Scarface," she drawled. "First, if Deuce don't think Jay can take him down, he's one sad, sorry mothafucker."

She glanced toward the condos. "Second, your boy's tied up inside."

Then her dark gaze turned back to him and she smiled just a little too sweetly. "Third, honey, ain't no man ever pulled a gun on me and lived happily ever after."

She leaned in a few inches. "I will hurt you," she whispered. "Count on it."

As they stared at each other, it took every ounce of his willpower not to pull the trigger and blow this bitch straight to hell.

"Lookin' forward to it," he growled softly.

No one said a word as she walked off.

"Tap," he barked. "Stay out here in case she comes back." Glancing at Cox, he jerked his chin in the direction of the condos. "Let's go, chief."

"This is fucked," Cox muttered, stepping in line beside him.

"Yeah."

"You think Prez is gonna go to war?"

"Yeah." Deuce didn't mess around. It was how the man had gotten where he was today. That and most people were scared shitless of him. Had been for a long time now. Ripper hadn't been around when Deuce had his old man, Reaper, offed, but the circuit still buzzed about it. Fuckers were still whispering about how Deuce had posted the hit with the explicit instructions to make Reaper's death as long and as painful as possible.

Ripper couldn't picture wanting to kill his own father, but then again, his old man had been a good guy. Both his parents had been quality stock. He often wondered where he'd be if he hadn't lost them at such a young age. Still surfing? Skating? Beach bumming it with his friends and an endless supply of blonde-haired, blue-eyed hotties?

A wave of longing hit him, a homesickness he hadn't felt in years, and suddenly he found himself thinking about home, eating his mom's pot roast and apple pie, watching TV with his old man, listening to him bitch and moan about the declining morals of modern society. Both of them constantly complaining that his hair was too long, that skating was too dangerous, but he saw the secret smiles when they'd thought he wasn't looking. They'd been proud of him.

He was fairly certain if they were still alive, they wouldn't be proud anymore.

Jesus Christ, what the fuck was wrong with him lately?

He needed to find a way to turn off this all of a sudden "give a shit" switch that had been turned on inside of him.

"Shit's gonna get messy," Cox mused.

"Yeah."

Reaching door number one, they pulled their pieces,

glanced at one another, and Cox kicked open the door. There was Marcus. The dumb as shit, hairy, Italian motherfucker was tied up in a corner. Dumbass.

"Please," Marcus said hoarsely. "Please . . ."

"Please fuckin' what?" he yelled, stalking forward. "You lost an entire shipment! To one fuckin' woman!"

"The bitch jumped me," Marcus rasped, struggling against the ropes. "Took everything, took the rest of the shit, took all the cash. Did you know she's got throwing stars?"

Eyebrows raised, Cox glanced at him and he shook his head in response. Marcus had made a big mess and he had to go to ground. It didn't matter if Mama Vi had used a motherfucking cannon to gank him, Marcus had one responsibility and he'd failed. Now he was deadweight.

Sighing, he bent down and pressed the muzzle of his nine to Marcus's temple.

Knowing he was worm food, Marcus began thrashing in earnest. "Dude! Please! Gimme two weeks and I'll make back what I owe ya! Please, man, I got fuckin' kids!"

Ripper snorted. Marcus knew the game, had been living in it his whole damn life, and knew having kids didn't mean jack-fucking-squat.

About to pull the trigger, the front right pocket of his leathers started vibrating.

"Gimme a sec," he said, tucking his gun back in his pants and reaching for his phone.

"Wat up?"

"Where are you?" Deuce barked.

"Edge of town, at the abandominiums." Using his shoulder, he held his phone to his ear while he pulled his smokes from his cut and lit one up. "'Bout to do Marcus in."

"The woman?"

"Ain't no woman, Prez," he said around an exhale of smoke. "Big Jay's little sister outta LA."

Deuce cursed. "You square that shit?"

"Yeah."

"What's that costin' me?"

"War. And more than likely me goin' to ground."

Because Mama Vi wasn't kidding around. He knew a sociopath when he saw one; that bitch had the same cold, dead eyes Frankie had. Eyes that lit up with a whole lot of crazy only when blood was involved.

"You ain't goin' to ground," Deuce growled. "Not on my watch. They want a war, they're gonna fuckin' get one. Put the word out, club's goin' on lockdown."

"On it."

"And Ripper?"

"Yeah?"

"Spoke to Dimebag earlier. Eva's at the club, so's Cage, and Danny ain't, meaning she's home alone. So I need you to grab her on your way back."

What? No. Fuck no.

"Can, uh, someone else get her—"

"You got somethin' else to do?"

Fuck.

"No."

"Yeah, well, the boys got families they gotta get, you don't. And the less traffic in and out of the gate, the fuckin' better. And I ain't real sure why I gotta explain shit to you that you already motherfuckin' know. So shut the fuck up and go get my daughter."

"Yeah," he muttered. "On it."

He shoved his phone back in his pocket, dropped his smoke onto the dirty carpet, stubbed it out with his boot, and pulled his piece.

"NO!" Marcus screamed. "No! No! N—"

The bullet cracked through Marcus's skull. Instant quiet.

"'Bout fuckin' time."

"You coulda done it, so stop fuckin' whinin'."

"Fuck off. Was that Prez?"

Ripper nodded. "We're on lockdown. Go grab your kids and that crazy bitch of yours."

Cox gave him a sideways glance and grinned. "Jealous."

After tucking his gun back into his leathers, Ripper used his forearm to wipe Marcus's blood spatter off his face.

"Dude, ain't no one jealous of you. Dumpin' Anna for Kami was like tradin' in a sweet little kitty cat for a bloodthirsty tiger."

"Yeah," Cox drawled, grinning. "Half the time I don't know whether to come or cry or both, but fuck me if she ain't worth it."

He watched Cox walk off, wondering what bitch on earth would be worth Kami's level of bullshit and came up empty. That bitch was on a level all her own.

CHAPTER 10

I WAS CURLED UP ON THE COUCH WITH MY PINK FLEECE blanket, wearing Hello Kitty pajamas, just flipping through the channels when the doorbell rang. I glanced over at the clock. 1:34 a.m. Which meant one of two things—either Eva had lost her keys or there was urgent club business. I was betting on the latter, since Eva hadn't come home after my father had left her naked and crying on their bedroom floor, leaving me to clean up another one of his messes. Tossing aside my blanket, I shuffled quickly through the family room, the living room, and into the foyer, where I simultaneously flipped on the hallway and porch lights.

On my tiptoes, I squinted into the peephole . . . and froze.

Ripper.

What was he doing here?

I placed my suddenly shaking hand over my pounding heart and tried not to hyperventilate.

Was he here to see me? Or had he been sent here?

And if he was here to see me, for what? To make sure I hadn't told anyone about what happened at the lake? To have sex with me again?

I squeezed my eyes shut, mentally berating myself for that errant thought, and how my body had warmed at the mere suggestion of his body . . . and my body . . . and—

"Danny," Ripper called out, sounding annoyed, knocking loudly on the door. "I know you're standin' there and I ain't got time for this bullshit. Club's on lockdown and I'm here to bring you in."

Oh.

Oh.

Feeling stupid and strangely hurt, I flipped the lock and swung open the door. With his stature—those broad shoulders, his legs spread, thickly muscled arms folded across his chest—he practically took up the whole doorway.

"I need to change," I muttered, quickly turning around before he had the chance to see my embarrassment.

I had one foot on the bottom stair when Ripper's large, warm hand wrapped around my bicep and squeezed gently.

"We should talk," he said quietly.

"Okay," I whispered as tears unexpectedly formed. I knew what was coming and I didn't want to hear it. The past year of my life had been nothing but one disappointment after another and I wasn't sure how much more I could take. The night at the lake had broken the seemingly never-ending cycle of letdowns. I'd felt free and happy and young again for the first time in a long time, and now he was going to ruin it.

I hated that Ripper had that ability. That somehow what had happened between us had given him power over my emotions. I wanted to take it back, I wanted not to care, but more than that, I wanted to understand why I did care so much.

"Hey," he muttered, roughly turning me around to face him. "Why the fuck are you cryin'?"

Feeling pathetic, I blinked up at him through blurry eyes. "I hate lockdown," I mumbled.

His brow rose. "You're cryin' 'cause you hate lockdown?"

Oh my God, this was the single most horrible conversation I'd ever had in my entire life. I wanted the floor to open up and suck me into another dimension. A dimension where Ripper didn't exist.

"Yes," I said, trying to pull away from his hold on me but his grip only tightened.

"Danny, fuckin' talk to me," he said gruffly. "I'm goin' crazy not knowin' what the fuck is goin' on."

I gaped up at him. He was what? Crazy? Why? And what did that mean? Crazy as in he wished it never happened? Or crazy because he wanted it to happen again? Or crazy because—

"Danny!" he yelled, shaking me. "You on drugs?"

I snapped back to the present. "No. I was thinking."

"Care to share?" he growled.

No, I did not.

"No."

"No? Are you fuckin' kiddin' me?" He glared down at me. "First you're trickin' me into fuckin' you and then you're leavin' me in the dark, scared shitless that your old man is gonna be breakin' down my fuckin' door any goddamned second, and now you're burstin' into tears and still not tellin' me what the motherfuck is goin' on!"

My mouth fell open. Did he actually just say that? Did he seriously just say that I—

"Tricked you!" I screamed, yanking out of his grip and scrambling backward up the stairs, slapping at his hand as he tried to grab for me again. "You dragged *me* out of the lake!"

"Only 'cause you were fuckin' beggin' for it!" he yelled.

My mind raced to keep up with my quickly rising anger. Ripper, it seemed, had a knack for stripping me of all self-control, leaving me unable to manage my thoughts in his presence both sexually and emotionally. He somehow had the ability to bring out the very worst in me and magnify it times a million, leaving me irrational, saying and doing things I normally wouldn't.

It was completely and totally unfair.

"You are insane!" I screamed. "Just because you regret it doesn't mean you have to put all the blame on me!"

He was on me before I had the chance to blink, forcing me into a sitting position on the stairs and slapping a hand down on either side of me. He leaned down until our noses were practically touching.

"Baby," he growled. "I ain't puttin' all the blame on you. I'm blamin' that killer fuckin' body and beautiful as fuck face, too."

I opened my mouth but quickly closed it. What did someone say to that, anyway? Thank you? Screw you? Not that I could speak. I was too busy concentrating on the proximity of our bodies, touching in some places, nearly touching in others, and before I knew what I was doing, I was arching up and pushing myself against him. Almost instantly he shot away from me, muttering curses and running his hands wildly through his unbound hair.

"Don't look at me like that," he said through his teeth, glaring down at me.

My face heated. Could this get any worse? I didn't think so.

"That's what that bikini bullshit was all about, yeah? You were tryin' for me again, weren't you. You that hard up for cock, Danny? You coulda just said something. You already know, baby, I ain't hard to get."

Apparently it could get worse. As humiliation flooded me, tears burned in my eyes. "Could you be any more disgusting?" I said bitterly.

"Yeah," he shot back. "I could. So why don't you clue me in as to why a girl like you is tryin' for a disgusting fuck like me?"

"Because I liked it!" I shouted, raising my arms in frustration. "Because up until a minute ago when you decided to be a total jerk, I liked you too!"

Ripper went from shifting irritably to standing completely still. "You liked me," he repeated dumbly.

"Not anymore!" I yelled, jumping to my feet. "Now I hate you!"

He blinked and I bit down on my bottom lip, angry at myself for putting my feelings out there, knowing he was going to stomp all over them.

"Say something," I whispered. "Please."

Years passed, it seemed, before Ripper spoke again.

"You're a liar," he said quietly, watching me closely. "I don't get it and I'm thinkin' that you might actually be on drugs or maybe you took a blow to the head recently, but either fuckin' way, baby, you ain't hatin' on me. Not at all."

I felt my entire body deflate with painfully embarrassing defeat. Why was he doing this to me? I'd done nothing to him.

"You actually want it again," he continued, smirking. "Don't you?"

My voice was a hoarse whimper. "Stop making fun of me."

His amusement vanished and he shook his head. "No, baby, I'm not. I'm tryin' to figure out whether I'm gonna slap some sense into you or fuck the shit outta you."

My mouth fell open. Now, what did that mean? God, he was so confusing.

"Shit," he muttered, scrubbing a hand over his face. "Shit, I shouldn't have said that . . ." He trailed off, mumbling a rainbow of curses.

His hand dropped listlessly from his face and my stomach fluttered nervously. Ripper had just admitted that he wanted me again.

He wanted me.

And I wanted him.

Judging by the look on his face, he wasn't going to say anything else. Whatever happened next, if anything, was going to have to be on me. He was purposely leaving himself open, vulnerable, to what I wanted.

I just needed the courage to jump way out of my comfort zone and make the next move. Something I had never, ever done before.

If I didn't take advantage of this opportunity, I doubted I was ever going to get another chance like this one.

Oh my God, I couldn't do this.

Anabeth could do this, but I couldn't.

I didn't know how. What did I say? How did I say it?

I wiped my sweating hands on my pajama pants and swallowed hard.

What would Anabeth say?

Ha. What wouldn't Anabeth say?

"Fuck me," I blurted out breathlessly.

Ripper's nostrils flared and I didn't waste time waiting for his answer. I jumped down the last two steps and grabbed his shirt.

"I want you," I whispered, closing my eyes, just breathing him in, letting the leather and cigarette smoke and the light undertone of soap-scented skin fill my nostrils.

"Fuuuuuck," he groaned, pulling away, pushing me backward. "I . . . shit . . . your old man . . . baby, I—"

"He won't find out," I said quickly, slapping his hands away and returning to my position pressed firmly up against him.

Even as he hesitated, his hand lifted, hovering near my cheek. Making the decision for him, I leaned into his touch, feeling both exhausted and relieved. What I'd said had taken every ounce of my willpower.

He stared down at me and I stared up at him, knowing the exact moment he made up his mind. His hard, tormented expression eased infinitely as the tension holding his body captive instantly evaporated.

"Jesus," he whispered, running his thumb along my mouth, tugging it open, gently stroking my bottom lip.

"Why can't I say no to you?"

My breath caught. *Oh my God, was it going to happen? Were Ripper and I going to happen again?*

His hand moved, sliding slowly back over my cheek, my ear, and then his fingers were gliding through my hair and his other hand was traveling down my spine, mesmerizing me into thoughtless submission, making me half delirious with this single-minded need.

Then his hand was moving up my side, along my ribs, sliding over my breast. He brushed his thumb across my nipple and . . .

All over my body, nerve endings flared to life. I wanted this; I wanted this suddenly so badly, my body had begun to ache for more of him.

"We do this," he growled softly. "Means you're in my bed and no one else's, yeah?"

The trapped air shuddered through my lungs and exploded into my quivering stomach.

He wanted more . . . after this? Or . . . he wanted only me? Or he wanted me to be with only him while he did . . . what? Is that what that meant? God, I really needed to start asking some of these questions out loud so I didn't just stand there staring at him like some sort of speechless freak. But then again, did I really care what he meant? This was what I wanted, right? I wanted him and this and I wanted it right now and everything else was just details that could be worked out later. Or not, because at this precise moment I didn't care about the details but instead about the hands on me, all over me.

"Ripper," I whimpered, arching my back, pushing my flesh into his hand. "Please—"

His mouth crashed down on mine and, oh my God . . . his tongue and my tongue and . . . Oh God, oh God, oh God . . .

Suddenly, Ripper pulled away from me and turned around. I panicked, feeling confused and worried until I saw him pull his cell phone from his leathers and bring it to his ear.

"Yo . . . Yeah, I'm here now . . . yeah . . . yeah . . . She's packin', Prez . . . fuck . . . yeah, I know what the fuck lock-down means, I'm gonna get her there."

Prez. He was talking to my father.

I winced, feeling like we'd been caught red-handed, that somehow my father would know what we'd been doing.

"Danny!" Ripper hissed. My eyes shot to him. He was holding the phone away from him and gesturing wildly to the stairs. Oops. Whirling around, I bolted up the stairs, burst into my room, and quickly changed out of my pajamas and into a short pink sundress and my cowboy boots. After throwing some clothing and makeup into my shoulder bag, I checked my reflection, smoothed my hair, and darted back down the stairs.

Ripper had already gone outside. I could hear the rumble of his Harley pipes from the foyer.

Hurriedly, I punched in the house alarm, flipped the lights off, and locked the door behind me.

He watched me rush down the walkway toward him, his expression disconcerting. Had he changed his mind already? Had talking to my father triggered his guilt?

Anger toward the man who'd taken a backseat role to my life the second his own had hit a road bump, surged to the surface. He kept ruining everything and now he was going to ruin this for me.

"Ripper?" I whispered, stopping beside him. His hard gaze met mine and my stomach flip-flopped. He looked a million times different than he had inside the house. Nothing remained of the hungry expression he'd been wearing only moments earlier.

"Fuck," he muttered, startling me as he reached out and wrapped his arm around my waist. I stumbled forward as he hauled me up against him.

"Meant what I said," he said, dropping his head, pressing his forehead to mine. "You're with me, you're with only me. I ain't gonna share you with some teenage asshat whose dick ain't full grown."

Teenage asshat? Ha. Fat chance. My father had ruined any chance of me dating any male my age when he'd threatened my one and only boyfriend. No one wanted anything to do with me after that, leaving me to wonder what sort of pain and torture my father had threatened him with. But Ripper didn't need to know any of that. He was jealous and I liked him that way.

"What about you?" I asked, before I could remind myself that the details didn't matter, that this was what I wanted and I'd no right to be demanding anything from a man like Ripper. But damn it, I was fooling myself if I thought I was going to be okay being with him again, if he was just going to turn around and be with other people.

I did not want to share.

I would, *that was how much I wanted him*, but I didn't want to have to. Even more so, I didn't want him to want to.

I wanted to be enough for him, but at the same time I wasn't stupid. I knew what the boys did at the club, or on runs while their old ladies were at home with their kids.

If I wanted this man, I already knew what would be expected of me. Was I prepared for all that came with it? No. But I was a fast learner and everything about Ripper had my body screaming *he's worth it, he's worth it.*

He pulled away from me, his expression serious, yet full of unabashed need.

And just like that, seeing that, knowing that look was for me, that it was all mine, the details no longer mattered.

"I ain't never did this shit before," he said quietly and I could hear the internal hesitation, the insecurity lacing his words. And, *God*, it only made me want him even more.

"But I ain't never wanted pussy like I want yours and . . . Danny, I ain't gonna touch another bitch, don't even wanna. Fuck, baby, since that night at the lake, I haven't done shit but jerk myself off, thinkin' of you."

How could someone so gruff and crude be so soft at the same time? Ripper was perfect. Perfectly flawed and everything I hadn't known I'd wanted in a man until this . . . him . . . us.

He only wanted me. Only me.

"Wish I knew what was goin' on in that head of yours," he said quietly.

"Nothing," I whispered. "I'm just . . . I think, I'm . . ."

Just say it. Say it, you chicken! Just say it!

"Happy," I finished breathlessly. And excited and nervous and pretty close to bursting at the seams.

CHAPTER 11

RIPPER LOVED RIDING. IT WAS ONE OF HIS FEW ESCAPES from thinking about the hours of torture he'd spent at the hands of Frankie. So when he wasn't working or sleeping or eating or fucking, he was riding. Constantly. No plan, no destination, no schedule . . . just him, his bike, and the open road. Riding gave him the peace of mind that nothing else could, not green, not booze, not pussy, nothing. Riding cleared his messed-up head and cleaned his shit-stained soul. For a little while.

With nothing but road stretched out in front of him and more road behind him, it was just him and his baby, completely in tune with each other. The past didn't exist, his future didn't matter; it was only right then, right there, she was him, he was her, they had melded together, had become not man and machine but one entity, lost to an endless stretch of road.

It was freedom and there wasn't anything more beautiful than freedom.

And all that freedom had just been flushed down the shitter.

All he could feel was her arms wrapped around his middle, her hands resting just above his groin, her tight little body pressed into his, her muscular thighs locked around his hips.

From the moment Danny had climbed on behind him, he'd been hyperaware of everything about her, every slight movement, every part of her that was touching a part of him.

His heart pounded as wave after wave of heat rolled through him, blurring his vision, leaving him fairly certain he was going to run them off the road if he didn't get his shit together.

Fuck me, she'd said.

He was ninety percent positive that had been the first time Danielle West had dropped the f-bomb, making those two little words even hotter than they would have been without that knowledge.

Then Deuce had called and torn him a new one because he hadn't gotten Danny back to the club yet. That's when he decided this shit between them, whatever it was, whatever was going to happen, was going to have to wait until after lockdown, until they could be alone again . . .

. . . until her thighs clenched and her fingers began creeping down his abdomen, to the edge of his T-shirt where she paused, fingering the threadbare material.

His dick went rock solid. Probably punched a hole

straight through his leathers; he was that hard.

No. No, no, no. Not now. He had to get her to the club before Deuce called again. If she kept this shit up, he was going to throw caution to the wind and be inside of her in about three seconds.

No? Who was he kidding? He was so fucked. Done for and completely fucked.

He wasn't going to make it to the club. He wanted that pussy so bad he could fucking taste it. And he couldn't keep pretending this was just about pussy either. It was more than pussy. It was Danny. Her pussy, yeah, and there was something else.

Ripper had been walking around life pissed off, not giving a shit about anything, until he'd made the mistake of fucking a girl he'd never given a second thought to before and everything had changed. Suddenly he cared about what was going to happen next, wondering when Deuce was going to find out, whether he was going to get killed or not, wondering where Danny was when she wasn't at the club . . . what she was doing, if she were hanging out with some other dude, and feeling murderous at the thought. Wondering if she were going as motherfucking crazy as he was.

He wasn't pissed off anymore, either. He was something else entirely. He was . . .

What the fuck was he?

Fuck it. Whatever he was feeling, he didn't want to ignore it. He wanted more of it; he wanted to own it.

Right. Now.

Fuck that black bitch, fucking threatening him. Fuck lockdown.

He wasn't losing this.

Caution met wind and he pulled off the dark, deserted highway onto a patch of grass and cut the engine.

Neither of them spoke.

Or moved.

They just breathed.

Hers, quick and short.

His, loud and heavy.

Just breathing.

"Ripper?" she whispered.

Aw, Jesus, that sweet, sweet voice . . .

. . . and the angelic face and the fucking body that owned that voice.

"Yeah, baby?" he asked, his voice hoarse.

Her hands slipped under his shirt, her nails dug into the skin on his stomach, and he stopped breathing altogether.

"Please," she whispered.

Ripper moved fast, jumped off his bike and hopped back on facing her. She pulled up the material of her dress and he yanked open his leathers, lifting her over top of him, moving her underwear to one side and positioning himself at her entrance.

There was just some shit you didn't get a say in.

He knew that better than most.

He'd lost his parents at seventeen, his only family.

At twenty-seven he'd been captured by Frankie, tortured for twelve hours. He'd lost his eye, a lot of fucking skin, and pretty much all of his self-respect.

Both of those events had drastically changed the course of his life, each one a wrecking ball that had come crashing into his world, forcing him to watch as everything around him shattered and fell to pieces at his feet.

That's how this shit was with Danny.

It was an accident, a mistake, it was the wrong place at the wrong time kind of shit that had quickly turned into a catastrophe of epic proportions.

If she'd just been pussy, if he'd fucked her at the lake then forgotten about it . . .

But Danny was different.

A game changer.

She wasn't pussy, she was damned beautiful and everything he'd ever wanted in a woman but hadn't realized until he held her in his arms.

She was the reason his world was about to shatter again.

"Ripper . . . *oh my God*." She pushed back against him, trying to take all of him inside of her in one thrust.

Yeah, she wanted him, the looming wrecking ball.

And fuck him, he wanted her more than he'd ever wanted anything else, and the wrecking ball swung.

So he took her, grabbed her thighs, and slammed her down onto him . . . and that wrecking ball came crashing through.

God, sweet fucking Jesus; it was better than he'd remembered. She was tight, wet, and warm and fit him like a fucking glove, kissing him and touching him as if he didn't have scars, not avoiding them, not lavishing attention on them; he was starting to think she couldn't see them.

She was making him feel whole again.

Yeah, no way was he losing this.

"Ripper," she cried. "*Ripper* . . ." Her head lolled to the right and her eyes rolled back.

Knowing she was about to come, he gripped her

hips, digging his fingertips into her backside, and began slamming up into her, harder and harder, rocking against her faster and faster until her body locked up tight and her cries turned into breathy, panting whimpers and her pussy clenched around his cock, again and again. He kept going, hard and fast, milking her orgasm.

And . . . *ah, God*, she was coming again, her muscles were contracting around him, the incredible feeling spurring him into increasing his already ball-breaking pace.

That's when it happened.

His hair was soaked with sweat, his jaw locked, his teeth clenched, his grip on her bruising, his hips powering back and forth, his cock slamming up into her, again and again.

It was so motherfucking good; she looked like a goddamn sex angel, face flushed and breathing hard, whimpering and crying as he took her hard and fast and she felt like heaven, tight and soft and smooth.

He felt the walls of his world start to shake and the bricks began to fall . . . one by one until it was a free-for-all and suddenly he could breathe again when he hadn't even realized he'd been holding his breath. Breath he'd been holding for the last five years.

Free from the ropes, cupping his right eye socket, Ripper staggered to his feet. Blurrily he looked around the empty warehouse until he locked on a door. Limping, his right leg dragging, he hobbled as fast as he could across the dirty floor and collapsed against the door. Trembling, he tried the handle and nearly fell over when the door pushed open. Looking around, he had no idea where he was. The last thing he remembered, he'd been overseeing a drop-off in Vegas when Frankie nabbed him, coldcocked him, and he'd woken up here.

Cursing, he dragged himself outside onto the gravel driveway.

A creak sounded from inside the warehouse and, gripping his right thigh, he tried to walk faster.

"Frankie!" a voice bellowed. "Horseman's on the loose!"

Fuck, fuck, fuck! He limped faster.

Footsteps pounded behind him, growing closer.

A road. He could see a road. Crying out, he amped up his speed, bit straight through his lip trying to stave off the pain.

He'd just breached the tree line, could see a pair of headlights off in the distance, when he felt the barrel of a gun jammed into the back of his skull.

"Where you think you're goin'?" Frankie laughed. "Date ain't over yet. Haven't even gotten to the best part. Where you're beggin' me not to end you."

The headlights grew closer, the rumbling engine of the truck louder.

He'd never beg for anything. Not a motherfucking thing. Not even for his life.

"Turn around slow," Frankie said. "And—"

Ripper, with the last of his quickly waning strength and pure determination to die on his own terms, leaped into the road, directly in front of the approaching truck and impact was immediate. As his body flew through the air, he closed his eyes and thought, Fuck you, Frankie.

He was jumping in front of that truck again, only this time he wasn't trying to die on his own terms.

He was trying to start living again. So he dug his fingertips even deeper into her skin, kissed her harder than he'd ever kissed, fucked her with a determination he didn't wholly understand and . . .

. . . and something inside of him began to ache. It was painful, yeah, but it was painfully . . . good.

He wanted more.

More and more until there was nothing left of his old world until everything felt as good as she felt and fit as perfectly as she fit him, and so he closed his eyes and thought, *Fuck you, Frankie.*

That's when it happened.

He lost control for the first time during sex and finished hard, still inside of her.

What the repercussions of that were going to be, he surprisingly didn't care. He was too busy staring at the beautiful girl sitting astride him, feeling clearer and freer than he'd felt in a very long time.

Danny's eyes blinked slowly open and, Jesus Christ, she was covered in sweat, had tears streaming down her cheeks, her makeup smeared and her face flushed from sex, and she was smiling, the sweetest dimpled smile he'd ever seen.

She was strikingly beautiful and sexy as shit and . . . good; she was a good, good girl. She was everything a man like him didn't deserve to be inside of.

"I like you, Ripper," she whispered, sliding her arms over his shoulders, threading her fingers through the hair at his nape, causing a ripple of tiny, pleasant tingles across his skin and a warmth inside of him, the likes of which he'd never felt before.

"Yeah, beautiful girl," he whispered. "I'm feelin' you too."

He meant it too. He was over his head into her and he

knew it. He didn't just want to fuck her, he didn't just want her in his bed . . .

He wanted her on the back of his bike.

Yeah, he wanted to lay claim to Danielle West, ink his name on her body and slap an old lady patch on her ass. And worse, he wanted the world to know it.

It was at that precise moment that Ripper knew his world had shattered for a third time, had crumbled and turned to dust at his feet.

Nothing from here on out would ever again be the same.

CHAPTER 12

I HATED LOCKDOWN. EVERY SINGLE ONE HAD ALWAYS completely sucked.

Brothers, their old ladies, their kids, young and old, all piled inside the club, filling up every nook and cranny. There was no seat unoccupied, no bed not taken, and in a warehouse roughly the size of a department store, most of which was used for locked storage, there wasn't a whole lot of room.

But this time . . .

It was day four of prison by Hell's Horsemen association and there wasn't anywhere else on earth that I wanted to be other than right there, locked up in a crowded, overheated building . . . with Ripper.

Seated at the U-shaped bar, my elbows on the counter, chin propped in my hands, I was watching Ripper move across the room. He was shirtless, barefoot, wearing only his half-buttoned leathers and his cut. His blond hair was pulled back midskull in a messy ponytail and a cigarette dangled from his lips. My gaze traveled down his big body, lingering on the trail of blond hair that disappeared inside his pants, and my heart started beating faster.

I'd never been so intensely attracted to a man before, never felt so aroused in all my life, and it wasn't just when he was touching me, it was all the time. All I had to do was think about being with him, and I was crossing my legs and squeezing my thighs together.

He was an incredibly beautiful man. The scars just forced you to look a little harder to see what was still there, and what was still there was the squared, strong bone structure of a Greek god, the heavily muscled stature of a boxer, and a deviously sexy smile.

We'd spent the past three days sneaking off together, deftly avoiding the club security cameras, and finding secret places to be together. The kitchen pantry, the communal showers, the shed behind the clubhouse . . .

I was waiting for Ripper's signal, eagerly anticipating day four of being together.

"This sucks." Tegen pouted, walking up next to me and folding her arms across her chest. Startled out of my Ripper stare-a-thon, I glanced over at her and winced.

Even her attempt at dressing like a girl had somehow gone hideously wrong. Her plain black sundress hung loosely on her, the straps had fallen off her shoulders revealing two white bra straps, she'd spilled something on the skirt of the dress earlier and hadn't bothered to wipe it off, and . . . I looked down at her feet. She was wearing flip-flops. Not cute, stylish ones but a plain pair of black foam flip-flops that I wouldn't have been caught dead wearing, not even at the beach.

"What does he see in those fucking sluts?" Tegen hissed.

Knowing she was talking about Cage, I started rolling my eyes until I saw where she was looking. It wasn't just Cage talking to a pair of club whores, it was Cage and Ripper. I shot into an upright position. He wasn't giving me the signal because he was too busy talking to . . . those *whores*?

Jealousy swamped me, followed closely by panic. He'd lied. He was still interested in other women and here I was forced to sit and watch it happen right in front of me, just like Dorothy had to watch Jase with his wife while she pined for him from afar. Oh God, I couldn't do this. I couldn't be an old lady or, even worse, a secret old lady that no one knew about.

Without warning he glanced my way, a small smile on his face that instantly fell the minute we locked eyes. I bit down on my bottom lip and attempted to school my expression, hoping my inner turmoil wasn't showing through.

I knew I'd failed when his eyes narrowed.

The next thing I knew Ripper was crossing the room, heading toward the bar, toward me. Taking the space to the left of me, he leaned forward, placing his forearms on the counter top. I went rigid, suddenly completely at a loss as to what I should be doing with myself, where I should be looking. God, I didn't even know what to do with my hands or how I should be sitting. He'd made a point to never be less than twenty feet away from me, and this new development had caught me completely off guard.

"Yo," he said, nodding at ZZ who, as usual, was playing bartender while he kept an eye on the security monitors.

ZZ lifted his chin. "Tequila?"

"Naw, dude, gimme a brew."

Nodding, ZZ reached below the bar and pulled a bottle of beer from one of the small refrigerators underneath. Popping the cap off on the bar, he handed it to Ripper, who took a prolonged swallow during which I moved my hands from the bar to my lap and back to the bar again. Twice.

"Uh, are you okay?" Tegen asked, eyeing me queerly. The expression on her face clearly showed that she thought I'd completely lost my mind.

I nodded jerkily. "Yes."

Her nose wrinkled. "Yeah, sure. So, you're suddenly acting like you have Tourette's for no good reason?"

I glared at her. Just because I wasn't dressed like a secondhand clothing reject who'd had her hair done by an electrical socket, and didn't pout in corners staring at a guy who'd never give me a second glance, didn't mean she had to hate on me.

"I'm fine," I gritted out.

"Right," she muttered. "Fine, whatever, no need to give me your prissy angry face."

I gaped at her, furious, Ripper's close vicinity instantly forgotten. Who did she think she was?

"What is wrong with you?" I demanded. "Why can't you ever just be . . . *normal*?"

Her eyes narrowed. "Normal?" she asked, her tone scathing. "What the fuck is normal, Danny? This? The club? My mom crying in the corner, staring at Jase and Chrissy? Or Adriana over there," she said gesturing to where Mick's wife was sitting. "She's talking to her husband's favorite club whore and she doesn't even know it. Is that normal?"

Whether Tegen actually cared about the virtueless bikers and the lack of morality that went on inside the club was debatable. Her bad moods, as often as they were, nine times out of ten were usually related to only one biker. My brother. If she wasn't angry, which was rare, she was just outright sad.

"Girls."

Ripper's voice was low but harsh and both our heads swiveled toward him. Using his bottle of beer, he gestured between us. "Lockdown's wearin' on everyone, yeah?"

Tegen sighed noisily. "If by wearing on us you mean driving us all to the brink of insanity from having to watch you all drink yourselves into oblivion, belch and fart and whore it up with whatever walks by, then yes, I'm a little worn."

Both ZZ and Ripper burst out laughing. Leaning over the bar to ruffle her hair, ZZ grinned at her. "You're one badass little motherfucker, you know that?"

She swatted at his arm, trying to duck away from his hand. "Piss off!" she yelled, throwing a stack of bar coasters across the bar, missing ZZ by several feet.

"Danny."

Swallowing hard, I glanced over at Ripper.

"You're thinkin' again," he said quietly. "And whatever you're thinkin' you really ain't likin'."

"I'm not," I protested. "I'm totally, completely, one hundred percent fine."

"You're not," he said. "You're readin' into shit you shouldn't and makin' up all sorts of crazy inside that head of yours."

Damn him.

"Fine," I hissed, slapping my hand down on the bar. "You want to know what I'm thinking about, I'll tell you. I don't like being a secret, that's what. I don't like that those stupid sluts can just walk up to you, thinking they can touch you. If they knew about me, that wouldn't happen when I was around."

Realizing what I'd just said, and that I'd said it not so quietly in a room full of people who would undoubtedly be interested to know why I was having such a personal conversation with Ripper, I slapped my hand over my mouth and shut my eyes in dismay.

When I braved looking up again, I found the club exactly as I'd left it. No one was paying me any attention, Tegen was still yelling at ZZ, Ripper was still beside me, still leaning over the bar, still looking right at me. Smiling.

"You tryin' to tell me you're my old lady, Danny?"

Yes.

"No," I whispered and watched his smile turn into a full-fledged grin.

"Liar," he whispered back.

"I hate you."

"Liar."

"Now I really hate you."

Standing up straight, he slid his empty bottle across the bar toward ZZ, using the action to lean into me. "Five minutes," he breathed over the top of my head. "Your room."

Then he left me sitting there, staring after him, feeling like a complete moron for freaking out.

For the next five minutes I stayed where I was, my

stomach fluttering with anticipation, watching the clock on the wall. After the longest five minutes of my entire life had gone by, I slid slowly out of my seat and began navigating through the groups of people. Once I'd cleared the hallway, filled with exhilaration and anticipation, I started running to where I knew he'd be waiting. My bedroom. I don't know how he did it—avoid the cameras, somehow knowing where to step and how to time it so his entrance to my room wouldn't be recorded—and I didn't care. All that mattered was that he was there in my room waiting for me and I was—

I burst through my door and nearly crashed into him. Grabbing my arm, he swung me further inside and kicked the door shut with his boot, locking it quickly.

"Why do you do this shit?" he demanded, looking me up and down as he walked me backward.

"Do what?" I asked, playing dumb.

"You know what," he muttered, shoving me backward, already unzipping his leathers.

I scooted backward over my bed, bunching my skirt up around my waist, then quickly wiggling out of my underwear.

"Shirt off," he growled, staring at the bared lower half of my body, slowly stroking himself. I watched him touch himself, growing harder as he continued to gaze at what I was freely offering him, turning myself on by doing so.

Once my camisole was gone, Ripper took a long, leisurely look up and down my naked body, further propelling my hormones into overdrive.

"Don't know why you're thinkin' I want club ass when I got all this waitin' on me."

"Sorry," I said. "I just . . . got jealous."

"Yeah," he muttered, using his body to push me onto my back again, then he was propping himself over top of me and pushing a finger up inside me. "I know."

Moaning, I reached up, wrapped my arms around his neck, trying to pull him down to kiss me but he turned away.

"I wanna watch you," he said softly, adding another finger.

Pure lust shot from the apex of my thighs and straight up my body, exploding in my stomach and lungs, making me shiver and clench tightly around his fingers.

The things this man made me feel just by speaking was unreal. At times I wanted to weep from the sheer sensation of never before experienced feelings that I knew had already wrecked me for any other man.

"Fuck, you're beautiful," he muttered, increasing the speed of his finger thrusts.

"Are you going on the run to North Dakota?" I panted.

"No."

"Mick said my father's going once he gets back from New York."

"Yeah . . . Danny?"

"Hmm?"

"Can we not talk about your old man right now?"

"But I was thinking . . ." I trailed off, breathless.

"Never good," he muttered and added another finger.

My eyelids fluttered as I tried to stay on task.

"Eyes on me," he growled.

"Mostly everyone is gonna be gone," I whispered, trying to focus on his face. "So I was . . . *oh my God* . . ."

My orgasm hit me hard and for a moment I forgot all about what I was talking about. I'd never had an orgasm before Ripper, before that night at the lake, that hadn't been a result of using my own hand. The difference between a self-induced orgasm and an orgasm given by a man is like comparing a rainy day and a rainstorm. Rain was a sure thing, you knew exactly what you were going to get: a clean and crisp, both sweet and refreshing experience. But rainstorms were unpredictable, they were riddled with surprises, messy and wet; they were something you had no control over.

Rainstorms brought you to your knees, soaking you in uncontrollable need, lightning flashing before your eyes while you dug your fingers deep into the earth, trying to hold on; unable to tell which was louder . . . the thunder roaring in your ears or the pounding of your heart.

Ripper was my rainstorm, my skin-drenching frenzy, where you couldn't tell right from left, where all you could feel was the phenomenon exploding throughout your body, feverishly burning through you even as it pleasurably cooled.

I came back to awareness as he rolled me onto my stomach and lifted my hips.

"You were thinking?" he asked, laughing softly as he positioned himself at my entrance.

I had to work fast. He was nearly inside me and once he was moving inside me, all would be lost.

"That we could spend a couple days together at your house and—"

I cried out as he slammed inside of me and his hand slapped down across my mouth.

"Shh," he whispered, pulling out of me only to slam back inside. I cried out again, this time the sound mostly muffled by his hand, only to end up crying out again and again as his body repeatedly met mine, harder and faster and harder still until I was screaming against his hand, another orgasm pulsing through my already over-sensitized flesh.

Flipping me over, he slid back inside of me, but before I could react, his tongue shot out, stealing all sound from my mouth and the breath from my lungs and we kissed and kissed, faster and harder, as he worked my body into a needy hysteria, leaving me begging to be sated.

. . . And he did just that.

Staring down at me, Ripper was growling—honest-to-God throaty growls were erupting from deep within his chest, vibrating against my breasts, and I was pretty sure it was the most wonderful sound I'd ever heard in my entire life—as I stared up at him feeling . . .

Just feeling.

I felt dizzy, drunk with need, and beautiful and wanted and alive.

I never wanted it to end.

"Goddamn," Ripper groaned, feeling his orgasm closing in. "Good goddamn, Danielle."

"Oh my God," Danny panted, grinding her hips upward into him, grabbing at him, driving him fucking nuts with how crazy into him she was. "Oh my God . . ."

His grip on her hair and ass tightened. "Gonna . . . come . . . baby, gonna . . ."

Biting down on Danny's lower lip, he swallowed her

whimpers and cries as he finished hard, still thrusting.

He waited there a moment, still deep inside of her, watching her beautiful blue eyes blink up at him, her nostrils flare with heavy, needy breaths, felt the moisture of her mouth against his.

When his breathing had returned to normal, he pulled out of her, watching while her soaked pussy clenched, as everything he'd just released inside of her began sliding out onto her pink comforter. No matter how perversely narcissistic, it was hands down the hottest thing he'd ever seen in his entire life.

And fucking without a condom. Fuck him, it felt so damn good, wasn't anything he'd ever done before or been able to do with the dirty bitches who hung around the club. But with Danny he wasn't worried; the girl was clean, an idiot with half a brain would know that, and she was on the pill. Which apparently was some big, bad secret that only she and Eva knew about and after telling him, made him promise not to spill the beans to Deuce or Cage.

Yeah. Right. That was the first thing that had gone through his head. *Tell the brother and father of the bitch I'm fucking that she's secretly on birth control.*

Sure . . . Maybe if he had a death wish.

Rolling off her, he fell onto his back beside her. "Jesus," he muttered, staring up at the ceiling. "That was—"

"Awesome?" she suggested.

He glanced over at her and smirked.

"It is always like this?" She sighed happily, smiling at him. "So . . . so . . . sexalicious?"

He almost laughed but a wave of realization knocked him straight on his metaphorical ass. No. It wasn't always like this. It wasn't ever like this.

Sex had never been this goddamn good before.

"Because the other guy I—"

"No," he growled, frowning at her. The last thing he wanted to think about was some asshat up inside what was his. "It ain't ever like this."

Her smile widened. "Then we got lucky," she whispered.

Ripper stared at her, feeling all kinds of weird shit happening inside of him, shit that was going down a whole lot faster than it should be, shit that should be scaring the ever-loving crap out of him.

But it wasn't.

"Yeah, baby," he whispered back, pulling her into the crook of his arm. "We sure as fuck did."

"So, can we go to your house?" she asked, kissing her way up his chest.

Threading his fingers through a handful of her hair, he closed his eyes, enjoying the feel of her mouth on him. His house? His house, or rather his one-bedroom cabin in the middle of the mountains, was his sanctuary. Where he went when he couldn't take one more second of the bullshit always surrounding the club, the constant noise, people always coming and going.

Cupping the back of her head, he kissed her hard. "We'll talk about it later," he muttered against her mouth as he debated on whether he wanted to fuck her doggy first and then have her ride him, or make her ride him first and then flip her onto her knees. "Got more important things to do right now and not a whole lot of time."

CHAPTER 13

Uncomfortable, Deuce shifted irritably in one of the two high-back wooden chairs Preacher had in his office.

With his hands steepled in front of him, his elbows propped on top of his monstrous, archaic, wooden desk, Preacher nodded gravely. "I agree. Big Jay's gotta go. I've 'bout had it with his fuckin' games and now this shit, hittin' the Horsemen up when I've been payin' them more than enough just to let our boys cross the fuckin' street in their territory."

Deuce stared at him, his head not really into the conversation but instead wondering how his boys would feel about him handing them over to Preacher and consolidating both clubs. Preacher was a strong leader; he took good care of his boys and their families. He would do the same for the Horsemen.

He could leave then. Take to the road knowing Eva, his kids, and his club would all be looked after.

"I'll kill you," Preacher growled and his head jerked up.

"What?"

"I said, I'll fuckin' kill you if you hurt either of them girls of mine."

What the fuck? How the fuck? Was the guy a fucking psychic?

"What the fuck are you talkin' about?"

"You think I don't know what a man looks like when he's thinkin' 'bout runnin'? Seen it a hundred different times on a hundred different men. Life starts takin' its toll, they've seen too much shit, done too much shit, and suddenly they're drownin' their bullshit in booze and pussy, and their marriages are fallin' apart, and they're hittin' the bottle even harder, and then they're dippin' into shit they shouldn't. All they wanna do is get on their bike and hit the road, start over, or find a quiet place to curl up and die."

Deuce didn't say anything. He didn't have anything to say. Preacher was dead-on and he was too goddamned tired of everything to argue with the man.

"You think I didn't wanna run?" Preacher shook his head. "You think I wanted to raise a little girl without her mama in a club full of assholes? And after I found out what Frankie had been doin' to my baby, right under my nose? But what fuckin' choice did I have? The day I put this patch on . . ."

Preacher slapped his hand over his "Prez" patch on his cut.

"The day *you* put that patch on was the day you handed

over your life. You ain't just the prez, Deuce, you ain't just runnin' a club, leadin' those boys. It ain't just a responsibility.

"It's *you*, brother; your club, your boys are you. You start bleedin' and they're all gonna bleed with you. The club comes first, you know it, I know it, every man who gets patched in knows it. Don't matter how bad shit gets with your old lady, your girls on the side, your fuckin' kids, you gotta keep goin'. Those boys of yours and their families, *they are your family too*. They ain't just respectin' you or lookin' up to you, they're countin' on you to do right by them. You know this shit, Deuce, the club always—"

"Comes first," he growled, interrupting Preacher. "I fuckin' know."

"Yeah, you know it, but preachin' it ain't livin' it. Time to get back to livin' it."

Fuck. As much as he hated Preacher, mainly because the fucker had shot him twice, he couldn't dispute a single word the man had said.

"Don't get me wrong, I don't like you any more than I liked you when I first saw you pawin' at my underage daughter," Preacher growled. "But for some fuckin' reason she loves you, meanin' I'm keepin' my mouth shut."

Deuce narrowed his eyes. "You call this keepin' your mouth shut?"

Preacher shrugged. "I'm keepin' my finger off the trigger, ain't I?"

Jesus Christ, if Eva ever decided she hated her old man, he was going to be first in line to put this asshole to ground. He might do it anyway, tell Eva he had no clue what happened to Preacher and for all he knew, aliens from outer space had kidnapped the slick bastard.

"You know," Preacher continued, "me and your old man go way back. Knew him when I was just a kid. Knew your mother too, had a goddamned crush on her . . . and those fuckin' dimples of hers—"

"Is there a point to this fuckin' bullshit?" he spat. The last thing he wanted to hear about was Preacher's crush on the mother he'd never gotten to meet.

"Yeah, asshole, and I was gettin' to it. Woulda gotten to it by now if you woulda kept your fuckin' mouth shut."

The two of them glared at each other until Preacher gave first, shaking his head and sighing.

"My point is, Reaper didn't give a fuck about the club, didn't give a fuck about your mother, or your brother's mother, or any of you. All he gave a fuck about was himself and what the club or what his bitches could do for him. He wanted power and money, he used the club to get it, he wanted kids to pass the gavel to, and he used those little girls to get 'em. But when it came down to it, he ain't never gave a fuck. And Deuce, that ain't you. I know you got love for your boys and your family and that's why you're thinkin' runnin' is what's best for 'em all, but I'm tellin' you it ain't. You leave and those boys are gonna fall apart. As for those kids you'll be leavin' behind, you tell me how it felt growin' up with an old man who didn't want ya? All you had was your little brother and when you lost Cas, then what the fuck did you have?"

Fucking shit, thinking about his old man, his mother, and his dead little brother was making it hard to breathe. Deuce rubbed the heel of his palm over his chest in a large circle.

"You had the club," Preacher said. "And you took the

mess your old man left behind and you turned that shit into a brotherhood. You tossed out the garbage, you had your boys pull their shit together, and then you started pulling in more strays then any MC I've ever known. Done my homework on all your boys; I know Dirty and Hawk were starvin' on street corners before you found 'em. Know Cox was stealin' cars for his next meal, and Ripper, seventeen, no family, didn't know jack shit about bikes, and what'd you do? Brought them all home with you and gave 'em all a family. You leave them, you'll be rippin' out the rug from underneath them all and your kids won't even have the club to fall back on. Nobody will have nothin'."

With his arms folded across his chest, Deuce gave Preacher a half-lidded glare. "I really fuckin' hate you," he growled.

His knowing eyes trained on him, Preacher pulled a smoke out from behind his ear and lit it.

"Deuce," he said, exhaling. "The feelin's mutual. Now, I'm gonna tell you what I tell all my boys when they're actin' like fools. Go grab a bottle and a bitch and fuck all that poisonous bullshit outta your system. Then you go home to my daughter and my grandbaby and your kids and your boys, and you fix whatever the fuck is broken. And if you don't, I'm gonna come collect my girls, maybe grab Kami away from that dirty fuckin' spic she married while I'm at it, but as for the rest of 'em, brother, that's your problem."

"Yeah?" he said dryly. "And while I'm drinkin' and fuckin', what the fuck are you gonna be doin' 'bout Big Jay?"

Preacher took another drag off his smoke and shook his head. "I'm postin' the hit tonight. You don't gotta do a damn thing."

With her sleeping toddler straddling her hip, Eva attempted navigating through the front of the club toward the back hall, wanting to leave behind the din of several ongoing conversations, the children crying or complaining, men laughing, women giggling. After five days, the constant noise was painfully bouncing around inside her skull, making her head ache for peace and quiet, and making her stomach churn with constant anxiety.

She'd never before minded lockdowns. In New York, she'd usually spent them in her bedroom, listening to music with Frankie or later, when they were older . . .

Her eyes started to burn and her grip tightened on Ivy.

Frankie.

Turning away from everyone, she closed her eyes . . .

Leaning back against the outside of the Demons' brownstone, tall and broad, his thickly muscled, heavily tattooed arms folded over his chest, stretching the material of his black T-shirt, his long brown hair pulled tightly back, his head cocked to one side, his dark, hungry eyes focused on her, a smile playing on his lips.

"Baby," he said in a low, harsh voice as he crooked two fingers. "Come here."

A cry bubbled up from her aching heart and lodged painfully in her throat. She covered her mouth with her hand, stifling the loud release of air.

No. She wasn't going to think about Frankie. That chapter of her life was over. She'd made sure of that when she'd put a knife through his throat. There hadn't been any other option. Frankie had been too far gone, causing too much pain to everyone he came into contact with; he'd been a walking time bomb.

Somehow Eva had managed to overcome the crippling guilt that killing him had caused. She'd pulled herself out of her pain, and taken control of her life again.

It was Deuce that refused to let it go.

Frankie had done the worst thing he could possibly do to a man like Deuce—a man who would have taken any sort of physical punishment Frankie could have meted out, preferred it actually. But Frankie had known that and instead had rendered Deuce immobile, forced him to watch the woman he loved being fucked by another man, then to take her, leaving him wondering if he was ever going to see her alive again.

To a man like Deuce, what Frankie had done was a punishment far worse than death.

It was also something a man like Deuce wasn't going to forget.

She'd tried . . .

And tried . . .

But she couldn't do it anymore. When it came to Deuce, it felt as if she'd been running in circles her entire life.

It wasn't just her anymore; she couldn't afford to be selfish, to do as she pleased, to let the man in her life do as he pleased. To keep waiting on something that might never happen. She had a daughter who deserved the very best life Eva could give her.

She was leaving.

The decision had been made the night Deuce had left for New York. She was going home, back to her father and the Demons, back to what she'd thought she'd left behind for good in exchange for a life of happiness with the man she loved. She hadn't told anyone yet, hadn't had a chance to. The very next night the club had gone on lockdown, and now she was stuck here.

"Do you want me to take her for a while?"

Dorothy appeared beside her and held her arms out. Grateful, Eva smiled as she passed Ivy, who blinked sleepily as she was shifted between them, but settled instantly back to sleep on Dorothy's shoulder.

"I need something to keep my mind off Jase and Chrissy," Dorothy whispered, rubbing small circles on Ivy's back. "She's out there talking about their upcoming anniversary—"

Eva stopped listening. Dorothy was a broken record when it came to Jase. Constantly upset yet still holding out hope that Jase would someday leave his wife, when it was clear to everyone except Dorothy that he never, ever would.

Lost to her own thoughts, she watched as Ripper came through the swinging kitchen doors and hooked a left toward them. She braced herself for his usual death glare.

"Yo," he said, passing by her and a still chattering Dorothy.

Her eyes widened in surprise. It wasn't friendly but . . . it wasn't horrible either.

Was he finally ready to forgive her for being married to the man who'd hurt him? She hoped so. It devastated her seeing his scars, what Frankie had so callously done to him.

My God, how had she not realized what her own husband had been capable of until it was too late?

Eva shook her head, still trying to clear Frankie from

her thoughts, when the kitchen doors swung open again and Danny walked out, headed in the opposite direction.

"Hey you," she called out and Danny spun around, a startled look on her face.

"Uh, hey," Danny stammered, her cheeks pink.

Studying her, she noted that the girl wasn't just flushed but sweaty . . . and disheveled. Really disheveled. As in her pink tank top was on inside out and her jean skirt was partially unzipped.

Drawing her brows together, Eva glanced over her shoulder to the end of the hall where Ripper had paused to talk to Mick and Bucket, and then she looked back at Danny. Her heart did a nosedive down into her stomach.

Danny and . . .

Oh my God, she couldn't even think it, it was just too bizarre. Bizarre and . . . Deuce was going to flip his shit. All she could envision was bullets and blood and bodies piled sky-high.

Okay.

Okay.

Okay, okay, *okay* . . . she had to think about this . . . about what she going to do about this.

Yeah, right. What the fuck was she supposed to do about this?

One thing was for sure, she couldn't leave Danny with only her brother and father in the middle of whatever mess she'd gotten herself into with Ripper.

God, how had that happened?

And what the fuck was Ripper thinking?

If Deuce ever found out, he would kill him. *Kill. Him.*

For the second time in the span of only a few minutes,

her heart dropped.

Ripper wanted to die. He'd finally lost his very last shred of give-a-damn and jumped off the cliff of no return. She'd seen it coming, everyone had seen it coming, but everyone had been holding out hope that after enough time had passed he'd eventually pull himself together.

Instead, the opposite had happened. He'd grown worse over time, bitter and cold.

What was Danny doing with a man like him? An angry, broken, older man, who was in all probability using her to get himself killed.

She squeezed her eyes shut.

She wasn't in any position to judge Danny. She'd made her share of mistakes over the years, some far worse than anything Danny would ever do.

And Danny was legally allowed to have sex with whomever she wanted.

But Danny was still a teenager, a deadly combination of immaturity and feelings. A big, fat, messy bank vault full of female emotion that you needed a jackhammer just to breach the surface of.

Who obviously wasn't thinking clearly. Or at all.

"Shut up, bitch!" Cox roared, startling everyone as he appeared at the end of the hallway.

"Never!" Kami screeched, her heels clicking heavily on the cement floor as she marched after him. The second Kami caught sight of Ripper, Eva cringed, knowing exactly what was coming next.

"Ripper," Kami purred, headed his way. "Hey, baby."

"Stay back!" he yelled. "I refuse to get shot because of your crazy ass!"

She grinned. "You did prefer my ass, didn't you, baby?"

Behind Cox, Danny made a small choking noise and Eva watched Ripper's gaze shoot to her, his jaw clenching.

"Ripper!" Cox bellowed. "I'm gonna fuckin' bury you!"

Sighing, Ripper grabbed his gun from the back of his leathers and waved it around in the air. "Either of you take another step in my direction and I'm cappin' you in the knee."

"You want me on my knees?" Kami said silkily. "You got it."

"Kami!" Eva hissed, grabbing her best friend's arm before she could get any closer to Ripper. "Stop it!"

"Christ," Ripper muttered. "You touch me, Kami, I'm gonna put a bullet in each of those bony knees."

Ignoring Eva, uncaring that Ripper had no problem shooting her and Cox was ten seconds from strangling her, Kami continued smiling sensually at Ripper.

"You're so fuckin' crazy, bitch!" Cox yelled, yanking Kami out of Eva's grip and pinning her up against the wall.

"And you're a fucking whore!" she screamed.

"I smiled at her, bitch! That's all I fuckin' did! For fuck's sake, you insane fuckin' whore, I fuckin' married you! I haven't been inside another bitch in forever!"

Kami brought her knee up straight into Cox's balls and he went down like a sack of potatoes, cupping himself and groaning. Hands on her hips, Kami glared down at him. "Do you want a medal, Cox-sucker?" she hissed. "I already know you haven't touched another woman! I have you followed!"

"You . . . crazy . . . bitch," Cox gasped. "As soon . . . as I can . . . I'm gonna . . . fuck . . . you . . . to death!"

Kami snorted. "Promises, promises."

"Did you two forget to take your meds today?" ZZ asked, poking his head around the corner.

"SHUT UP!" they yelled simultaneously.

Spinning on her heel, Kami stormed off, leaving Cox in a fetal position on the floor.

"I hate lockdown," Dorothy muttered.

"Me too," Cox said with a groan.

ZZ burst out laughing. "Dude," he called out. "You brought this shit on yourself. You marry crazy, crazy is what you're gonna get."

Ripper nearly knocked over Dorothy as he stormed past them, cursing as he headed in the direction Danny had since disappeared. She supposed now that Danny had just crudely found out about Ripper and Kami, he had some damage control to contend with.

Frowning, Eva stared down the hallway after him. No, she couldn't leave. Not in the eye of a major shit storm. If she went home now, who would be here to buffer between Danny and Deuce when the shit hit the fan? Cage? No. Cage loved his sister, but he was about as articulate with emotional confrontations as his father and preferred using his fists when things got heated. Deuce and Cage would only end up beating the hell out of each other, and Ripper would still end up dead, and Danny . . .

Who would be here to pick up the pieces of Danny's broken heart if Ripper ended up breaking it?

She was going to have to shelve her own problems for a while and make sure the family she loved—but was eventually going to have to leave—stayed together after she was gone.

CHAPTER 14

RIPPER JUMPED OVER COX AND TOOK OFF DOWN THE hallway after Danny. Motherfucking crazy, ass-less Kami. Always running her mouth. Using him to try to make Cox jealous over something that happened ten years ago. And it worked. Every damn time. If that was his bitch using another dude to make him jealous, always kneeing him in the junk when she was pissed off, he'd slap the fucking shit out of her.

He found Danny fumbling with the key to her room. One glance at him stalking her way and she amped up her fumbling.

"Danny!" he growled, increasing his pace. "Fuckin' wait!"

He caught up just as she turned the key. Grabbing her arm, he yanked her down the back hallway and into a dark corner, unseen by the cameras mounted on the walls.

"I know what you're thinkin'," he whispered, "but it ain't like that. Me and Kami—"

"Shut up!" she hissed. "I heard exactly what you did with Kami!"

His grip tightened on her arm, squeezing the limb. "Don't do this," he gritted out. "Not now, not here in the fuckin' club. What happened with Kami was ten years ago, Danny. What the fuck were you doin' ten years ago?"

Her cheeks turning pink, she glanced down, refusing to make eye contact.

"Yeah, baby," he whispered. "So cut me some fuckin' slack."

"Sorry," she mumbled. "I guess I wasn't thinking. I thought—"

He cut her off with a kiss he knew he shouldn't be risking, not with so many people cooped up inside the club. But, shit, he didn't want her hating on him and with Danny, it seemed need was always overpowering sense.

Her free arm slid around his waist under his T-shirt and her nails scraped lightly over his skin. He closed his eyes and kissed her harder.

"We should go to my room," she whispered, moaning softly as his lips descended down her neck and his hands up her ribcage. "Or back in the pantry."

They should. They should at least get the fuck out of the hallway. But he couldn't wait that long. The dim lighting, his size compared to her, all convinced his lust-addled brain that if someone happened to come down this hall within the next five minutes, unable to see Danny's face, whoever it was would just think he was fucking a club slut and leave him the hell alone. It wasn't the first time he'd fucked a bitch in the hallway.

Not by a long shot.

"No," he rasped, cupping her ass. "Now . . ."

"Ripper . . . *no* . . ."

He'd already lifted her, was pulling her underwear, still soaked from their last encounter, to the side and pushing inside of her.

"You can't say no," he growled, slapping his hand across her mouth. "It ain't allowed."

"Yes, I can," she mumbled. "I can say . . . oh God . . . *oh God* . . ."

Male arrogance slammed into him like a battering ram and his hand tightened, further muffling her cries and whimpers. He smiled to himself; she couldn't say no to him any more than he could say no to her.

"Baby," he said softly during a series of small, hard, hip thrusts up into her. "Made up my mind. I'm takin' you home with me. Sick of fuckin' you with my hand over your mouth. I wanna be goin' deaf hearin' you screamin' my name, yeah?"

She couldn't answer but he could feel the curl of her lips underneath his hand and, fuck, if that didn't turn him on to the point of internal combustion.

Ripper slammed his hips forward, rolling them as their bodies connected, his cock pulsing against her walls as he ground painfully into her. Eyes wide, she was panting hot, wet breaths against his hand, her heels were digging into the backs of his thighs, her nails piercing the skin on his neck.

It was so fucking hot, fucking her out in the open where anyone could find them. She was always so fucking hot, just letting him take and take and take from her, from her mouth and her body, from her sweet pussy, he took it all, he took *everything*, chewed it up, spit it back out, and then took her all over again.

He. Took. It. All.

He wasn't giving it back.

Danny was his.

Now he just had to figure out how he was going to convince her father of that.

"Stop looking at me like that," I whispered, feeling flustered and blushing as I yanked my skirt down.

Ripper, who hadn't had to right his clothing because he hadn't had to do much except unbutton his pants, was grinning down at me, watching me try to reassemble myself.

"Shirt's on inside out." He laughed. "Musta been from the pantry."

I looked down and, damn it, my tank top was on inside out. Embarrassed, I closed my eyes, thinking about everyone who'd seen me after I'd left the kitchen. Did they know? Had it been obvious what I'd been doing? Had I waited long enough after Ripper had left the kitchen? I didn't know. Who knew how long Eva and Dorothy had been standing out there.

"Ripper."

I nearly jumped out of my skin but Ripper, upon hearing his name, had gone still, his smile slipping off his face. It took him all of a second to steel his expression and then he turned around and facing Hawk.

"Yeah?"

Hawk's narrowed eyes landed on me and I swallowed hard. How was one supposed to look nonchalant when they felt like anything but?

"What's up?" Hawk asked warily, glancing between the two of us.

Pulling his cigarettes from his cut, Ripper lit one up and shrugged. "Not a whole fuck of a lot. You?"

Hawk flexed his jaw, his hard stare now on Ripper.

He knew.

He so knew.

"Just hopin' you know what you're doin', brother."

Ripper's fist clenched around his lit cigarette. Ash and tobacco fell through his fingers, drifting down to his feet. I stared at his hand, in shock that he didn't seem to care that he was purposely burning himself.

"How's D doin'?" Ripper gritted out. "Good? Or is she still throwin' dishes at your head?"

My head shot up. D? And throwing dishes? What did Dorothy or dishes have to do with anything?

Hawk's response was nearly imperceptible, just a small flinch, a twitch really and an extra blink, something I wouldn't have even noticed if I hadn't been staring directly at his face. Something was going on, something involving Dorothy and Hawk.

The two men said nothing as they continued to stare at each other.

Then Hawk gave a slight nod. "Fair enough," he said gruffly. "Ain't none of my business anyways."

As Hawk walked off, Ripper turned to me. "Go to your room, baby. I got this shit."

I did as he said, nervous yet confident that Ripper knew

what he was talking about, and called Anabeth.

She answered after three rings. "Are you still on lockdown?"

I sighed. "Yes."

"Ew."

"Yeah."

"So, what's up?"

"I need a favor."

"A sexual favor?"

I rolled my eyes. "Shut up."

"Well, what then?" she asked, sounding bored.

"After lockdown, I want to spend a few days at Ripper's. Will you cover for me?"

"Actually," she said, snapping her gum. "If it's next week, it works out perfectly. It's the annual fam' trip to the Poconos."

I grinned. That was perfect. Anabeth would be gone for an entire week, which meant for that entire week I could be alone with Ripper. *Alone.*

Envisioning all the things we could do while alone, without worry of being caught, my stomach flip-flopped.

"Thank you," I said, unable to keep excitement from bleeding into my voice.

Her gum snapped. "I want something in return."

I made a face. "What?"

"I want to know how big Ripper is."

"Anabeth," I said, exasperated. "Why do you even care?"

"Because," she said pointedly. "If you ever get sick of big, scarred, and sexy, I want to know if he's worth my time."

Just thinking about Ripper with another woman, let alone one of my closest friends, made me sick to my stomach. But as much as I wanted to tell her to go to hell, I knew she wouldn't let up.

"He's big," I admitted. "But I don't have much to compare him to."

"I want inches and circumference," she said, her tone matter-of-fact.

"Oh my God, Anabeth, seriously?"

"Seriously."

"Fine." I sighed. "He's, um, like as long as . . ." I trailed off, looking around my room, trying to find something to compare Ripper's penis to. "The DVR remote. Or, almost as long," I finished, picking the remote up off my bed and studying it.

"Mmmm," Anabeth murmured. "Nice. What about girth? When you hold it, do your fingers overlap?"

"*Oh. My. God.*" I groaned. "I hate you. No, they don't overlap, they don't even touch."

"Perfect," she purred. "Does he eat you out?"

"I'm hanging up now!"

"What? It's a legitimate question and a deal breaker for me. If a guy isn't going to go down on—"

I hung up.

Two seconds later my phone vibrated, signaling a new text message.

Anabeth: What about stamina? Is he a one, two pump?

CHAPTER 15

I WAS IN HEAVEN.

Two days ago my father had come back from New York, officially ending lockdown. The club had gone into secret meeting mode and I'd gone home with Eva and Ivy. The next morning my father and Cage, along with half the club, left for North Dakota.

And now . . . I was in heaven.

And my heaven consisted of the bare bones of a home, if you could even call Ripper's tiny, one-bedroom log cabin in the middle of nowhere, a home. He didn't even have real dishware, only plastic plates and cups and, yes, plastic sporks. There were no curtains or carpets, no pictures or paintings on the walls, nothing was personal except a small picture of his parents he had on his bedside table. They were conservative-looking people, well dressed with an air of importance about them. His mother was a strikingly beautiful woman and his father, an older, clean-cut version of Ripper minus the long hair and scars. They looked nothing like I'd thought the parents of my gruff and overbearing biker would have looked.

My biker.

My biker, whose hands—beautifully large and covered in deliciously rough, hardened skin—were groping me as I lay naked on my back. Sneaking past the slats of the window blinds, warm rays of sunlight heated my skin wherever they landed. Heaven.

"You hungry?" Ripper whispered, licking at the side of my neck.

Was I hungry? Oh my God, who cared about food? I was sore everywhere, I was excited and nervous and insanely happy and scared out of my mind and . . .

"Baby," he said, grinning, "you gotta be hungry. I know I'm hungry. We haven't left this fuckin' bed in twenty-four motherfuckin' hours. Let's get you in the shower, and then you can make us somethin' to eat."

"Mmm," I murmured, hooking my arms around his neck. "Whatever you say."

"Whatever I say?" He laughed as he dragged me out of bed and into the hallway. "Careful, beautiful girl, I might take you up on that."

Like I'd care. Whatever he wanted me to do, whatever he wanted to do to me, I already knew the answer would be a thousand times yes. I was at the point of no return, falling hard for a man I'd had more sex with than conversations. But for some reason, it didn't seem strange to me.

Every time he moved inside of me, looking up into his

gaze, it felt as if we had already spoken a million words at a million different times.

We existed in a world where words weren't needed. Everything I needed to know, everything he was feeling, I could already see on his face and feel through his touch.

And what I saw, what I felt, was . . .

He loved me.

I don't know how I knew, because I'd never been loved by a man who wasn't my father or my brother, loving me only out of familial obligation. Never, ever like this, nothing in my life had ever felt like this, but somehow I knew . . . I just knew.

In the bathroom, inside the large tub shower, my eyes closed, I reveled in his touches, his kisses, as the hot water poured down over us, washing away hours upon hours of sweat and sex that I was determined to put right back on us.

"You're killin' me." He groaned as I cupped him and began stroking him back to life.

"Ripper," I begged, feeling like I would burst if I didn't have this man inside of me. Right. Now.

"Please . . . now . . . please . . ."

I couldn't get enough.

I would never get enough.

Pushing me up against the wall, he gripped my side with one hand; his other slid down my leg and grabbed a hold of the back of my knee. Lifting my leg, he situated it high around his waist and then he was there, right where I needed him between my thighs, hard and ready and pushing inside of me.

Moaning, gripping his biceps, I let my body go soft and limp, letting Ripper take complete control.

"Baby." He groaned, sliding inside of me. "Ah, God, Danny . . . I gotta see your face, baby, please . . ."

He stopped, paused to brush several thick clumps of wet hair out of my eyes, and with heavy lids and water-blurred vision, I blinked up at him.

"That's it," he whispered, pulling out. My hips jerked up, not wanting to lose him. "You look right at me, beautiful girl. I need to see you, I gotta see that way you fuckin' look at me."

He thrust back inside and my eyes closed as all the air left my body.

"Eyes," he demanded, pulling out and slamming back inside. "Look at me, Danielle."

I kept my gaze locked with his. Even when it was nearly impossible to do so. Even when my womb was burning, quivering, and clenching with my release, even when he took me harder and faster, even when my legs were shaking, my body jelly, my mind nothing but mush, still I kept my eyes on him.

"Ripper," I whispered, clinging to his neck as he carried me from the bathroom into his bedroom. "I think I love you."

Laying me gently down on his bed, he climbed over top of me and covered me with his body.

"Yeah, baby," he whispered, sliding back inside of me. "Ain't no other explanation for what a girl like you is doin' in bed with a man like me."

She was trying to kill him. She was trying to fuck him to death.

Or maybe he was already dead and this was heaven, or hell, depending on how you looked at it.

"More," Danny whimpered, writhing on top of him.

Jesus, he couldn't. He wasn't even hard. They'd done nothing but fuck since they'd gotten to his place.

And now his cock was dead.

"Shh," he whispered against her mouth, kissing her lips, kissing the corner of her mouth and both her cheeks as he moved her off him and pulled her up against him, her back to his front.

"Please," she whispered, trying to twist around. "I can't . . . I need . . ."

Ripper bit down on her neck and sucked her soft skin into his mouth. "I'm broken, baby," he said, licking where he'd bitten.

Moaning, she arched her neck to give him better access, and he kissed his way across her neck and down her shoulder.

Flipping around in his arms, Danny looked up at him, grinning. Her hair was matted with sweat, her face flushed, her blue eyes shining, and he just stared. She was the most perfect thing he'd ever seen, ever touched, felt, kissed. She was the most perfect thing he'd ever known.

Pulling her over top of him, he buried his face in her neck and squeezed her tight. Fuck, he hadn't felt like this in . . .

Fuck him, he'd never felt like this.

She shrieked as he flipped her off him and onto her back.

"Baby," he said, smiling, climbing over top of her, straddling her hips. "I'm dead."

Threading her hands through his hair, she pulled his face down to hers. "You're not," she whispered.

"Get some sleep," he said softly, rolling off her and pulling the covers up to her chin.

"Just once more," she whispered, kicking the covers off her and reaching for him. "Please . . ."

"Fuck, Danny, no," he muttered, even as his spent body responded to her touch.

Unwittingly he found himself rolling her over, sliding down her body and spreading her legs wide open. Looking his fill, his head dipped forward and he gave her a long, slow lick, wetting her further. Then shoving himself back up, he positioned himself, gripped her thighs and, exhausted and sore, surged inside her.

"Hurts," she murmured, her eyelids fluttering.

Yeah, it did. He was so damn sore and yet . . .

"Harder," she whispered.

He complied; she both whimpered and moaned.

"Faster," she demanded.

Harder . . . faster . . . harder . . .

Sweat beaded on his forehead and his muscles burned, his breath raw. But he didn't give a fuck. The only thing he gave a fuck about was beneath him, gripping his sheets, breathing in small, ragged hiccups and staring up at him with a beautiful pair of wide, unfocused blue eyes.

"I wanna rip you the fuck open," he said, breathing harder as his thrusts became brutal. "I want all of me inside all of you, not just my fuckin' cock, baby, but all of me. All of you."

"Yes," she whimpered. "I want all of you."

Christ. Yeah, she did. Danny wanted him bad, so bad he

could fucking feel it, feel her need all around him, cloaking him from his living hell and comforting him in her soft and silken, pure fucking sweetness.

He couldn't lose her.

The wayward thought horrified him.

Losing her would end him.

A man like him, a girl like her . . . Ripper knew there would be no going back for him. Not after her. He'd hit the fucking jackpot and no bitch that came in her wake would ever measure up.

Determined to keep her, to make her irrevocably his, he fucked her with everything he had left inside of him.

But he couldn't get deep enough, he couldn't fuck her fast enough, hard enough . . . nothing he did seemed to be enough.

He was still trying when the sun set again; no longer capable of an erection, he was still trying. Trying to leave a piece of himself behind, one that couldn't be erased, one that would stay with her always, one that would make it so Danny was forever his. Only his.

Jesus . . . he loved her.

She'd said it already. More than a few times, most of which he'd doubted she'd even been aware of, faulting delirium from exhaustion and tear-inducing orgasms. But then there had been the other times where she'd been looking right at him, her eyes clear, her voice strong.

He hadn't known what to do. It wasn't the first time a bitch had told him she loved him, but it was the first time he'd wanted to say it back.

Only . . .

It had all happened so quickly and was still so confusing.

They barely knew each other.

Only . . .

It didn't feel that way. He suddenly couldn't remember a time he hadn't been staring into those beautiful icy blue eyes and not feeling completely at peace. Or maybe he just didn't want to remember anything before her because nothing before her was worth remembering.

Gripping her face, Ripper forced her to look at him.

"I love you," he rasped then froze, waiting for the nauseating regret to wash over him.

When it didn't, when he only continued to look down at her, feeling nothing but a peaceful exhaustion, the kind only garnered from an entire day spent inside of a beautiful woman, his woman, he knew it was true. Erik Jacobs had finally fallen for a woman. And he'd fallen motherfucking fast and hard.

The smile he received in return caused his heart to split into a million different pieces. Then, as the organ began to knit itself back together, feeling fuller and stronger than before . . .

He got it.

Just like that, he finally got it.

He knew now why Cox was such a bumbling moron when it came to Kami. He understood why Jase refused to let Dorothy go even though he knew their fucked-up relationship was slowly killing her. He got why Deuce had never been able to stay away from Eva . . . despite the age difference . . . despite Preacher's trigger-happy hands, despite her being married to a crazy motherfucker.

Why they never could forget them.

Because once you had a taste of a good woman,

suddenly nothing else mattered but her.

Nothing.

Yeah, he got it now. There wasn't anything sweeter. Not even riding.

It was that very moment, a mere pittance in the span of his lifetime, that after he'd lost Danny would become his happiest memory, the one Ripper would hold closest to his heart and cherish above all others. The one he'd lay awake at night playing on repeat.

Wishing . . .

Wishing . . .

Wishing . . .

. . . she still loved him.

CHAPTER 16

ON THE COUCH, LYING ON TOP OF RIPPER'S BACK, wearing a holey Metallica T-shirt five sizes too big for me, I smiled at the television as Johnny offered Baby his hand and pulled her out of her seat.

Nobody puts Baby in a corner.

"I love old movies," I said with a sigh. "*Dirty Dancing* is my favorite."

Ripper's big body shook with laughter. "Old movies," he repeated. "You do realize this shit came out when I was a kid?"

Pressing my lips together, I buried my face between his shoulder blades, directly over the words hell's horsemen tattooed on his back. He had his fair share of ink, although not nearly as much as Cox who, aside from his face, probably didn't have any skin left that wasn't tattooed.

From his left wrist to his elbow Ripper had a beautiful montage of his parents' faces, their birth and death dates swirling around them with a heavily detailed headstone as the backdrop.

A bare-breasted pinup girl took up the space from his right shoulder to his elbow, that had since been slashed through several times and filled in with scar tissue. On his knuckles, in gothic lettering, when he put his clenched fists side by side, spelled out R-I-P-P-E-R-4-1.

Lastly, on his right wrist he had a sparsely beaded rosary wrapped several times, the cross falling in the middle of his palm.

When I'd finished counting the beads, seventeen total, I'd looked up at him.

"Are you religious?" I asked.

He laughed. "Naw, baby, I ain't. It's just a reminder because sometimes I need remindin', yeah?"

"Reminding of what?"

He lit up a cigarette and took several long drags before answering. "Of what kinda man I am."

At the time, I hadn't understood what he'd meant, but because of the sudden change in him, from silly to serious, I'd dropped it and moved on.

"You look pretty good for an old man," I whispered against his warm skin, trying hard not to laugh.

"Brat," he whispered back and I heard the smile in his voice.

It was our fourth day together in Ripper's home, yet it was the first time since arriving that we'd left the bedroom for something other than a bathroom trip or a food break.

"You wanna watch an old movie, we can put in *The*

Wild Bunch. Great fuckin' movie."

I wrinkled up my nose. "The what?"

"Pike?" he asked. "Old Sykes?"

"Who?"

"Jesus, Danny, it's only the best Western ever made."

I rolled my eyes. "Westerns are lame."

"Yeah, and *nobody puts Baby in a corner* isn't."

"It isn't!" I protested, smacking the back of his head. "It's romantic. Best quote ever."

Ripper snorted.

"Yeah, it's real fuckin' deep. Try this on for a change," he said, clearing his throat. "'The land had changed. They hadn't. The earth had cooled. They couldn't.'"

"What does that even mean?"

"Means shit was changin' all around them but they were stayin' the same. Men who had a certain way of livin', their own way of gettin' shit done, wasn't gonna fly anymore 'cause they were livin' in a world full of pussies makin' rules."

"Kinda like the club," I mused, thinking about my father and Mick, about Bucket and Freebird and their rants about society and living by their own rules, the code of the road and brotherhood.

And speaking of my father . . .

Before I could speak, Ripper reached behind him and hooked his arm around my neck. In one swift move, he'd reversed our positions and had me pinned underneath him.

"Smart girl," he said softly, cupping my chin, tilting my head back as he moved in for a kiss.

"Wait," I said, turning my head away from him.

"No," he growled, biting down on my exposed neck.

I swatted at his head. "Yes!"

He lifted his head and scowled at me. "What the fuck, Danny, make it quick."

"My dad's gonna be back soon," I said, dodging another kiss.

"Yeah?"

"Are you going to talk to him? Tell him about us?"

After spending so much time with Ripper, alone, I knew I wasn't going to be able to go back to sneaking around the club just to be with him. I wanted to be with him everywhere and I wanted everyone to know it.

Ripper moved off of me and into a sitting position. I pushed myself up and reached for his arm.

"I ain't gonna tell him shit," he said, shrugging me off him.

I gaped at him.

"But why not?" I whispered.

"Why?" he bit out, his expression hard. "Because the club comes first, you fuckin' know that. And shit between your old man and Eva is fucked-up, meanin' your old man is fucked-up. I spill this shit between me and you to your old man, and shit's gonna go bad real fuckin' quick, for me, for you, and for the club."

The club. The club comes first.

God, I'd heard it enough over the years and even if I hadn't heard it, I'd certainly felt it. My father had always spent more time at the club than at home. He'd almost never come to school functions and not once had he come to a game to watch me cheerleading or to a single gymnastics competition. His excuse? Club business.

"You said you loved me!" I yelled. "I should have known you were no better than him! Making me think you care about me, but really all you care about is your stupid club!"

Ripper shot to his feet, startling me. "STUPID CLUB?" he roared. "You got any fuckin' idea what's been feedin' you all these years, what's been keepin' you rollin' in all that stupid pink shit you're always wearin'?"

My mouth fell open.

"Yeah, bitch, that'd be the club you been livin' the good life off of."

I jumped to my feet, furious. "I hate it when you call me a bitch! And if you consider having a drunk for a mother and a father who was never home, who prefers hanging out with Cage over me, living the good life, then you have a seriously messed up view of what the good life is!"

"This ain't about your cunt of a mother or your old man or your brother. This is about me and you and the club. You bein' in my fuckin' bed means you're my old lady and you bein' my old lady, you tellin' me you fuckin' love me, means you're lovin' the club too. And right now, lovin' the club means we ain't tellin' your old man jack shit."

"Then maybe I don't want to be your old lady," I snapped.

"Stop actin' stupid, Danny. You don't get to decide that. I do. So wise the fuck up and get rid of whatever crawled up that hot little ass of yours."

Don't smile, don't smile, don't smile.

Just because he thinks your ass is hot doesn't mean you've forgiven him for not wanting to tell your father about you and him.

"Why you makin' that face, baby? You gotta take a shit or somethin'?"

My eyes flared wide. "You are sooooo gross!" I yelled,

no longer able to stop the grin that shot out across my face.

Ripper scoffed. "You like it."

"Don't," I shot back.

"Do."

"Don't."

"You do, beautiful girl. You like me dirty and the dirty shit I do to you."

"That's different," I said, my gaze dropping to his waist where, beneath his tattered jeans, he was quickly hardening.

He grinned. "Like when you're kissin' me hard after I've been eatin' at that beautiful pussy, and you're suckin' yourself off my mouth like you're starvin'. Or when I'm fuckin' you, got two fingers up inside that perfect ass and you're movin' those hips, fuckin' those fingers, cryin' for a third—"

I put my hand up. "Okay!" I shouted, my neck suddenly hot from embarrassment. "You've made your point!"

He took a step toward me, still grinning. "You want me to drive that point home?"

I did. I so did. Just looking at his big, beautiful body made me crazy, but I was still mad.

"No," I snapped. "I do not."

He sighed. "Don't fuck around, Danny. I don't like playin' these stupid games women are always playin'."

My jaw dropped. Next to my father, Ripper was hands down the most infuriating man I'd ever met.

"I hate you," I spat, pushing him out of my way.

"No you don't," he called out.

"Now I really hate you!" I yelled over my shoulder.

"Don't."

"Do!"

Ripper watched Danny stalk out of the living room, wondering what the fuck she'd expected.

How the fuck did she think he could explain this mess to Deuce? Without getting killed?

No matter what he said or how he said it, Deuce was going to flip his fucking shit.

Prez, I'm feelin' Danny and I thought maybe you'd be cool with me takin' her out?

He could almost hear the gun discharging.

Prez, Danny and I been hangin' and I'm wantin' more.

Yeah. Right.

Jesus, what the fuck was he supposed to say?

Dude, I've been fuckin' your daughter since her prom night and I just wanted to give you a heads-up 'cause I ain't gonna stop fuckin' her.

Yep, he'd die.

He knew Deuce deserved his respect; he'd owed it to his prez to tell him the truth. In fact, he owed Deuce a lot more than that. The man had taken him in when he was still a kid, gave him a place to live and a family, a way to financially pull himself together. Deuce had been a father to him after he'd lost his.

And how was he repaying him? He was fucking his daughter behind his back, something Deuce had made explicitly clear to all the boys they were not to do. They were not even to think about doing it.

And he wouldn't have.

If it hadn't been for Frankie fucking him up and the

drunken wallowing that had followed, he would have never touched Danny.

Too late, he thought.

Not only had Ripper touched her many, many times inside and out, she was firmly rooted inside him now. He wasn't giving her up. Not only that, but he didn't want to have to keep her a secret.

It wasn't ever going to happen, but that didn't stop him from fantasizing about her hanging off him at the club, wearing leather and heels, her eyes trained on him, looking at him in that hungry way she did. He wanted everyone to see her hands on him, her nails digging into his skin, claiming him. He wanted them knowing that her thoughts . . . were always on him.

He wanted every motherfucker out there knowing her pussy was his, that when he went to sleep at night, he did it with her in his arms.

Yeah, he wanted the whole fucking world to know that eighteen-year-old Danielle West, the most beautiful female he'd ever laid eyes on, loved . . . *him*.

Jesus, he was hard again. As if he hadn't already fucked himself into oblivion. That fucking pussy of hers was Viagra in the form of sweet and soft pink flesh.

But there was no way . . .

"What the fuck!" he bellowed, seeing Danny exit his bedroom, fully dressed in head-to-toe pink, her stupid bag with some weird cat on it slung over her shoulder, heading for the front door. Moving fast, he made it there before she could.

"Move," she ground out. "I'm leaving."

"Nope, and no you're not."

"Fine," she hissed, spinning around. "Then I'll call my dad for a ride!"

Ripper gritted his teeth. Bitches. Crazy. All of them.

Dumping her bag out on the floor, she bent over, reaching for her cell phone, forcing her skirt up and giving him a first class view of her ass.

"You wanna play it that way, Danny?" he growled, fighting the urge to slam her up against the refrigerator and take her from behind. "Fine. You either do what I say or you can act fuckin' stupid and let your old man in on the secret. And if you choose actin' stupid, you can take to the fuckin' bank that I'm gonna be tellin' your old man this shit was your fault, that you'd been beggin' me for cock all summer."

She went still and for a moment he thought he'd won whatever round of stupid female shit she was forcing him to play.

Then, standing up straight, she slowly turned around. "Go ahead," she spat. "And I'll tell him everything you did to me! In detail!"

Holy hell. If she was anyone else pulling this shit, he'd slap that attitude right the fuck out of her.

"You do that, baby," he gritted out, "and it's my funeral. Is that what you fuckin' want? Me goin' to ground?"

"I'm sure Kami will be devastated," she hissed.

"Jesus Christ, bitch!" he yelled. "Who's fuckin' talkin' about Kami! The only pussy I'm wantin' is yours, you crazy shit, only right now I'm wantin' to slap it!"

"You're the one who doesn't want anyone to know about us!" she cried and he half-expected her to stomp her feet like a cranky toddler.

He was going to kill her. Right now. She was going to be

dead in about five seconds.

"Ripper!" she cried out as he barreled into her, hefting her over his shoulder. "Let me go!"

"Did you hear what I fuckin' said?" he yelled, slapping her ass. "You ain't leavin'!"

"You can't tell me what to do!" she shrieked.

In his bedroom, he threw her on the bed and bent over her, bringing them nose-to-nose.

"I can and I will, 'cause you actin' crazy like this isn't gonna do nothin' but get us caught and me sent straight to ground. And bitch, if your old man caps me, you better be front and center at my fuckin' funeral, cryin' your goddamn eyes out."

She went quiet and the angry lines in her face disappeared.

The next thing he knew she was giggling.

"Laugh it up," he bit out angrily.

And the crazy bitch started laughing even harder.

Since it didn't look like she was going to stop anytime soon, he figured he had two choices to shut her up. Knock her out or . . .

He slammed his mouth down on hers and kissed her hard, ignoring her protests and pathetic attempts at fighting him off, until she was kissing him back with equal desperation and turning him on something fierce.

"You're gonna drive me motherfuckin' crazy, ain't you, baby?" he mumbled against her mouth as he pushed her thighs open and settled his hips between them.

"Excuse you?" she demanded, digging her nails into his back. "Me? Drive *you* crazy?"

Ripper grabbed the hem of her T-shirt and yanked it

up to her neck, baring her upper body. "Are we fighting or fucking?" he growled, roughly fondling one firm, perfect breast. Quivering, covered in gooseflesh, her nipple peaked, begging him to suck it inside his mouth.

Her blue eyes positively burned holy hell fire and his cock swelled at the sight of them. Danny was going to drive him crazy, but fuck him, if she wasn't going to be worth every crazy moment of it.

"We're fucking," she hissed.

"Damn straight," he muttered and slammed up inside all that eager sweetness.

CHAPTER 17

"WHERE THE FUCK IS RIPPER?" DEUCE DEMANDED, glancing around his office at all his boys. He pinned Mick with a glare. "I told you to have everybody here when I got in."

Arms folded across his chest, his VP shrugged. "Called him six fuckin' times, Prez. He wasn't even tryin' to pick that shit up."

"He got outta here pretty quick after lockdown," Hawk said from across the room. "Probably shot outta town and is shacked up in some no-tell motel, stackin' pancakes as we speak."

Deuce shook his head. "If he can't drag his sorry ass outta bed when I call a meeting, I ain't repeatin' jack shit for him. One of you assholes will have to tell 'im."

"This about Big Jay?" Tap asked.

He nodded. "Hit went down last night. Demons took him out clean, half his crew too. The rest scattered, some were caught, are bein' interrogated as we speak, and some got away. Way it goes."

"What about his bitch of a sister?" Cox growled, his hand automatically going to the piece he kept under his cut.

Deuce eyed him; Cox and Ripper had always been tight, only a year apart and had been brought into the club around the same time, no family, no friends. They'd grown real close, real fast, and Mama Vi had specifically threatened Ripper.

He shook his head. "No one knows. But she hasn't surfaced as of yet and Preacher doesn't think she's gonna, not without backup. She wasn't the brains of the operation, just the muscle, and by muscle I mean a big bag of crazy willin' to do whatever's necessary. Ain't too much she can do without the big man tellin' her which way is up, but still keep your eyes out for her or anyone else outta LA who might be nursin' a revenge hangover."

"That's it, right, Prez?" Jase asked, his eyes on the door, obviously itching to see Dorothy after a week on the road.

"Respect your prez much, asshat?" Hawk muttered. Jase's narrowed gaze shot to Hawk and the guy met him stare for stare.

"Brother, what the fuck is your problem?" Jase asked, jerking his chin up.

"I ain't your brother," Hawk shot back.

The occupants of the room went eerily still. It was a low blow for any Horseman to say that to another, even worse because these were two of his lifers, patched in and loyal to the fucking bone. Whatever was going on between them wasn't going to fly, and needed to be reeled in right the fuck now.

Cursing under his breath, Deuce pushed his chair away from his desk and got to his feet.

"Explain yourself," he directed at Hawk. "Now."

Just as Hawk's mouth opened, Dirty was suddenly beside him, shoving the guy toward the door.

"Hawk's been pukin' his guts up the whole time you fuckers were gone," Dirty said over his shoulder, smacking Hawk's head forward when the guy kept trying to glare at Jase. "Had a fever and shit. I've been sitting by his side, holding his hair up and rubbin' his tummy and shit, and he still ain't feelin' so hot."

The door slammed behind them and Jase turned to him. "What the fuck?" he shouted. "Prez, you gonna let that shit stand?"

Feeling more like an elementary school principal than an MC president, Deuce turned to his VP. "Somethin' go down around here that I need to know about?"

Mick gave him a blasé shrug. "Fuck if I know what these fuckers are doin' with themselves. I got kids and shit, can't be babysittin' grown-ass men all the time."

"Get out," he said irritably, gesturing to his office doors. "All of you, get the fuck out."

One by one his boys left until only Blue remained.

Deuce eyed the old man. "Somethin' you need?"

"Worried 'bout you, boy," Blue said quietly.

He gaped at him. Who the fuck called a fifty-year-old man a boy? But then again, nobody knew Blue's true age. Never had any of the brothers known Blue without a full head of long white hair and an equally white beard. The man's eyes were a milky cataract-infested mess, his teeth long ago rotted out, and his skin nothing but a mass of mottled wrinkles. Yet, he was healthy as a horse and could throw back a bottle like he was twenty-five, when in all likelihood he was a hundred and sixty.

"You're hurtin'," Blue continued. "And ain't no one blamin' you for that. You and Eva sure done been through some shit. But, Deuce, this shit ain't your fault, it ain't Eva's fault, it ain't no one's fault 'cept for Frankie and he's long gone."

Used to these longwinded bullshit speeches from Blue, Deuce sat down heavily in his desk chair and prayed it would be over soon.

"I get you, always have," Blue said. "Reaper was a special brand of bastard, we all knew it, and we all watched you growin' up fightin' for your next breath. You never knew nothin' else, always fightin', even with Eva you were still fightin'. You don't gotta be fightin' anymore."

"I ain't fightin' nothin'," he growled. "You—"

"You got ghosts," Blue interrupted. "I know it. Hell, we all fuckin' know it. You got 'em followin' you everywhere you fuckin' go. You got Reaper breathin' down your neck and now Frankie's back there too. You ain't gonna move forward unless you dig yerself a hole and throw that bullshit six feet under, set it on fuckin' fire, and bury that shit. Otherwise you ain't no good to no one, least of all yerself."

Fuuuuck this shit.

"Shut up, old man," he bit out. "I've had enough motherfuckers tellin' me what I should and shouldn't be doin' lately."

"She loves you," Blue continued, ignoring him. "A fuckin' dumbass could see that. You're pushin' her away again and she's leavin' this time, mark my word, Deuce. She's leavin' you this time."

"She ain't leavin'," he said through his teeth. Was she? Did he even care?

His jaw clenched. Yeah, he did, and no way was she leaving.

Blue shook his head again.

"You stupid? Ain't no woman gonna walk away from a man just 'cause he's crazy or 'cause his job ain't all sunshine and roses. Fact, you bein' crazy, this life bein' what it is, is probably only makin' her love you more. Women are stupid like that. But you're fuckin' yourself. You don't start givin' that girl what she needs and she's gone, and listen to me when I tell you, you ain't never gonna find a woman who loves you like that one does."

Deuce closed his eyes, remembering.

Bending down in front of Eva, he looked into her eyes. "What do you want, babe?"

She turned away from him and hid behind her hair, but not before he saw her turn bright fucking red.

He filled with primal male satisfaction. She wanted him. Her, a fucking angel in a mess of demons, wanted him, one of the biggest fucking demons he knew.

"Say it," he said harshly.

Fuck. What the fuck was he doing?

She turned back to him and tucked her hair behind her ears. God, that face. That sweet, perfect face.

"You a virgin, Eva?" He already knew the answer.

"Yes," she whispered. Christ.

He leaned in closer, close enough to smell the nicotine and beer on her breath. "You ever been kissed, darlin'?"

She sucked in a sharp breath. "No," she breathed.

Good. So fucking good.

He turned his head and rubbed his cheek up against hers, inhaling the fragrance of her strawberry-scented hair.

"You wanna be kissed?" he whispered in her ear.

He licked the skin just behind her ear and she shivered. He sucked on her skin, bit down lightly, and rolled it between his teeth.

She was breathing hard, the pulse in her neck fluttering wildly against his mouth. He started sucking with vigor and her legs fell open. He took advantage and shoved himself between them.

He spread kisses across her neck and under her chin, up to her cheek, kissing a line to her mouth. His lips met hers. She trembled.

"One more time, babe," he said, low and raspy. "You wanna be kissed?"

"Yes," she whimpered.

Yeah, he'd fallen hard, been forever ruined by a goddamn sixteen-year-old in the stairwell of the Silver Demons MC. Not a day had gone by since that he hadn't thought of her, and still nothing had changed. Next to the club, Eva was his whole world.

Blue shrugged. "But what the fuck do I know. My old lady died over thirty years ago. Hardly remember what lookin' at a woman worth lookin' at feels like."

Deuce barely remembered Gladys but he'd seen the old black and whites of her and Blue from back in the day when Reaper still ran the Horsemen and Blue still had teeth. She'd been damn beautiful. Dead ringer for Natalie Wood. Way too good-looking for an asshole like Blue. Cancer took her in her fifties and Blue hadn't gotten back on a bike since. In fact, he was surprised Blue had even gotten off the barstool for the meeting.

"Go home, son," Blue said as he shuffled toward the door. "Go home and take back your woman."

Dropping his head in his hands, Deuce closed his eyes. Blue was right. The stupid fucker was always right. And Preacher, that stupid fucker, had only been half right. Telling him to go fuck away his problems had been a catastrophe.

"My name's Heather," the whore slurred.

"Clothes," he barked, unbuckling his belt. "Off. Now."

Grinning, she swayed drunkenly and tried to salute him. "Aye, aye, Captain. Or should I call you Mr. President?"

"How about," he growled, shoving down his boxers, "you shut the fuck up, finish takin' your clothes off, and then you get down on your fuckin' knees."

Laughing, she pushed down her jeans and kicked them away, leaving her in a purple T-shirt and a matching thong. And that was good enough.

Grabbing her, he bent her over the railing and kicked her legs apart. Reaching between them, he pulled her thong aside and then palming his cock, pushed up against her and tried to push inside.

"Fuck," he muttered as his partial erection went completely flaccid. "Fuck!"

Grabbing the back of her neck, he swung her around and shoved her down on the floor. "Suck it," he said, pushing her face in his crotch.

Gripping his thigh, she grabbed his cock, filling her mouth, and he closed his eyes, trying to think about anything other than Eva.

Frankie grunting on top of Eva.

Eva whimpering.

Eva crying.

Eva . . .

Coming.

Frankie grinning.

Grinning.

Fuck.

Eva.

Eva.

Eva.

Fuck him.

"This ain't workin', honey."

He glared down at the whore.

No shit, it wasn't working. Nothing in his life was working.

Grabbing his boxers and jeans, he dressed quickly.

Still buttoning her jeans, she staggered by him. "I wouldn't worry 'bout it, baby," she said. "Happens to all you old dudes all—"

Anger at Frankie, at Eva, anger at the whole goddamn world powered through him and he reacted, grabbed the back of her hair and yanked her backward, then thrust her forward, power-slamming her face into the drywall. Still holding her hair, he dragged her away from the wall and with a hard shove, sent her sprawling down the hallway.

"What the fuck!" she screamed, scrambling to her feet. Tentatively she touched her lips and nose and her hands came away bloody. Seeing them, seeing the blood, she looked up at him and started to scream.

Jesus motherfucking Christ.

"SHUT UP!" he roared, pulling his gun from the inside of

his cut and aiming it at her. "JUST SHUT THE FUCK UP!"

She didn't. The bitch just stood there, covered in the blood from her broken nose, screaming, sounding like something out of a bad horror movie. Fuck it. She was annoying him.

Thumbing the hammer, he slipped his pointer finger over the trigger, cocked and—

"Deuce!" Preacher shouted, jumping in front of him. "Put the damn gun away!"

He didn't. He couldn't.

He wanted someone else to hurt.

Someone who wasn't him.

Grabbing his shoulders, Preacher leaned in close. "Deuce, lemme take care of this bitch."

When he didn't respond, Preacher gave him a hard shake. "Go home, brother," he said firmly. "You need to go the fuck home."

He did.

He needed to go home right the fuck now and take back his woman.

Eva stared down at her cell phone, at the text message Deuce had sent her only moments ago.

Deuce: You home?
Me: No. At Kami's. Why?
Deuce: Meet me at home.
Me: Why?
Deuce: GO. HOME.

"Foxy?"

Startled, she glanced up and found Cox looming over the couch she was sitting on.

"When did you get home?" she asked.

"Just now." He nodded at her phone. "That Prez?"

She could sense anger in Cox's tone, see it in the tight lines of his face, and didn't understand what she could have possibly done to warrant any sort of negative reaction from him.

"Yes," she said warily.

"What's he want?"

"Cox, I'm not sure that's any of your business."

At his sides, Cox's fists clenched. "The fuck it isn't," he hissed. "You think I'm stupid? You think I don't know you're ready to split? Don't get me wrong, Eva, I don't fuckin' blame you, but bitch, you take off and I know Kami's gonna follow you. I ain't gonna let that happen."

"Cox," she said quietly. "Kami married you. You have a son together. She isn't going to leave."

His nostrils flared. "The fuck she isn't. I know her. She loves you more than she loves me and that's fine, I fuckin' accepted that shit a while back, but no fuckin' way am I gonna let you take her from me. I've been watchin' this shit comin' from a mile away and I can't keep my mouth shut no more. Fix this shit with Prez and fix it quick because I swear to fuckin' God if you don't, bitch, and I lose—"

"Cox!" Kami screamed, stalking into the room. "Shut your stupid Mexican mouth!"

Cox glared at her. "Bitch, I'm Puerto Rican!"

She waved her hand dismissively. "Whatever. Don't you have some lawns to mow?"

"I'm Puerto fuckin' Rican!"

"What! Ever!"

"Bitch! Don't you got some rich boy cock you need to suck off for a new pair a fuckin' shoes?"

"Fuck you!"

"No, bitch, fuck you! I'm fuckin' Puerto Rican! Say it, Kami, say Puerto Rican!"

"No!"

"Say it!"

"American Indian!"

Eva quickly got to her feet. "I'm, um, going to—"

Cox spun on her. "You're gonna to go fix this shit!" he bellowed. "Before it ain't just Prez who's fallin' apart, but my fuckin' family and the whole goddamn club!"

"Don't you dare blame her for anything!" Kami hissed.

"See!" Cox roared. "You're always sidin' with her! You'd jump off a fuckin' bridge if she did!"

"Yes, I would!" Kami shrieked. "Did you actually think there was a chance I'd choose some hot Cuban piece of ass over my Evie?"

"PUERTO RICAN!"

While they were busy screaming at each other, Eva was able to slip from the living room unnoticed and head down the hall toward Devin's playroom. She found both kids on the couch, sharing a handheld video game and a pair of circumaural headphones stretched out over top of both their heads. She paused in the doorway, watching them, unable to stop the memory that assaulted her . . .

On top of a picnic table, she and Frankie were sitting side by side sharing a pair of earbuds. Her Discman was wedged between them, and their heads were pressed together while they rocked out to Led Zeppelin's "Dazed and Confused." She had her arm slung over Frankie's broad shoulders, his hand was sliding up and down her thigh, his fingers tapping out the beat of the song.

"Miss Fox?"

Eva blinked at Devin's nanny, Kajika.

"Are you all right?" she asked.

"Sorry," Eva murmured, shaking herself out of the memory. "Just thinking."

"We can learn much from children," Kajika said, smiling at Devin and Ivy. "They view the world as it is, innocent and waiting for them, like a playground ready to be explored."

"Yes," Eva whispered, staring at her daughter. "They do."

"Can I share something my grandfather once told me, Miss Fox?" Kajika quietly asked.

Eva nodded.

"There is an old story passed down through the generations of a Native American grandfather counseling his young grandson, telling him that he has two wolves living inside of him, constantly fighting each other for dominance. One is the wolf of peace, love, and kindness. The other represents fear, greed, and hatred. The boy asks, 'Which wolf will win, Grandfather?' and the wise old man replies, 'Whichever one I feed.'"

Eva stared at her, wondering what the woman was talking about.

"I'm sorry," Eva said, "but I don't under—"

"May I be frank?" Kajika asked.

"Of course."

"It's no secret you are in pain; it is also no secret why. Not in this house."

Eva snorted. Nothing was secret in Cox and Kami's house. Both of their neighbors, each a mile away in opposite directions, could hear the two of them screaming at each other. Eva was surprised Kajika had stayed as long as she had.

"You're afraid," she continued. "And if I know it, he does too."

He being Deuce, Eva guessed.

"And your fear is perpetuating his, a vicious cycle that unless stopped will do nothing but continue to grow. Before you know it, you will no longer know each other."

Kajika's dark eyes looked kindly upon her. "You must feed the wolf of peace some love before it is too late."

Eva said nothing; there was nothing to say. Kajika was right. She was afraid. Afraid and ready to run, just as she'd always done where Deuce and she were concerned.

After planting a kiss on Devin's cheek and gathering up Ivy, Eva gave Kajika a small smile and headed outside.

Once she and Ivy were settled inside her truck, she called Deuce back.

He answered after only one ring. "Where you at?"

She swallowed hard. "Still at Kami's."

He cleared his throat, something he never did. He was hesitating. Her stomach dropping with dread, Eva held her breath and waited for what would come next.

"You headed home?"

"Do you really want me to?" she whispered.

"Yeah," he said gruffly. "I do."

Don't be afraid, she reminded herself. Don't be afraid. But she couldn't help it. She was terrified of what might happen, but more so of what might not happen.

"Deuce—"

"Just do it, Eva. We gotta talk."

Biting her lip, she looked out the window, across the beautifully manicured field that constituted Cox and Kami's front yard. She couldn't handle another failed attempt at being together. It would break her.

She took a deep breath. "Okay," she whispered. She had barely gotten the word out before he hung up.

"Mama?"

Shoving her phone in her purse, she glanced over at her daughter. "Yeah, baby?"

"You sad?"

Eva swiped at the tears running down her cheeks.

"Just a little bit, baby," she whispered, leaning over the bench seat to place a kiss on her daughter's chubby, dimpled cheek, then ran her fingers through her tight blonde curls. "But mama's gonna be okay. I promise."

With a heavy sigh, she put the truck in gear and headed home.

CHAPTER 18

TWISTING THE DOORKNOB, DEUCE PUSHED OPEN THE side door and walked inside the house. Closing the door softly behind him, he locked it, set the alarm, kicked off his boots, and walked quietly through the dark kitchen, headed for the stairs.

He found Eva on his side of the bed, her body curled around his pillow, sound asleep. He stared down at her for several moments, his hand hovering just over her head, wanting so badly just to touch her, to feel her again without thinking about . . .

He could do this. He could touch her and it would only be about her and him and no one else. Just her, just him . . . just her . . .

Fuck.

He spun away, cursing, and headed for the bathroom.

Turning on the shower, he stripped off his clothes, stepped inside, and stood under the spray of hot water, his eyes squeezed shut, wishing, praying for the strength to put his family back together.

Preacher might be the biggest dick to ever walk the earth, but he'd been right about one thing. If he took off, left in the middle of the mess Frankie had made of his club, everything would fall to ruin in his wake.

He had to fix this shit.

He just didn't know how.

Deuce had never been any good at cleaning up messes. Usually he just ignored them, moved the fuck on, and eventually forgot about them. Or at least tried to forget about them. There were some he'd never been able to let go of. The biggest one being the beautiful woman sleeping on his side of the bed. Eva had been the best mess he'd ever made and now . . .

He was still making a mess of things between them.

Then, as if she knew, as if she could feel how badly he was aching for her, the shower door clicked open and Eva stood naked before him. His eyes skimmed her body, her heavy breasts and perfect curves, and he hardened instantly, wanting her.

"Can I join you?" she whispered.

He nodded, moving aside to let her in and she stepped inside, filling the small space he'd allowed her.

They stared at each other. Her looking up at him with those big gray eyes filled with pain and confusion and so much wanting, and him, looking down at her, watching her hair flatten against her cheeks and shoulders as the water poured over her.

"I fucked up, Eva," he hoarsely blurted out. "I got into it with your old man. I was feelin' shitty and pissed off and I tried to fuck some bitch but—"

He never saw it coming.

Eva's fist slammed into his jaw with an audible crack and his head whipped right.

"Fuck," he muttered, cupping his jaw.

"You fucking piece of shit!" she screamed, spinning around and kicking open the shower door.

He lunged for her, grabbing hold of her wrists as he propelled them both across the bathroom. Belly first, he pinned her up against the wall and bent his head to her ear.

"I couldn't do it," he growled. "I didn't even want to."

"You're never going to stop!" she cried, struggling against his grip. "You're never going to change!"

"I didn't fuckin' do it!"

"Did you touch her? Did she touch you?"

He fell silent and closed his eyes. "Baby," he rasped. "It was only—"

Eva went screaming crazy in his grip, thrashing and kicking and shrieking nonsense at the top of her lungs.

"STOP!" he roared, trying to keep a good hold on her but they were both wet from the shower, and Eva managed to twist a hand free of his grip. She spun around, her hand flew through the air and he had only enough time to flinch before her palm cracked down on his cheek and already sore jaw.

"Motherfuck!" he yelled, grabbing for and missing her hand. She slapped him again, this time, on his ear.

"You wanna hit me?" he roared, curling his hand into a fist as she continued slapping and shoving him. "Then fuckin' hit me, EVA! FUCKIN' REALLY HIT ME! FUCKIN' HURT ME, BITCH. *FUCKIN' HURT ME*!"

He slammed his own fist into the side of his head and he swore he felt his brain do a goddamned backflip.

He hit himself five more times, swift punches, each to his face, one right after the other, *bam-bam-bam*, before he realized Eva had fallen silent, staring up at him with tears streaming down her face.

"It's never going to end," she whispered. "Is it?" Reaching up, she cupped the side of his cheek and ran the pad of her thumb under his eye. "We were doomed from the start, weren't we, baby?"

Years of heartache and pain grabbed hold of his balls and twisted like a motherfucker.

"No," he growled, slapping her hand off him and grabbing her face, squeezing her cheeks. "You ain't leavin', don't even think it."

She tried to shake her head in protest and he squeezed harder, refusing to let her interrupt him.

"Shut up and listen to me," he demanded. "Everything's all fucked-up right now but that don't mean it's always gonna be that way. Shit's been bad before and we figured it the fuck out, didn't we?"

When she didn't respond, he glared at her. "Didn't we?"

She nodded.

"Yeah, we fuckin' did. And we're gonna do it again. I'm gonna fix it, Eva. I came home tonight to start fixin' it and I'm tellin' you that I didn't fuck the bitch. I couldn't fuck her, not when all I want is you, darlin'."

He watched more tears pool in her eyes and spill over.

"I'm gonna fix it," he said fiercely. "And then I'm gonna

fix it again and keep on fixin' it until the bad stops outweighin' the good, until there ain't nothin' but good left.

"You feel me, Eva?" he asked, releasing her face.

She nodded again. "Promise?" she whimpered in a small, child-like voice, full of pain and desperation that gutted him straight to his soul.

"Promise," he growled, grabbing the back of her head and crushing his mouth to hers. A breath, a blink, a heartbeat passed and Eva was gripping him, grabbing at his hair and climbing up his body, wrapping her legs around his waist.

He fought desperately against the images that assaulted him while battling the rising nausea in his gut as he tried to give her what she needed, what they both needed . . . and failed.

"Fuck," he whispered, pulling away from her mouth, tears burning in his eyes. "I can't . . . not yet."

"*No*," she cried, gripping his face, forcing him back. "No, no, no, please, Deuce, please . . . I'm yours, baby, I've always been yours. Please, baby, please make me yours again . . . please make it good again."

His tears spilled over and he gritted his teeth, feeling pathetic, hating the fact that he was crying, hating being helpless, just fucking hating everything and everyone.

"Please don't stop," she choked out, her own tears falling. "Please."

He grabbed her before he could think twice about it, determined to make good on his promise. He grabbed her and kissed her and she kissed him back, hard and fast, and in turn he kissed her harder and she gripped him tighter and it became a battle for control, for power, but not power over each other, power over their life together, power to regain control of what had been so brutally ripped away from them.

"Say it," he rasped. "Fuckin' say it, Eva, say it right the fuck now."

"I love you," she cried softly. "No one else, baby, not like this, not the way I've always loved you."

"How much do you love me?" he asked hoarsely, cupping her breast and squeezing.

"You already know," she whimpered. "You're everything to me, everything, you always have been, baby . . ." She trailed off and peeked up at him with those damn eyes of hers. Staring straight into his rotted-out soul, supercharging him with need.

He needed to lay claim to her once and for all, to strip her of that beautiful spirit, to keep it safe, protected inside him so that no one, not one single motherfucking thing or person could ever take her away from him again.

"You're my reason, Deuce," she whispered through her tears. "You always have been."

He stopped moving and stared at her.

Her reason.

Him.

The knowledge propelled him forward and he found himself pushing inside of her, fat tears rolling down his cheeks, splashing against her chest as he shuddered through the onslaught of both unwanted memories and wanting, needing to be inside of her for so long now and not being able to.

And then . . .

He groaned as she quivered, moaning as she stretched

for him.

Fuck, she was tight and wet and his, she was all his.

"I love you," she whimpered, her head falling backward. "I love you so, so much, Deuce."

Fuck him.

"Eva," he rasped, cupping the back of her head and forcing her to look at him. "Marry me, darlin'."

A sob escaped past her beautiful lips and her eyes filled up again. He took her mouth with his and kissed her softly, slowly, making his way across her cheek to her ear, where he paused.

"One more time, babe," he whispered. "Marry me?"

"Yes," she breathed out.

He closed his eyes.

He was home.

It had taken him nearly half a century to get there, but he'd made it.

He was finally, finally fucking home.

"Deuce?"

"Yeah?"

"You're gonna have to call Christine."

His eyes flew open and he glared down at Eva, wondering why the fuck she was talking about his ex when he was balls-deep inside her, asking her to marry him.

"Why the fuck do I gotta—"

She placed a finger over his lips and smiled. "In case you forgot, baby, you're still married. Kinda makes it hard to marry me."

"Fuck," he muttered, closing his eyes again. "Fuck, fuck, fuck."

"She's going to want money," Eva mused.

“Yeah.”

“A lot of money.”

“Yeah.”

“She’s—”

“Jesus Christ, woman, shut the fuck up. Here I am tryin’ to fuck you and you’re tryin’ to make me blow a fuckin’ hole in my skull.”

“Sorry.” She giggled.

Deuce glared down at her until he couldn’t continue glaring at her perfect, smiling face and ended up smiling like a damn fool himself.

“Eva?”

“Yeah?”

“I’m gonna fuck you now.”

“Okay,” she whispered, running her index finger underneath his bottom lip. “But, Deuce?”

“Babe?”

“I want it slow.”

He grinned.

Then he gave it to her slow.

CHAPTER 19

"HELLO?" I SAID BREATHLESSLY, NEARLY FALLING out of bed trying to grab my cell phone off the nightstand.

"Eva's tellin' me you're campin' with Anabeth and her family?"

My brain stalled out.

Father.

My father was on the phone.

And I'd completely forgotten about everything other than Ripper and the past week we'd spent together.

"Yes," I choked out, my hand over my pounding heart, trying desperately to swallow the sudden anxiety that, at the sound of my father's voice, had lodged itself in my throat.

"Yeah, well, I'm back, so when you comin' home?"

"Tomorrow," I said quickly.

There was a long pause. "Like to spend some time with you, baby girl," he said gruffly. "I know I've been—"

"Don't," I whispered, squeezing my eyes shut, counteracting my burgeoning tears.

"Danny girl," he said softly. "I—"

"Please, Daddy, don't do this now, not over the phone."

I could absolutely not listen to his excuses and apologies right now, not while I was happy for the first time in over a year. I wasn't going to let him ruin this for me too.

He cleared his throat. "I just wanna see my daughter, Danny, that's all. I know I got some time to make up for."

Between his recent parental absenteeism and his inability to salvage his relationship with the only woman on earth who'd ever truly loved him despite his many faults, he suddenly wanted to do some father/daughter bonding?

What had changed?

But no matter how much I wanted to scream at him, to tell him he didn't deserve to spend time with me, I couldn't. He'd taken Cage and me when our mother ran off, no questions asked, and never once complained about it. He'd always made sure we were cared for in his absence. Yes, there were a lot of absences, and yes, he could be a hard man, a brooding, miserable man, a man who was better at running and hiding than expressing his feelings.

But he was my father.

And I loved him.

"Eva's home," he continued when I didn't say anything.

She was? With him? Had he found his missing heart in North Dakota?

"Are you . . . together?" I asked, hoping and praying they were.

I felt Ripper's arms snake around my middle and pull me backward, feeling his thick, ropey scars as his chest slid up my bare back. He pressed a kiss into my hair and a tear snuck through the corner of my closed lids. I quickly swiped it away.

"We're together," my father said quietly. "Asked her to marry me last night."

All breath fled my lungs.

"What did she say?" I whispered.

"What the fuck do you think?"

I smiled. Now that sounded more like my father. "Yes?"

"Yeah, darlin'," he said gruffly. "She said yes."

I sucked in a deep breath. She'd said yes. *She'd said yes.* Things were going to finally get back to normal. I was going to have my family back. No more lonely nights spent eating dinner alone and watching bad television.

"I'll be home tomorrow," I said, my voice firmer.

"Good," he said and hung up.

I pressed end and set my phone back down.

"Your old man?" Ripper asked.

"Yeah," I whispered, turning in his arms and snuggling into his embrace. "He asked Eva to marry him."

"No shit? Damn. Didn't see that shit comin'."

I scattered kisses along the largest scar on his chest. One of his hands found the small of my back and the other slid up into my hair, gripping my head. "Neither did I," I murmured. "But you know what this means?"

"We're gonna fuck again?"

"No," I whispered. It meant if my father was happy again, Ripper might be able to tell him about us without worrying about flying bullets.

"Baby," he said, studying me. "You're thinkin' again."

"I'm not."

"Nose is all scrunched up, eyes unfocused, lips parted. Yeah, you're thinkin' again."

I scowled at him. "You think you know everything."

"No," he said softly. "I don't know shit, never did. But, baby, for some fuckin' reason, I know you. Crazy, yeah?"

"Ripper," I whispered, staring up into his eyes, a deep beautiful blue, one real and one made of glass, thinking about how right it felt to be with him. "We can tell him now," I said, feeling hopeful. "We could wait awhile but then—"

Ripper let out an exasperated sigh as he pushed me away from him. Rolling onto his back, he glared up at the ceiling.

"No, Danny, how many times I gotta tell you, no one is tellin' him nothin'. It ain't gonna matter if Eva and him are doin' better, he ain't never gonna let me be with you. I get smacked in the head just for lookin' at you. What do you think is gonna happen if he finds out I've been doin' a whole lot more than lookin'?" Shaking his head, he grimaced. "And on your prom night. Jesus, I'm a fuckin' dirtbag."

"Thanks for the self-esteem boost," I muttered.

"Baby," he said, turning to look at me. "Bein' with you is worth winnin' dirtbag of the year, yeah? Now, shut the fuck up about tellin' your old man, it ain't happenin'. Not until you're at least thirty."

"Fine." I sighed, knowing after spending nearly a week with him that it was pointless to keep arguing.

"Good, glad we agree. What you need to be doin' is gettin' your own place."

"Um, don't you sort of need money to have your own place?"

"Yeah. Get a fuckin' job."

"Hello? I start college in the fall. I won't have time."

He shook his head. "Spoiled," he muttered.

Offended, I punched him in the shoulder, earning myself a loud snort. "Ow," he said mockingly.

"I hate you."

"No, you don't. Now go make breakfast. I'm fuckin' hungry."

"There's no food, Mr. Bossy. We ate it all."

"There's tequila."

"Tequila isn't breakfast."

"Says you."

Ripper was happy.

It had been so damn long, he almost hadn't recognized the light, airy feeling.

Almost.

But then he remembered the way it had felt his first time catching a wave and not falling off his board, or his first ollie where he'd landed upright instead of on his head, or his parents' twentieth wedding anniversary party during which he'd gotten his first blow job.

Or the first time he'd gotten on a bike and put the road behind him.

He smiled into his pillow. He was actually looking forward to the future. As long as it included Danny.

Which, at present, was going to be difficult, but . . .

If she couldn't afford her own place, he'd help her out. Not sure how she'd explain that to Deuce, but Ripper needed her out of that house and more accessible to him. Maybe if one of her friends roomed with her . . .

That could work.

They could make this work. Yeah, it was going to suck sneaking around, but it was doable and it wouldn't be forever. Just ten, maybe twenty years. Or until Deuce was too old and feeble to do anything about it. Or maybe they could just hold out until Deuce kicked it. The dude was getting up there, and in their line of work, no one usually made it to eighty. Except Blue.

"Fuck," he groaned. He didn't want Deuce to die. He wanted Deuce to accept him as Danny's man.

Which wasn't ever going to happen. Deuce knew all his dirty secrets, including how many bitches he'd fucked and how many lives he'd taken. There was no way he was going to want a man like him with his daughter. It was hypocritical, but Ripper understood it. If he had a daughter, he wouldn't want her shacking up with some trigger-happy asshole, who'd once made it his goal in life to fuck as many women as he possibly could.

Fuck it. They'd have to sneak around. There wasn't any other way. Danny was going to have to get her own place, her own car, maybe even move a town over. She could go on a few runs with him, so they could be out in public together somewhere far away from Montana without having to worry about being caught. He'd do what he could to make her happy and keep Deuce from finding out.

"Ripper?"

He flipped onto his back, expecting to find Danny carrying something resembling breakfast. Instead he found her standing just outside his bedroom doorway, trembling and wide-eyed with fear.

"Baby?" he asked, sitting up. "What's the—"

Danny stumbled forward into the room and Nikki appeared behind, her heavily lined, angry eyes trained on him, the gun in her hand pressed into Danny's side and . . .

Everything stopped. Everything. His brain, his breathing, his heart.

"You fuckin' scumbag asshole," Nikki hissed. "You've been ignoring me, not answering my phone calls, and I'm thinking something's happened to you! I was actually worried about you!"

Using the gun, she shoved Danny further into the room. "But instead I find you at home? And with her!"

Again she shoved Danny and his entire body twitched as he fought the urge to leap off his bed and beat Nikki to death.

"Nikki," he said, trying to keep his voice low and even. "What the fuck are you doin'? Let her go," he bit out through clenched teeth. "This ain't what you think."

Nikki's eyes went wide. "It ain't what I think? So you're not shacked up with Deuce's fuckin' daughter?"

"She was just stayin' over," he said quietly. "It ain't like that."

"Bullshit!" Nikki spat. "You haven't touched me in months! And now I find Danny in your kitchen, half naked, and you're tryin' to tell me it ain't like that? I heard you callin' her baby, Ripper! It *is* like that!"

"So, what're you gonna do, bitch?" he growled, his patience quickly waning. "You gonna blow a hole in Deuce's fuckin' daughter? You do that, you know hell is gonna be rainin' down on you."

"I don't give a fuck!" she yelled. "I've put up with your

bullshit for how long? Since I was twenty-two years old, Ripper, waiting to be your old lady! And instead, this is what I get in return? You fuckin' little girls behind my back!"

Fuck. Jesus fucking fuck. He wasn't just going to kill this bitch, he was going to make it hurt.

"I've been fuckin' girls behind your back since the beginnin'!" he yelled.

"Whores!" she screamed. "You've been fuckin' whores and Danny ain't no whore! I ain't stupid!"

He glanced at Danny and his heart constricted. She was terrified. And it was all his fault.

"DON'T LOOK AT HER!" Nikki screamed. "YOU LOOK AT ME! I DESERVE THAT MUCH!"

His eyes shot back to Nikki, whose shaking hand was two seconds away from accidentally blowing a hole in the woman he loved. So he did what he had to do, to get the focus of that gun off Danny and on him.

"You're fuckin' crazy, thinkin' whatever you're thinkin'. Yeah, Danny ain't no whore but that don't mean I give a fuck. She's hot pussy and, bitch, you're shot. Fuckin' used up and lookin' old." He shrugged. "Ain't feelin' you no more."

Both women sucked in sharp breaths but he kept his gaze on Nikki and forced out a hard laugh. "Fuckin' crazy bitches, thinkin' I give a fuck about either one of you."

Just as he'd expected, any remaining shred of sanity left inside Nikki fled. Her arm shot forward and . . .

Ripper leaped off the bed and to the left, hoping to avoid the bullet but he wasn't fast enough and searing pain sliced through his side. He stumbled sideways, slamming into the wall just as two more shots rang out.

He whipped around, expecting to find Danny shot, or

worse, but instead found Nikki crumpled in a heap on the floor, choking as blood gurgled up out of her mouth.

And standing above her was Danny, Nikki's gun in her hands.

CHAPTER 20

Ripper pushed open the door to Deuce's office where he found his prez sitting behind his desk, Cox was perched on the side of it, and across the room Mick and ZZ were at opposite ends of a leather sofa.

His stomach firmly lodged in his throat, Ripper closed the door behind him and crossed his arms over his chest.

Deuce's eyes fixed on him. "Freebird said you needed to talk to me?"

He nodded, feeling like an asshole for what he was about to do to Deuce and the club. But he didn't have much of a choice.

He'd given it a shitload of thought. Sat on the bathroom floor for twelve straight hours, just smoking and thinking.

This needed to be done.

For Danny's sake.

For Danny's future's sake.

Eventually she'd get over it, without him hanging around like a dark cloud, reminding her every other second that she'd killed a woman. Because of him. She'd grow to hate him and the thought of those icy blue eyes looking at him with anything but love in them made him sick to his stomach.

Clearing his throat, he said, "This ain't fuckin' easy for me, Prez. Known you since I was seventeen, been with the club a long time now—"

Cox shot to his feet. "What the fuck you doin', Ripper?"

He looked at his friend. His brother.

"I gotta go," he said quietly.

"Fuck that!" Cox yelled. "You tell me why you gotta go, 'cause I ain't seein' it!"

As if he'd been kicked in the balls, his breath caught, nausea powered through him and his vision swam. Christ, Cox wasn't going to let him go easy. There was too much history, they'd been friends too long, fucked a lot of shit up together . . . hell, they'd fucked a lot of girls together too. Cox wasn't just his brother, Cox was his best friend, for fuck's sake.

"Prez," he gritted out through clenched teeth, ignoring Cox. "I can't do my fuckin' job, I'm not right in the fuckin' head, and . . . I gotta go. I gotta get my shit under control."

"Ripper," Mick said, leaning forward, resting his forearms on his knees. "You haven't exactly been right since Frankie fucked you up. Why are you decidin' this now?"

He didn't say anything. What could he say? He couldn't tell them about being with Danny; Deuce would kill him on the spot, and no one but Cox knew about Nikki. Either way, if anyone found out about either, it wouldn't take them very long to realize the events were related and he could absolutely not let that happen. He would not let that shit fall on Danny in any way. This shit was on him, all of it; just another fucking check mark on his long list of sins.

The through and through on his side burning like a motherfucker, Ripper grunted in pain as he gently set Danny down on his bed. He knelt in front of her and she looked up at him with tears in her eyes.

"I . . . I . . . I killed her," she whispered hoarsely, her eyes wide, her expression a mixture of utter disbelief and horror.

"No!" he yelled, grabbing her arms. "No, you did not! This shit was my fault, baby! I shoulda ended shit with her a long time ago. Me bein' stupid killed her! Do you understand me?"

She shook her head. "No . . . I shot her . . . she—"

"No!" he roared. "Fuckin' listen to me! I. Killed. Her. Me. Not you."

She didn't say anything, just stared at him, violently trembling.

Cursing, he got to his feet and grabbed his cell phone off the nightstand.

Cox answered immediately.

"Got a problem," he said.

"Got one of my own," Cox said and Ripper could hear Kami yelling nonsense in the background.

"Cox, brother, I wouldn't ask but I got a dead Nikki on my bedroom floor and a hole in my side."

Silence.

Then, "Gimme an hour and I'll be there. You need Z?"

ZZ, the only brother who could sew them up nice and neat when shit got ugly.

"Naw, it's just a flesh wound."

"And Nikki? Two-man job?"

"Yeah . . . and, Cox?"

"Yeah?"

"You know what you gotta bring, yeah?"

"Don't worry, I got you covered. Ain't nothin' about that bitch will be left to find."

No shit. He was not going to allow one shred of evidence to remain that could in any way, shape, or form be traced back to Danny.

Ripper blinked back to the present as Deuce stood up, placed his palms on his desk, and leaned forward. "This is my club, you're my boy, and that makes you a part of my motherfuckin' family. So this is how shit's gonna go down. Frankie Deluva is done fuckin' up my family. So, yeah, you take some' time, ride it out, and then you get your ass back here where you belong."

Ripper lowered his eyes. For the first time in a long time, he wasn't thinking about what Frankie had done to him. In fact, he hadn't been thinking about Frankie at all lately.

"SHUT UP!" Cox roared, startling everyone in the room. To everyone's astonishment, Cox bent over the desk and shoved his face up in Deuce's personal space.

"I get why you're lettin' him go, but if you let him go and some shit goes down and we're not there for him, then what the fuck is gonna happen?"

Fuck him. As if this wasn't hard enough.

His expression sad, Deuce lifted his arm and grabbed the side of Cox's face. "Say good-bye to your boy," he said quietly, giving Cox's cheek a soft slap. "Then go home to your family."

Family.

Ripper's throat closed up. He was leaving the only family he had.

Before he broke down, he shrugged off his cut, pulled his dagger from its sheath on his boot, and started slicing through the stitches that held his sergeant-at-arms patch on the vest. By the time he was finished, all eyes were on him. Stalking forward, he slammed his patch down on Deuce's desk and with a sinking feeling in his stomach, turned to leave.

"Ripper," Deuce growled.

Reluctantly, he turned back around.

"This is still your club, brother. This will always be your club and you are still my boy, ain't no shit ever gonna change that. You get your shit together, you come back, your patch will be waitin' on you, you feel me?"

Jesus Christ, he had to get out of this room.

"Yeah," he muttered and left the office. A handful of brothers playing pool all stopped to watch him walk away. He quickened his pace, headed for the door.

"Ripper," Cox said, grabbing his arm.

He closed his eyes and let out a frustrated breath. Brother wasn't going to make this easy on him.

"Don't do this," Cox said quietly. "Don't run just 'cause shit went down bad with Nikki. I ain't gonna say a word and you know, sure as shit, she ain't never gonna be found. Not after what we did."

He wasn't running away and he couldn't give two shits about Nikki. Nikki had been fill-in, like an old pillow he'd only kept around just because it was there, had been for a long time, and what the fuck, it was a pillow, he needed a pillow, and she'd fit the bill.

Until Danny.

And like everything else in his life, that had gone to shit real fucking quick.

If Ripper had learned anything in his thirty-something years of life, it was that dark roads only get darker if you stay on them, and his road was pretty damn dark.

So he was giving Danny the only good thing he could give her, what he couldn't give her if he stayed here. The sooner he left, the sooner she could go back to being a normal girl, having a normal life, one without his inner demons and *his* dead girlfriends. A life without a man who could kill without a second thought. Yeah, his girl deserved better and so better was what he was going to give her.

"Brother," he choked out. "Right now me and the road, we got some reconnecting to do, yeah?"

Cox stared at him, his dark eyes narrowing.

"I need to go," he said firmly.

Shaking his head, Cox released him.

And he left.

Left his brothers.

Left the club.

Left Miles City.

Left Montana.

Left . . . Danny.

CHAPTER 21

"DANNY GIRL," CAGE WHISPERED, SOFTLY BRUSHING my hair out of my eyes. "Danny."

I blinked several times, trying to blink back sleep and dried tears and memories I didn't want.

"Gotta get outta bed, little sister."

"Go away," I whispered hoarsely.

I shoved his arm away from me and rolled over on my side.

Two weeks. Four days. A handful of hours.

Ripper had been gone for two weeks, four days, and a handful of hours.

At first, when he hadn't answered my text messages or phone calls after dropping me at Anabeth's house, unable to sleep or eat or do much of anything except pace and shake, the next day I'd tagged along with Eva and Ivy to the club.

And that's when I saw the sad faces, heard the whispered conversations. That's when I knew.

"Ripper left."

I pushed my sweatshirt hood off my head and turned to Tegen.

"He just up and left," she continued, shrugging. "Didn't even give a reason. Isn't that, like, against the rules or something?"

"Wh-what?" I whispered, my voice cracking.

Tegen eyed me strangely. "You okay?"

I didn't answer her. I couldn't. Fuck speaking, I couldn't even breathe.

He'd left.

He'd just up and left me.

And now . . .

I was dying.

At least it felt like I was.

I could barely eat. When I did manage to sleep, it was riddled with nightmares, images of Nikki's dead body and blood . . . everywhere.

I always woke up crying or on the verge of crying. I'd never felt so awful, so alone, so desolate before.

So empty.

Aching.

Oh God, it hurt . . . so damn bad.

And it was all my fault.

I'd pushed for something to happen between us, and . . . and I . . .

I had shot Nikki.

Me.

I'd killed her.

Now Ripper was gone because I'd been a selfish little girl who'd wanted him so badly I hadn't cared about the repercussions my actions would bring down on him.

"Danny," Cage pleaded. "You're makin' yourself sick, please—"

"Get out of my room!" I screamed, yanking my blankets up over my head. I didn't want to get out of bed. I didn't want to do anything. I didn't want anything at all . . . except to stop feeling, to lie in bed and waste away. Or die, I didn't care.

Clutching the rim of the toilet bowl, Ripper's face fell forward. Gagging and dry heaving, he began expelling another round of tequila vomit. When he finished, he spit, stood, and gripped the edge of the sink. Pulling himself up, he fell forward and leaned over the counter. Swaying heavily, he managed to turn the tap on and wash his mouth out.

He wanted to go back. He wanted Danny. She was all he could think about. The only thing keeping him from turning his ass around was keeping a bottle with him at all times and pussy in his bed. It helped, gave him a minute sense of comfort, but just barely.

He needed something else, a bigger distraction and real comfort, the kind that only comes from familiarity.

The kind that came from family.

Family . . .

He could go home, back to California, back to the house he owned yet hadn't been inside of since he'd lost his parents.

For the first time since he'd lost the only two people in

the world who'd loved him unconditionally, Ripper wanted to go home. They wouldn't be there but his memories would, the foundation and four walls that he'd grown up inside of would be full of mementos and photos of everything he'd lost. And that was something.

Stumbling out of the bathroom, gripping the walls, he made his way back into the motel bedroom. Shielding his eyes, he cursed both the sun and the naked bitch sprawled across the bed he'd paid for like she fucking owned it. Seizing her arm, he haphazardly dragged her off the bed and dumped her on the floor, so he could take her place in bed. Another bitch, he couldn't remember their names for the life of him, rolled over and curled up around him with a sigh. He shoved her off him and grabbed the nearly empty bottle on the nightstand.

"You gonna share?" the bitch whined, reaching for him again, running her hand down his body and taking hold of his cock.

He elbowed her hard, shoving her off him and, because she was still hammered or crazier than shit, the bitch started laughing.

Annoying, high-pitched, drunken laughter.

His head throbbed angrily.

But he'd picked her for a reason. Because she was blonde, a real blonde, her hair nearly white and her body was toned and tight and her skin tanned, soft, and smooth.

"Too drunk to fuck." She laughed.

"Fuck off," he growled.

She laughed harder and he reached for her, grabbed hold of her hair, and yanked her face close to his. "Shut. The. Fuck. Up."

She didn't.

Still gripping her hair, Ripper rolled on top of her and dumped the last of the tequila over her face. "You gonna shut the fuck up now, you dirty fuckin' whore?" he yelled as she thrashed beneath him.

She didn't answer, because she couldn't.

Because he had her face shoved down in the pillows.

CHAPTER 22

A BLONDE NURSE IN PINK SCRUBS WITH SMALL WRINKLES around her deep brown eyes appeared in my line of vision. "How we doing?" she asked kindly.

Fighting my tears, I nodded jerkily and tried to focus on her instead of the cramping, rippling sensation in my abdomen and the dull roar of the machine that was sucking out the tiny little life growing inside of me. I should have opted for the drugs they'd offered me. But not having a ride home, I'd thought it best to have my head clear.

But having a clear head meant I was fully aware of what was happening to me . . .

To my baby . . .

I'd never given much thought to having children other than the passing, "I'd like to . . . someday." But now, even as terrified as I was, now that I had one inside of me, Ripper's baby, I wanted to keep it there, keep it safe, feel it grow, hold it in my arms. Be a *mom*.

Just not without Ripper.

And if this baby came out looking like a little version of him . . .

No longer able to hold them back, my tears began to fall.

"Almost done, honey," the nurse said, rubbing my arm. "Almost done."

Sucking in a breath, I squeezed my eyes shut and turned away from her.

I was a wreck, my life was a wreck, everything was just . . . wrong.

Irreparable.

And all I could think about was Ripper.

I loved him and missed him and *hated* him for leaving me. Leaving me all alone with my screwed-up family and both my beautiful and horrible memories of him and us and all the horrible pain and the gut-wrenching guilt that came with them. All of it had piled so heavily on top of me, I could barely stand any more.

I was tired all the time, physically and emotionally, and eventually I was just too tired to get my life in any semblance of order and back on track. I showered as often as I ate, which was nearly never because I couldn't seem to keep anything down.

Then, on top of everything else, two weeks ago I'd discovered I was pregnant. After sharing my secret with Anabeth, she'd given me the number and address of a clinic in Billings that accepted patients without health insurance, or in my case, patients who had health insurance yet couldn't use it without their father finding out.

So I'd borrowed some money from my father's bedroom safe and taken a bus out of town.

And all of this had happened in just three short months. Ninety days. It had taken a mere ninety days for my entire life to fall apart.

"Here we go," the nurse said, holding my elbow as I struggled to sit up. On shaking legs, I followed her out of the procedure room into the recovery room, and slid into the medical reclining chair she gestured to.

"Can I have some water?" I said hoarsely.

"You need juice, honey," she replied. "I'll go get some."

I nodded and she walked off. A quick survey of the room showed me three other women, also seated in recovery chairs, avoiding eye contact while several busy nurses walked back and forth. Closing my eyes, I let my head roll off to the side.

"Here's your juice," the nurse said, handing me a small paper cup. She began flipping through a chart while I sipped on apple juice.

"Remember that bleeding and blood clots are normal, as is cramping, but if you're bleeding excessively—"

I stared up at the kind nurse, not really listening, thinking about Ripper, wondering where he was and what he was doing. Wondering if he'd known that I was pregnant, if it would have made a difference. Would he have come back home? Wondering why he had left in the first place and why wouldn't he answer my phone calls.

Wondering if he'd been with another woman.

"Do you have a ride home?" the nurse asked, handing me several small squares of paper. I glanced at the prescriptions, wondering how I was going to fill them without anyone finding out.

I shook my head. "I'm taking the bus."

When the bleeding had slowed and I could stand without shaking, I was discharged. Exhausted and nauseous, I pushed through the front door of the clinic and stopped dead. Standing in the snow-covered parking lot, leaning against his pickup and smoking a cigarette, was my brother.

Seeing me Cage cursed, flicked his cigarette away, and strode quickly toward me. I tried to shrink away from him but he was quicker than me, bigger and stronger, and grabbed a hold of my shoulders. "Who?" he demanded. "I want to know who did this, right the fuck now."

Clutching my abdomen, I gaped at him. "What are you doing here?" I demanded weakly.

"Tegen told me," he gritted out. "Now fuckin' answer me!"

Tegen? Tegen!

"How did Tegen know?" I shrieked, my pain turning suddenly into mortification and terror that my father or Eva knew as well. Did the entire club know? The whole world?

"Ellie," he said, growing angrier by the second. "She was worried about you and called me this morning. Ana-fuckin'-slut let it slip and when Ellie couldn't get a hold of you, she called me."

I narrowed my eyes. "That still doesn't explain how Tegen found out."

"I was in the fuckin' shower and she answered my damn phone."

"She's gonna tell someone!" I cried.

"No she ain't, I made sure of it. Now, tell me who the

fuck knocked your ass up so I can find 'em and fuckin' kill 'em."

"Stop it!" I hissed. "It's none of your business."

"Like fuck it isn't!" he yelled.

"Cage." I sighed. "Just take me home, okay? I'm really tired."

He let loose a string of curses. "So you're not tellin' me, huh? You're gonna protect some sorry-ass motherfucker who let you deal with this shit all by yourself?"

"He doesn't know," I whispered.

Cage's brown eyes bored into me, watching me intently. I knew the exact moment he put two and two together. His entire demeanor changed and his expression turned hard and violent.

"You in bed with a brother, Danny? 'Cause if you are, Dad is—"

"Cage!" I yelled. "Don't you dare tell him anything! What I do is none of his business! Or yours!"

"Fuck!" he bellowed, spinning away from me, running his hands through his hair. "You are! You're fuckin' a brother!"

"Why was Tegen in your bedroom while you were showering?" I demanded, the only reason why Tegen would have been in my brother's bedroom suddenly occurring to me. "Does Dorothy need to know you're screwing her underage daughter?"

His nostrils flaring wildly, his jaw locked up tight, Cage looked every inch our father, the last person I wanted to be reminded of at the moment.

"I'll figure it out," he seethed. "Whoever it is, I'll figure it out."

No, he wouldn't. There was nothing left to figure out. Ripper was long gone.

"Are you seriously gonna keep yelling at me in front of an abortion clinic?" I asked. "Could we at least get in the truck?"

Cage let his head fall back as he sighed angrily. When he looked back at me, his expression had considerably softened.

"Coulda fuckin' told me, little sister," he said quietly. "Woulda never let you go through all this shit by yourself."

Grabbing my hand, he threaded his large fingers through mine and squeezed. "This is what big brothers are fuckin' here for," he said, pulling me toward his truck. "To pick their little sisters up when they fall the fuck down."

I said nothing while he opened the passenger door, aiding me as I climbed inside.

"You need anything?" he asked.

I pulled my prescriptions out of my purse and handed them to him. "Just these," I whispered.

Nodding, he shoved the papers in his pocket and closed the door.

I watched him walk around the front of the truck, big and broad, strong and tall, ready to take on the world if he had to.

I could tell him. I could trust someone with what had happened. I could finally unburden myself and my guilty conscience.

I just couldn't trust him not to tell our father. Maybe he'd keep quiet about my relationship with Ripper, but what I'd done to Nikki . . .

He'd tell.

I wasn't sure what my father's reaction would be, but he would undoubtedly blame Ripper for the entire thing when it wasn't his fault. It was mine. I'd wrestled the gun away from her, I'd pulled the trigger, and I'd killed her.

As Cage climbed into the truck, I sank back into the seat and closed my eyes. I couldn't tell a soul. I'd take the secret to my grave, even if it meant I'd have to bear the burden alone. Even if it meant my slow but certain, utter ruin.

Gritting his teeth, Ripper lifted the tire and hefted it up onto the rim of the vehicle when his cell phone started vibrating. Turning around, he pulled his phone out of his coveralls pocket and saw it was Deuce calling him.

Jesus Christ.

Why wouldn't they stop?

Why couldn't they just leave him the fuck alone?

His phone beeped, signaling a voice mail. Blowing out a heavy breath, Ripper stalked through the garage and headed outside.

"Jacobs!" Phil Marinetti, the auto body shop's owner bellowed. "Where the fuck you goin'?"

"Break!" he shouted and kicked open the door.

Lighting a cigarette, he leaned against the wall, pulled out his phone, and listened to his pileup of messages.

"Ripper, it's Deuce. Got a bead on Jimmy. Word is he's out in Cali. So, brother, the job's there if ya want it. Gimme a call."

And . . .

"Yo, Ripper, it's Cox, just wanted to know where the fuck you're at, brother."

And . . .

"Hey, asshole. Hawk here. Just checkin' the fuck in, makin' sure you're still breathin'."

And before he knew what was happening, his phone started playing his saved messages. All from Danny.

"Please, please call me back. I can't breathe, Ripper, I can't think straight, and I can't eat or sleep and everything is all screwed up. I miss you so much . . . why did you leave?"

He quickly hit end and shoved his phone back in his pocket. Finished with his cigarette, he stalked back inside the shop and back to the old Chevy he was working on.

Ripper had been home in Cali for several months now, cleaning out his parents' old house, selling their shit, working at Marinetti's Garage. He'd put away his cut, shaved his head, put his bike in the garage, and after fixing it up, he'd been driving around his old man's pickup.

He'd stopped fucking blondes that reminded him of Danny.

He was trying to move the fuck on.

But none of those motherfuckers back in Montana were letting him.

And Danny . . .

Jesus Christ.

She was killing him. The voice mails were getting worse. She was getting worse.

Twice now, after listening to her messages, hearing the raw pain in her voice, hearing her tears, the violent switch of emotions, he'd almost gone back. Almost.

But he couldn't.

Eventually, she'd get over him. She had to. That was the whole fucking point of this bullshit.

Him leaving so she'd move past what had happened with Nikki, pull herself together and meet a nice guy, one who didn't have a past worthy of a horror movie, one who could give her everything she deserved. A guy who would look good next to her, look like he fucking deserved a woman as beautiful as she was, inside and out.

A shudder rippled through him.

Fuck him, but he didn't want anybody else giving her jack shit.

He really had to get a new phone number.

It would get easier, he promised himself. Eventually, after enough time had passed, she'd let it go. Then he wouldn't be in a constant state of anxiety, ready to haul ass back to Montana every time she called him. Hopefully.

Aw fuck, he wanted her back.

Cursing, Ripper picked up an air ratchet and got back to work.

CHAPTER 23

Deuce glanced across the club to where Danny was lying on one of the leather sofas, staring blankly up at the ceiling. Her hair was a mess, her eye makeup smeared, she was still in yesterday's clothes, a baggy black T-shirt and dark jeans. The same clothes she'd worn the day before and the day before that.

He watched as Dirty approached the couch and gave her knee a two-finger tap. She lifted her feet up, allowing Dirty to sit down beside her, laid her legs over his lap, and went back to staring up at the ceiling. It wasn't as if Dirty was touching her, or even paying any attention to her at all. Instead, the guy propped his elbows up on the back of the couch, his gaze on a club rat standing by the bar.

Deuce turned to Eva. "She still won't talk to you?"

Eva looked toward Danny, then back to him and

pressed her lips together, shaking her head.

He sighed. “What about spring semester? Did she agree to sign up?”

“No, baby, she refused. Then not so nicely told me to ‘get the fuck away from her.’”

“Jesus Christ,” he muttered, running his hands through his hair. “What the fuck is wrong with her? She ain’t hangin’ with her friends, and the only person she isn’t shittin’ on is Cage. He ain’t sayin’ shit, and damn if that son of a bitch doesn’t know what’s really goin’ on.”

“He’s protecting her,” Eva said quietly. “It’s what big brothers do.”

“Yeah, well, he ain’t doin’ a very good job. She’s gettin’ booze and smoke from the boys; I can fuckin’ smell it on her. None of them are ownin’ up to it, but I fuckin’ know it. She’s always at the club, either sleepin’ or hangin’ ’round Dirty and Bucket.”

“They would never hurt her.”

“Yeah,” he gritted out. “I know. But they ain’t exactly the type I want my baby girl bein’ best fuckin’ friends with. Don’t know how she can even stand bein’ near Dirty, smellin’ the way he does.”

“I think they smell equally bad,” she whispered.

Deuce cut his eyes at her, frowning. “Babe. Not funny.”

“I didn’t say it was.”

“I could toss her ass in the shower,” he suggested. “Hold her down while you dump a bucket of dish soap over her head.”

Eva smiled wryly. “Somehow I don’t think that will go over very well.”

Yeah, he didn’t think so either, but he was sick of sitting

around, doing nothing but watching his oldest daughter wasting away, not knowing why or how to fix it.

He was motherfucking cursed, had to be. As soon as shit started getting better with Eva, the second he thought he'd gotten the chance to put his family back to rights, his eldest daughter had done a face plant into crazy town.

His eyes still on Danny, Deuce watched as she pulled a pack of cigarettes from her jeans pocket. Fucking shit, she was smoking now?

"Danielle!" he yelled, unable to stop himself. This shit was too much. He wanted to know what the fuck was going on and he wanted to know right the fuck now.

The club grew quiet as all eyes turned to him. All except for Danny's.

"God dammit," he growled.

"Deuce," Eva whispered, placing her hand on his arm. "I don't think this is the best—"

"Fuck that," he shot back, pulling away from her. "I'm not lettin' this shit go any further."

He stalked across the room, stopping beside the couch Danny was lying on, and glared at Dirty. The guy shot up and hurried off to the bar, but Danny's eyes stayed trained on the ceiling.

"Danny," he growled. "My office. Now."

No response.

"Did you hear me?" he bellowed. "Get your ass into my office!"

She still didn't look at him. Didn't even flinch.

Even as his anger rose, his insides were aching. He wanted his daughter back. His bouncy, easily excitable daughter who never shut the fuck up, who was always wearing pink shit or fuzzy shit or something ridiculously sparkly.

"Fine," he bit out. "You wanna do this right here, in front of everyone, that's on you, baby girl."

Danny turned her head ever so slightly toward him and his chest went tight. Dark circles ringed her eyes. She looked gaunt and the expression on her face . . . reminded him of Eva in the months after she'd killed Frankie. Pained. Sad. Lost.

"What do you want?" she said, her tone flat, devoid of emotion.

"What do I fuckin' want? I want you to get your ass off the couch and into the fuckin' shower 'cause, Danny, you smell worse than Dirty!"

"Hey," Dirty muttered from the bar. Deuce ignored him.

"Then I want you to get your ass over to the school and sign the fuck up for spring semester!"

Rolling her eyes, she turned away. "No," she said.

He was already fighting to keep control but, damn her, she was making it difficult.

"No?" he bit out. "You like livin' with me rent-free? You like free meals, free clothin', free fuckin' everything? You don't get your ass in gear, you're on your own!"

"Whatever," she said, and just as he was about to punch a hole in the wall behind the couch, Cage was suddenly up in his face, pushing him backward.

"Dad, leave her alone."

He shoved his son in the chest and glared at the twenty-two-year-old version of himself. "Leave her alone? She's my fuckin' kid, not yours, and I ain't leavin' her alone."

Danny burst out in humorless laughter. "Why not, Daddy?" she sneered. "You're so good at it."

Before he could explode, Cage was up his face again. "Dad, I'm askin' you to leave it be. She doesn't need this bullshit right now."

Cringing, Eva watched Deuce and Cage stare each other down, both of their expressions murderous, wondering who was going to throw the first punch. They were the same height now, both big and broad, Cage only slightly leaner than Deuce but equally as strong.

The club was silent, unmoving, waiting for the father/son explosion they all knew was about to happen.

The two of them didn't disappoint. They tore into each other, shouting insults, both of them trying to out-bellow the other. And through it all, the entire club was forced to listen to Danny's life story as the two men closest to her violently rehashed everything Cage had decided Deuce and Christine had done wrong over the years. And it was a lot.

From her drunk of a mother slapping her around, to cheerleading competitions and gymnastics meets no one had gone to, and even a salt map, her third grade social studies project that Deuce had promised to make with her but never had. Cage kept firing, sparing no details, even bringing up that Danny had gone to him, her brother, when she'd gotten her first period because she hadn't had anyone else.

Every woman inside the club flinched and Deuce, who'd gone rigid hearing this, lost his mind.

"You're in my fuckin' club, you little fuckin' shit! You need to reel your bullshit in before—"

"I give two fucks about your club! You do whatever you

gotta do, Dad, and if I gotta, I will take Danny far away from you and your fuckin' club!"

Appearing beside Eva, Blue whistled under his breath. "Gotta hand it to the boy," he said quietly. "He's got balls talkin' to Deuce like that."

"I HATE YOU!" Danny screamed, on her feet, pushing in between the two of them. "I HATE YOU BOTH AND I HATE OUR FUCKED-UP FAMILY!"

"You hate me?" Cage demanded, grabbing her arm and roughly bringing her nose-to-nose with him. "You fuckin' hate *me*?" he growled.

"You hate our family, Danny," Deuce yelled, "you can get the fuck out of it!"

Looking up at his father, Cage's eyes went wide with rage. "How about you get the fuck out of your bullshit club!"

Eva sighed. This was quickly spiraling out of control.

"You little shit," Deuce yelled, reaching around Danny to slap the name patch on the front of Cage's cut. "Talkin' shit to me is one thing but talkin' shit about the club? This is your fuckin' club too!"

"Fuck you," Cage spat. "I had a fuckin' club long before this one! It was called the Dad ain't never home, Mom's drunk and cryin' in her room, and Cage and Danny only have each other club!"

Okay, this was no longer spiraling, the West family was now well past any sort of control.

"Mick," Eva called out, quickly crossing the room toward the chaos. "Grab one of them." She pointed at Bucket. "You, grab another! And someone please grab Danny!"

"Let your sister go," Mick said, grabbing Cage's arm.

"This ain't your business," Cage growled.

"No," Eva said, stopping beside Deuce. "It isn't his business but it's mine, and Cage, you need to let her go."

"Not until she takes that bullshit about hatin' me back!"

"What are you?" Eva yelled. "Five years old? This isn't helping!"

"Fuck you, Eva!" Danny screamed. "We are not your business!"

"Shut your mouth!" Deuce bellowed just as Cage jerked out of Mick's hold and slammed his fist into the guy's face.

"I said this ain't your business, Mick!"

"You little fuckin' shit!" Deuce roared, lunging for Cage.

"Someone get Danny out of here!" Eva yelled, scrambling backward as father and son went barreling into each other.

ZZ got to Danny first, swept her off her feet, and tossed her up over his shoulder.

"Take her to her room!" Eva demanded. "And keep her there!"

She waited until ZZ disappeared around the corner, then turned to Mick. "You okay?"

Rubbing his jaw, Mick snorted. "Foxy, you know it ain't the first time one of those assholes has punched me. Ain't gonna be the last either. Runs in their blood."

Sighing, she turned back to the father-and-son leather-clad ball of flying limbs and pained grunts. "Anyone want to help me out here?"

Not surprisingly, no one answered.

CHAPTER 24

FOR THE SECOND TIME, I SLAPPED MY PALMS AGAINST ZZ's chest and tried to push him out of my way. "Let me out of my room!" I demanded.

He gave my hands an amused glance before looking up at me. "Sorry, Danny, lady of the house said to keep you here and that's what I'm doin'."

"Fuck you!" I yelled, spinning around, sweeping my arm across my dresser as I did, sending everything on it flying across the room. "I need to get out of here!"

And I did. I wanted out of my family, out of the club, out of Montana, out of the never-ending depression and nightmares. But the more I daydreamed about running away, the harder it seemed to find the energy to do anything about it.

"Where you gonna go?" ZZ asked quietly. "How you gonna get there?"

"Shut up!" I hissed as I grabbed one of my ridiculous pink throw pillows and whipped it across the room. "Do you really think I need you telling me how pathetic I am?"

"Don't think you're pathetic, Danny. Think you're hurtin' somethin' fierce."

The next pillow I threw, this one purple and fuzzy, hit him square in the face. He picked it up off the floor and examined it closely. "Why's it fuzzy?" he asked. "What's the point?"

Cursing, I flung myself facedown on my bed. "Just go away!"

"Can't. Orders are orders."

I turned my head so he could see me glaring at him. "Orders are orders," I mimicked. "Aren't you a good little sheep."

To my annoyance, ZZ burst out laughing, shaking his head as he reached into his cut and pulled out his cigarettes. He was still laughing when he took his first drag and ended up choking on it.

"Ha," I spat, smiling nastily at him.

"You know," he said, watching me with dark, knowing eyes, eyes I felt like gouging out of his head with a fork. "You could always talk to me. Tell me why you're actin' like a fuckin' maniac. Seems to me like you need someone to talk to."

"You know what you could do?" I shot back. "You could get the fuck out of my room!"

"Sorry, baby," he said, shaking his head. "Nothin' is gonna make me leave until either your old man or Foxy gives me the go-ahead."

I stared at him, my thoughts a violent mess, only able to

focus on what was wrong with my life and how I could make it worse. I was on autopilot, destined to destruction without a return ticket. No matter how desperately I wanted to turn this fucked-up ride around, to head back to what was good, to when I was happy, I didn't know how.

"Nothing?" I sneered, pushing up off my bed. "Nothing at all, huh?"

I deliberately ran my eyes up and down his body. And it was an impressive body. ZZ was six feet of solid, toned muscle that showed underneath his plain white tee and form-fitting leathers. On his right bicep hell's was tattooed in big, bold lettering, and below it, on his forearm, read horsemen.

His dark brown hair was pulled back in a ponytail, showing off his small hoop earrings, and wrapped around his neck was a black leather strip, identical to the ones on each of his wrists. All in all, ZZ was a big, sexy man package that I was about to try and exploit.

But however sexy ZZ might be, he wasn't dumb. Far from it. He watched me eye-fuck him, his lips twitching.

"Ain't gonna work," he said.

"Why? You don't think I'm pretty?"

He snorted. "I'd have to be blind or just straight up dumb not to, but I like my women a little less . . . ripe."

I shrugged off the insult even as it cut me. I wanted to shower. No, I wanted to want to shower. I wanted to want a lot of things. I just . . . couldn't figure out how.

"Okay," I said, shrugging nonchalantly, grabbing the bottom of my T-shirt and lifting it over my head. I tossed it across my room and watched ZZ's eyes drop to my bare breasts.

"Put your shirt back on," he said, his tone blasé, but the

subtle tightening in his jaw gave him away.

"How about I do this instead?" I shoved down my jeans and underwear and kicked them aside. Naked, I glared at ZZ. "Still nothing I can do?"

He took an extra long drag off his cigarette before answering. "No," he said tightly. "Put your fuckin' clothes on before your old man walks in here and sees you actin' like this."

"Like I care!"

"Do you care about me?" he shot back. "If someone walks in on this shit, they're gonna get the wrong idea and I'm gonna be takin' the blame for it. You want your old man to shoot me? Thanks a lot."

If your old man caps me, you better be front and center at my fuckin' funeral, cryin' your goddamn eyes out.

I squeezed my eyes shut, shuddering through the painful memory ZZ's similar words had stirred up inside me, and fought back my rising emotions.

"Then you better hurry," I hissed. "And fuck me before anyone walks in."

Muttering curses, ZZ dropped his cigarette on the floor and crushed it with the toe of his boot. Next, he reached behind him and pulled his gun from his leathers. After setting it down on my desk, he started for me, already unzipping his leathers.

My anger turned to panic. Oh God, why was I doing this? Why was I acting like a crazy slut? What was wrong with me? Why couldn't I stop it? Just shut it off? I didn't want to have sex with ZZ any more than I wanted to be lashing out at my family.

But everything hurt. Every heartbeat a knife to my chest, every breath more painful than the last. It hurt straight to my bones, freezing my blood and straining my muscles, making me ache . . . so . . . bad.

And I couldn't make it stop.

"You want to fuck," ZZ hissed, grabbing my biceps and pushing me. I stumbled, trying to keep up with him as he began forcing me backward. "I'll fuck you, Danny. That body of yours is worth an ass kickin' or two."

I wanted to scream, *NO*, that I didn't want this to happen but I couldn't, my pain keeping my mouth shut, demanding that I continue to hurt myself, my pain telling me that I deserved this, I deserved worse than this.

"But first," he muttered. "Your ass is takin' a shower."

I shrieked as cold water spiked against my skin, not realizing until that very moment he'd backed me into my bathroom and straight into the shower.

"Let me out of here!" I screamed, violently thrashing as he held me under the spray of water, now lukewarm. But he didn't. ZZ held fast, my punches, slaps, and kicks not fazing him in the least. And still I continued, hitting him harder and harder until I was crying, sobbing uncontrollably, relentlessly beating on him and the worst thing was . . .

He let me.

He just stood there and took it.

And when it was over, when I'd wrung the last tear from my exhausted body, when I could no longer stand on my own two feet, he wrapped me in a towel, picked me up, and tucked me into bed.

"You were never going to have sex with me," I whispered, blinking sleepily up at him. "Were you?"

"No," he whispered back, brushing a lock of wet hair out of my eyes. "I wasn't."

CHAPTER 25

Seven months later

BLASTING CANNIBAL CORPSE, RIPPER PULLED HIS TRUCK off the Harbor Freeway and onto Wilshire Boulevard. Shit was going good. He'd quit drinking hard liquor, stopped smoking green, and work was solid. He'd done a couple of hits for Deuce on the side, earning him a nice bankroll, and he was fucking some airheaded bitch named Colleen or Colette or whatever, that he liked well enough. Liked as in she had a pussy, he had a dick, and if he kept the lights off he didn't have to see a face that wasn't the one he wanted to see. You put two and two together and it added up to him not feeling the need to scope out other pussy for the time being.

Yeah, he was an asshole. But a dude's gotta do what a

dude's gotta do, yeah?

Yeah. Whatever. He was so full of shit, it wasn't even shit anymore; he was straight up pissing out of his asshole.

Shit wasn't going good. Shit was just . . . going.

Barely.

The more time that passed, the more Ripper found himself thinking about a lot of things. About his life before the club, his life with the club, Frankie. Even Eva.

All this free time away from everything he'd known had put a lot of shit into perspective for him. Like how he'd been able to get away from Frankie.

"Eva's blowin' up my fuckin' phone, brother."

Ripper heard Frankie jump to his feet, heard his heavy booted steps crossing the floor, heard a door creak open, then slam shut.

It took a moment to realize that he was alone.

Eva had saved his life and he'd done nothing but blame her. Maybe subconsciously he'd always known it was Eva who'd saved him, maybe saving his life was what he'd been blaming her for.

Either way, he was a first class asshole.

But mostly he thought about Danny and why she'd stopped calling him.

It bothered him at first. He'd thought something might have happened to her, and he didn't know how to ask anyone without making them suspicious of why he was asking. But then Deuce had casually mentioned her a few times, so he knew she was still breathing. And like everything else when it came to Danny, he let it drop.

And moved the fuck on.

It was for the best that she'd forgotten about him and

what had happened.

Yeah, it was for the best. He just had to keep telling himself that.

Hitting his turn signal, he made a right onto his parents' street and—

Cox, that stupid motherfucker, was standing in the middle of his driveway, grinning at him.

"Fuckin' hell," he said, laughing.

He'd barely cleared the truck when Cox surprised the hell out of him and pulled him into a hard hug.

"Fuck you," Cox growled, squeezing him hard. "Fuck you for makin' me look for you."

They pulled apart.

"Dude. Nice hair."

Laughing, Ripper rubbed his hand over his shaved head and shrugged. "Don't gotta shower as much."

Cox snorted. "Nice."

"Yeah, and what about you? Nice fuckin' tat," he said, nodding at the new tattoo of Kami that Cox had on his neck. "What's that now, your third one of her?"

Cox shrugged. "What can I say? She likes to look at herself."

He started laughing. "Brother, I need a drink. You want a drink?"

"Depends," Cox said. "I can't do strip clubs. Kami fuckin' knew last time. The bitch can smell a lie a mile away and I ain't gettin' locked out of pussy that I fuckin' own for two whole weeks again. I swear, Ripper, the bitch is psychic. Psychic and crazy and—"

Ripper held his hand up.

"Thanks for sharin' 'cause, really, I give two fucks about

your crazy old lady, but I was only talkin' brews that I got sittin' on ice in the kitchen."

Cox laughed. "Let's do it."

Once they both had a drink and were seated, Cox slapped his hand down on the table and grinned at Ripper. "Reason I'm here, brother, is Prez is gettin' married next week."

"So?"

"So? That's your fuckin' prez and I know you been talkin' to him. I know he hasn't said jack shit about you comin' home for the weddin', but we both know Prez and you fuckin' know he wants you there."

At the thought of seeing Danny again, Ripper's stomach tightened in anticipation. Even so, he shook his head. "Naw, I already explained this shit to you—"

Cox's fist came down hard on the table. "You didn't explain shit! You said you were fucked-up and left. You ain't lookin' all that fucked-up to me, and I'm tellin' you, it's time to come the fuck home."

Ripper couldn't help but grin. "Miss me, huh? Or does Kami miss me?"

For the first time since Cox and Kami got serious, Cox actually smiled at one of his Kami jabs.

"Brother," Cox said. "Shit has smoothed out back home. Things are good between Prez and Foxy, and whatever the fuck you think you're goin' through, you can come back home and go through it there. Where we are. Your fuckin' family. Havin' your back."

"So . . . everyone is good?" he asked slowly, only really caring about one person in particular.

Cox grimaced. "Prez and Foxy are good, but I'm pretty

sure Hawk's gone crazy, actin' like an angry hermit and hatin' on Jase somethin' fierce for some reason that he's refusin' to share with the rest of us."

Looked like Hawk was still hard up for D.

"Then," Cox continued, "there was the bullshit with Danny and seriously, brother, I thought Deuce was gonna have her locked up, it was that bad."

Ripper kept his gaze on his beer even as his entire body jerked to attention at the mention of Danny's name.

"What was wrong with Danny?" he asked quietly, picking at the label on his beer.

Cox shook his head. "Who the fuck knows? She just stopped talkin', started gettin' drunk and high and, get this, hangin' out with Dirty. She was makin' scenes left and right, cryin' and screamin' at everyone. Straight up, brother, I ain't never seen a good girl go bad so fuckin' quick."

Ripper swallowed thickly, feeling sick to his stomach.

"She good now?" he asked hoarsely.

Cox lifted his shoulder. "She's better. She ain't the same but she's goin' to college now and her and ZZ are all up in each other—"

Everything just stopped. Screeched to a motherfucking, backbreaking halt. His heart included.

"What?" Ripper interrupted. "Danny and ZZ, what?"

Cox snorted. "Yeah, dude, Danny and *ZZ*. In love. Fuckin' crazy, huh?"

Christ. Jesus fucking Christ. No. *NO*. Aw God, no. He went from feeling sick to pretty sure he was going to vomit.

"Don't even ask me how those two got together 'cause I don't know, but Prez is dealin' with it. He isn't happy but he's a whole lot happier than he was when Danny was actin' nuts. He knows it was because of Z that she stopped flushin' her whole fuckin' life down the shitter."

No. No. No. Just . . . no.

"And ZZ's been takin' some pretty bad beat-downs, which is a whole lot of fuckin' awesome if you ask me."

Ripper wasn't listening anymore. He was too busy trying to remember how to breathe. He'd wanted Danny to move on, forget about him, to meet a guy who would be good to her, give her all the shit he couldn't . . . he'd wanted . . .

How long had he been gone? Around a year? One motherfucking year and she was already in bed with one of his brothers. In love? They were in-motherfucking-love?

She'd lied. The bitch had to have straight up lied. She'd never loved him. He'd been a damn fool to think an eighteen-year-old with a foot still in the cradle had been capable of anything other than the selfish desire to fill the hole inside of her that her fucked-up family had caused.

So, yeah. He'd gotten what he wanted. Only now he knew the truth.

He'd never had it to begin with.

"Ripper?"

He had to clear his throat several times before answering. "Yeah?"

"You're comin' back with me, right?"

They stared at each other.

"Why the fuck not," he choked out, then picked up his beer and downed the remaining contents in one long swallow.

CHAPTER 26

One week later

"Danny," ZZ whispered in my ear. "Wake up, baby. I fuckin' want you."

Yawning, I stretched languidly, allowing ZZ to roll me onto my stomach. Spreading my legs apart, he situated himself behind me and began pushing inside.

I moaned softly as I stretched for him, enjoying the pleasurable burn as he fully seated himself. Spreading my legs farther apart, I dug my fingers into the pillows and arched my hips up, pushing back against him. One of his hands came down over my own, interlocking our fingers.

"Fuck," he growled, moving slowly in and out of me. "Fuckin' angel wings are hot as fuck, baby."

I smiled against the pillow. My angel wings were my

newest tattoo, taking up almost my entire back. It had taken eight separate sittings, but the heavily detailed and beautifully done wings, with tips that curled around my waist, ending at my belly button, were worth it. I absolutely loved them.

"Harder, Z," I whimpered, writhing under him.

His hips slammed into mine, over and over again, harder and harder but . . .

It was never enough. Sex with ZZ was always good, but something was missing. And no matter what I did to fill the hole, nothing worked. Most times, I didn't finish.

"Stop," I said, getting to my knees, pulling away from him. I scooted down on the bed on my back and held my arms out for him. Grinning, he covered my body with his and pushed back inside of me, groaning heavily.

"Go slow," I whispered, wrapping my arms around his shoulders and my legs around his backside, holding him close.

I kept my eyes tightly closed as ZZ began his slow, leisurely thrusts, picturing a different man in my arms, moving inside of me, loving me.

But no matter how hard I tried to pretend, reality always ended up winning.

Ripper was gone.

Pulling out of me, ZZ rolled onto his side. "Fuck, that was good. Love you, baby."

"Love you too," I whispered, brushing my lips across his shoulder. "Gonna go get something to drink, you want?"

He didn't answer me. He was snoring, already sound asleep with the condom still on. Rolling my eyes, I crawled over him and hopped out of bed, headed for the bathroom to clean up.

After filling up an empty glass with tap water, I leaned against his bathroom doorway and studied him.

I'd never had any intention of being with another man ever again, and after my embarrassing incident with ZZ, I'd certainly never expected to end up with him. I'm still not even sure how it happened. He just sort of started integrating himself into my life. Watching television with me, eating meals with me, finding excuses to talk to me about pointless, random things, things I'd known he wasn't interested in and to be honest, neither was I. Not anymore. In fact, I'd had little interest in much aside from sleeping, eating, and of course, breathing. That was an important one.

Then one day, in the middle of a particularly gruesome horror movie, he kissed me. It was an awful kiss; foreign lips and a taste I didn't recognize, belonging to a mouth I didn't love. After several emotionally brutal seconds, I had to pull away. But ZZ wouldn't let me go.

"I wanna be your man," he whispered.

Fighting tears, I looked down at my hands.

My man. He couldn't be my man, no one could.

I'd already had my man . . .

And lost him.

There would be no one else. It was a fact I could feel deep within me, one that made my body ache in remembrance.

"Already talked to your old man, Danny."

Surprised, I glanced up at him and noticed for the first time his black eye and a rather large gash on his cheek. Always so consumed by my thoughts, I'd somehow looked over the fact that ZZ had been badly beaten.

"Oh my God," I whispered. "He did this to you?"

ZZ laughed. "I'm fine, baby. It's worth it, anyway, if it means I'm gonna get what I want."

Me. He wanted me. He'd taken a beating just for the opportunity to ask me out.

Ripper hadn't . . .

Ripper hadn't ever wanted to tell my father.

"Kiss me again," I said hoarsely as my tears blossomed. And he did.

It was still awful. And wrong. But instead of stopping, I kissed him harder, I held him tighter, I encouraged him to touch me roughly.

I continued to torture my already broken heart; I made it hurt, more and more, until I didn't think I could bear the pain for one more second.

And then he was inside of me.

Like a bullet cracking out of its chamber, in an instant, the pain was gone.

In its place . . . a quiet numbness.

We'd been together ever since.

Did I love him?

I did love him, like I loved . . . my brother.

It wasn't his fault. He was a good man, kind and generous, and he truly cared for me. But no matter how much time passed, every time I climbed onto the back of his bike and put my arms around his middle . . .

It felt wrong.

He wasn't Ripper.

Turning away with a sigh, I grabbed a pair of ZZ's sweatpants and shoved into them, tying them tightly. Searching through the bedding, I found my black camisole and slipped it over my head. Grabbing ZZ's cigarettes, I lit one, shoved the pack in my waistband, snatched my keys off the dresser, and headed for the door.

Noise greeted me in the hallway, a mixture of happy shouts and clinking glass.

Knowing the boys and their exorbitant capacity for alcohol, I figured the wedding celebration had begun a day early.

Halfway down the back hall, I stopped, checked right, then left, making sure I was alone before unlocking Ripper's door and slipping quietly inside. After locking the door behind me, I tossed my keys and smokes on his unmade bed, flipped the lights on, and headed for his bathroom.

Three more drags and my cigarette was shot and flushed down the toilet. I undressed quickly, started the shower, and stepped inside, sighing happily under the stream of hot water.

Because he'd left his shampoo and soap behind, here was the only place I could still find a piece of Ripper. Not even his bed smelled of him anymore, and so I took advantage of this small retreat down memory lane whenever the opportunity to slip away arose.

I washed my hair first, breathing in the sharp, clean scent of his generic 2-in-1 shampoo and conditioner. The tiny sliver of soap that remained, I glided up over my arms and legs, up and down my body, slowly, slower, until I could feel the warming stirrings of arousal deep in my belly.

The soap slipped through my fingers as I pressed one palm against the wall and slid the other between my thighs.

Fuck . . . Fuck, Danny, fuck . . . I'm gonna fuck you so

hard . . . you're gonna scream, baby . . .

I want that pussy, baby, gimme that beautiful fuckin' pussy.

Here, now, I could pretend all I wanted. I didn't have the reality of ZZ smacking me in the face. Here I was surrounded by nothing but Ripper and my memories of him.

Here, I had no problem coming.

Picturing his big, beautiful body covered in scars, in tattoos, laden with heavy muscle, I cried out as my fingers increased their pace.

I was so close, almost there and I needed to finish, I needed it more than I needed my next breath.

It was all I had left.

The shower curtain suddenly ripped open with an audible snap. Startled, I spun around, nearly losing my balance and came face-to-face with . . .

Ripper.

Poof . . . he'd disappeared.

Poof . . . he was back.

Just like that. Standing there in front of me looking the same as ever. Well, he was bigger, his neck and arms were thicker, his clothing tighter. His head was shaved, only a layer of blond fuzz remained, showing off the two long scars on the right side of his skull that I'd never known about.

But still Ripper.

Just standing there looking at me as if the past year of my life hadn't been one long, bitter stretch of unbearable agony.

I tried to speak, to say something, to move, but all that happened was a large exhalation of shuddered air and a tiny, pathetic squeak.

Everyone had been happy to see him. More than happy. Fucking ecstatic. After nearly an hour of hugs and back slaps and enough shots to give him more than a good buzz, Ripper had finally managed to sneak away.

The first sign of something wrong was the fresh smell of cigarettes that greeted him inside his room. The second, the Hello Kitty key ring and nearly full pack of smokes on his bed. The third, the running shower.

He knew. He knew who was in there. There was only one bitch associated with this club who sported Hello Kitty bullshit.

What the fuck was she doing in his room, in his bathroom, in his motherfucking shower?

Was she in there with Z? Fucking fuck, he'd flip.

He stalked toward the bathroom, the sounds of soft moaning stopping him in his tracks. Nearly a year had passed yet he instantly recognized Danny nearing orgasm. Raw jealousy and ugly hatred flooded him.

They were fucking in his shower?

Was this a fucking joke? Did God hate him this much?

Or just Danny?

Crossing the tiny room, he envisioned his hands choking the life out of . . .

He ripped the shower curtain open and all his blood drained straight to his feet.

She looked . . . different.

Aside from the full back piece that initially spanked him in the face before she'd whipped around, she was thinner, less muscular, and softer looking.

And tired. She looked downright exhausted.

And still fucking beautiful.

Ripper stared at her; her blue eyes wide with surprise, her drenched body heaving with heavy breaths, her slim legs quivering.

He wasn't sure who moved first. But it didn't matter; they both were moving, crashing into each other and he took immediate control, wrapping his hand around her neck, shoving her up against the shower wall as he yanked open his leathers. With her arms wrapped around his neck, she hoisted up off the floor and locked her legs around his waist.

Fully clothed, soaking wet, full of seething, jealous anger and a longtime pent-up need for her, he found her entrance and in a single thrust, jammed himself inside of her. Her following scream of pain sent a perversely thrilling spike of pleasure straight through him.

They were fighting more than they were fucking.

He could both see and feel . . . fuck, he could taste the rage radiating off her. Yeah, well, fuck her, he was mother-fucking pissed off too.

It was frantic, desperate, thoughtless fucking. Each of them physically screaming for more, for as much as they could get from the other.

Amping it up, he powered into her, uncaring that her head was bashing repeatedly against the wall, uncaring that her nails had surpassed skin and were well on their way to puncturing his muscle, uncaring that instead of kissing him, she was biting him without restraint and blood was filling his mouth.

Grabbing a handful of her hair, he pulled her head to one side and sunk his teeth into her neck; shudders wracked his entire body as she cried out against his shoulder, again and again and again.

But she didn't try to stop him. In fact, later, when he stopped to really think about what had happened, he would realize that the more he'd hurt her, the more she'd hurt him, the more pain they'd wanted.

This wasn't love. It was hate. And love.

That fine line had been destroyed.

Mutilated.

He wanted to knock her fucking teeth out.

No, he wanted to take her to bed and fuck her the way he used to, feel the way he used to feel when he was inside of her. Not like this, never like this. This shit was nothing but an outlet for empty rage and bone-crushing heartache.

He wanted to cry.

Instead, he came.

"Fuck!" she screamed, shoving at him. "Get out of me! Ripper, pull out!"

He stumbled backward, bent over, groaning as he continued to finish.

"You fucking asshole," she hissed, kicking him in the calf. "You came in me!"

"Sorry, bitch," he gritted out, glaring up at her as he straightened out his body. "Didn't mean to piss all over Z's territory."

He should have expected it after the way they'd just fucked, that one wrong comment and she was going to go ballistic, but he was still in shock from finding her in his shower, from fucking her and then coming only seconds ago.

The moment she barreled into him, her nails going right for his face, his feet slipped out from under him and they both went down hard. Cursing, he tried to grab her, but she was flailing, soaking wet, and he couldn't get a good grip on her. Finally he just gave up, lay there on the bathtub floor, trying to shield his face until she tired herself out.

At least that had been the plan until something she said in between her bouts of cursing and hysterical nonsense shocked the ever-loving shit out of him.

Renewed strength born from heart-stopping rage had him grabbing her, throwing her carelessly over the side of the tub, and following her over. Pinning her arms above her head, he straddled her and grabbed her chin hard enough to bruise, forcing her to look at him.

"What the fuck did you say?"

"That I fucking hate you!"

He squeezed harder and she whimpered.

"Answer me," he growled.

"I was pregnant," she hissed. "And I had an abortion. Happy?"

Was he happy? Was he motherfucking *happy* she'd killed his kid? Never once during the five billion psychotic voice mail messages she'd left him had she mentioned being pregnant or having an abortion. He would have come home. He would have come the fuck home.

Releasing her, he got to his feet. "Get out," he snarled. "Get the fuck outta my room!"

Trembling with rage, Danny rolled over and jumped to her feet. "You left me," she vehemently accused. "You fucking left me!"

"All that cryin' you fuckin' did, callin' me all the time,

and not once did you mention bein' pregnant! Not once!"

"You left me!"

"Is that all you know how to say?" he yelled as he bent down to grab her clothing. Shoving it at her, he pushed her backward, out of the bathroom and into his bedroom. "GET OUT!" he roared, then slammed closed the bathroom door.

He waited until he heard his bedroom door open and close, then sank to his knees. Pregnant. *Pregnant.* She'd been fucking pregnant. And she'd killed it. She'd killed his baby.

His baby.

Jesus, he was going to throw up.

Staggering to his feet, Ripper sent his fist into the bathroom door, then his boot, then his fist again and his boot again, and again and again until he was tired of beating on the door and spun around only to be greeted with his fucked-up reflection in the mirror.

"FUCK YOU!" he roared as his fist shot out. The mirror shattered on impact.

Shattered.

Just like his fucking life.

He'd stay for the wedding but afterward he was putting miles of road between him and anything to do with Danielle West. And this time when he left, he was throwing his cell phone in a lake and making sure no one, not even Deuce, would be able to find him ever again.

CHAPTER 27

DEUCE WASN'T GONNA LIE. WITH HIS HAIR PULLED tightly back, dressed in his leathers, a clean white tee, and his Horsemen cut, standing there in the middle of a motherfucking gazebo decorated with motherfucking flowers, he felt damn uncomfortable. Didn't help that Mick, Cox, and Ripper were laughing at him, and standing across from them were Kami, Danny, and Dorothy, all dressed in matching black dresses, also laughing at him.

Yeah, real fucking funny. Bet they wouldn't think it was funny if he pulled out his Glock and took out their knees. Except for Danny. He wouldn't shoot his baby. Just glare at her until she ran away. Which she wouldn't because she never did, because she wasn't scared of him. His feisty little girl, during this past year, had developed her mother's tough-as-nails personality. Funny that Danny being the way she was didn't bother him nearly as much as Christine had.

Nostrils flaring, shifting uncomfortably, he glared at the minister, an older woman with long white hair dressed in white and purple robes, smiling serenely back at him.

He caught himself before he growled at her.

Why the fuck was he getting married?

Again?

Because he sure as hell fucked it up the last time. He didn't know the first thing about how to be a husband. All he knew, all he'd ever known, was how to be a provider. To make sure the people he loved were safe, well fed, and warm, and in Danny's case and now Eva and Ivy's, spoiled shitless too. Although, he figured the giant shoe pile of Chucks in his foyer was a pretty good trade-off for the woman he had in his bed.

But a husband . . .

He didn't do husband. What the fuck did husbands do, anyway? He sure as hell didn't do it right with Christine. She had wanted so much more from him than he'd been willing to give. Than he'd known how to give. She'd wanted to bend him to her will, own him even.

Aw, Jesus . . . he couldn't pretend to be someone he wasn't. He couldn't put a ring on Eva's finger. He couldn't fuck her up like he had Christine. Like he did everything.

"Prez," Mick whispered, leaning over.

His head snapped left. "What?" he snarled.

Mick's lips twitched. "Nothin', Prez, just thought maybe you'd wanna watch your bitch walkin' down the aisle." Mick's chin jerked left and Deuce's gaze followed.

Suddenly he didn't give two fucks about how he was going to fare as a husband or how many mistakes he was going to make, which was going to be a lot because, well . . . that was what he was best at.

No, he didn't care about anything else in the world except for his woman, the sweetest kid he'd ever met, the smartest too, a kid who'd turned into the sexiest woman he'd ever seen. A woman who didn't just love with her whole heart but with her body and soul. A woman who, time and time again, brought him to his fucking knees, had him praying to a god he didn't believe in just so he could keep her by his side.

A woman whose motherfucking smile made the world and his life seem somewhat livable. Even worth it sometimes.

On the arm of Preacher was his Eva. Her soft hair hung long in dark brown waves, her makeup was minimal, and her dress was a simple, strapless white cotton sundress that ended at her knees. His gaze traveled down her silky smooth legs to her feet and his chest constricted. Black Chucks. And not just any black Chucks but her oldest pair. Ratty, doodled on, coming apart at the seams, the same ones she'd been wearing the very first time he'd kissed her. Back when she'd been way too young for him and he'd lost complete control of himself and his better judgment.

Eva came to a stop at the bottom step of the gazebo and looked up at him, her big gray eyes shining, her luscious lips twitching something fierce, trying not to smile while Preacher straight up glared at him. Deuce glared back. If her old man wanted a fight, he was going to get one.

"Yo, Prez." Cox laughed. "You're gonna wanna go get her, right?"

Oh. Right.

He strode forward, taking all three steps at once, and grabbed Eva away from Preacher and started yanking her back up the stairs. The faster they could get this shit over with, the faster he could get her alone. And set to working on kid number two.

Preacher yanked her back and the two of them spent another good minute glaring at each other.

"You'll always be my baby girl," Preacher whispered, giving Eva a kiss on the cheek, shooting eye daggers at him.

Yeah, fucking right, he thought, dragging Eva up the steps. Eva was his. All his. Ain't no man, not even her father, should be thinking otherwise.

"I have a bra on," Eva whispered, unable to fight her grin any longer. "It's my something new."

He couldn't help himself and burst out laughing. She was just so damn . . . perfect.

"Something old," she continued, pointing at her feet.

"Something borrowed." She grabbed his gold Horsemen's tag around her neck. The one that had deuce inscribed on the back.

"Borrowed for fuckin' ever," he said gruffly. Ain't no way she was ever giving that back. Her grin grew.

"My dress is white," she continued. "And I'm wearing your blue boxers."

The entire wedding party roared with laughter.

"Oh, Evie." Kami sighed. "I told you not to do that!"

"Fuckin' hell," he muttered, grabbing her arm and turning her toward the minister. "Let's get this fuckin' circus over with."

Still smiling, although regarding Eva strangely, the minister ushered them closer. "Ready?" the minister asked.

"Fuck, yeah," he said gruffly. "This bitch is mine."

This time everyone in the entire yard erupted in laughter. Except for Eva. She was staring up at him, her smile wide, her eyes soft. Damn those eyes, drowning him in nothing but Eva.

"I, Eva Fox, take you, Cole West, to be my beloved husband," Eva softly repeated. "To have and to hold you, to honor you, to treasure you, to be at your side in sorrow and in joy, in the good times and in the bad, and to love and cherish you always. I promise you this, baby, from the bottom of my heart, for all the days of my life."

Deuce stared down at her, burning with a whole mess of emotions he was helpless to turn off. Burning because he knew he'd never get enough of her. Burning because he wanted to pick her up, take her inside the clubhouse, strip her naked, and knock her up again just to make sure she'd never leave. Burning because after all the shit they'd gone through—the pain, the loss, the heartache, the straight up evil brutality that made them question everything they'd thought to be true and had nearly driven them apart for good—he knew he'd do anything for her. Steal anything, kill anyone, be anyone.

Even a fucking husband.

"Baby," Eva whispered, grinning. "It's your turn."

He glanced over at the waiting minister, then back at Eva. "What she said," he grunted. Then he turned to their guests.

"This is it," he bellowed. "This here is me and fuckin' Eva and this is our fuckin' road and anyone who doesn't like it, anyone who's got somethin' fucked-up to say, can get the fuck off our road!"

The crowd—his boys, their family and friends, even Preacher—erupted in happy cheers and laughter.

"You may kiss your bride," the minister said, shaking her head.

He didn't waste any time. He grabbed his woman, his wife, his Eva and lifted her off her feet and crushed her to him. Her legs wrapped around his waist, her arms around his neck, and their mouths crashed together.

"'Bout fuckin' time!" Blue bellowed from his place at the bar just before "Born to be Wild" blasted through the outside speakers and drowned out the cheering.

Eva pulled away laughing, happy tears rolling down her cheeks. He curled his hand into a fist and ran his knuckles down the side of her face.

"There it is," he whispered.

"What?" she whispered back.

"You, Eva. Just fuckin' you."

They both turned to watch as Kami threw herself across the aisle at Cox. Beside them, Dorothy buried her face in her hands, her veil of red hair shielding her from view, and burst into tears.

Mick rolled his eyes. "Idiots," he muttered. "I'm surrounded by idiots."

And Danny . . . he paused to study his oldest daughter.

"Mama!" Ivy cried out, bursting out of the crowd, gunning for Eva. Eva turned away from him to bend down and catch their daughter as she toddled up the stairs and into her mother's arms.

Deuce looked back to Danny, worried about the strange expression on her face. He followed her line of sight to . . .

Ripper?

They appeared to be having some kind of staring contest, the rest of the world forgotten, no winner in sight.

What the fuck?

"Yo, Danny!" ZZ said, appearing beside his daughter, startling her. She turned to ZZ.

"You wanna dance?"

Danny shot one last look at Ripper, turned back to ZZ, and nodded. Deuce watched them walk off—already planning on how many different ways he was gonna beat ZZ to death—then got up in his former sergeant at arms' face.

"What was that?" he growled.

Ripper eyed him boldly. "What was what?"

His nostrils flared. "You. Danny. What. Was. It."

"Baby," Eva said, wedging herself in between them. "I wanna dance."

Of course she did. She always had him doing stupid shit like dancing. And for some reason he was always doing it, even though he fucking hated it.

"Later," he promised Ripper, and allowed his new wife to drag him off.

"When can we get the fuck outta here?" he asked her.

Laughing, she wrapped her arms around his neck and tucked her beautiful body against his. "I love you, Deuce." She giggled. "So, so much."

"Babe," he said softly, holding her tightly. "Fuckin' yeah."

"One more thing," she said.

"Yeah?"

"You're mine."

He grinned. He sure as fuck was.

With Deuce as far away from Ripper as she could get him, Eva thanked God she'd interrupted the two of them before Ripper said something out of anger and blood was shed. The guy looked strung out, both pain and fury deeply etched in his features, and he hadn't stopped staring at Danny since breakfast this morning. Glaring, really. He wasn't even trying to hide it. It was a wonder no one had noticed yet. Although . . .

She glanced around the crowded lawn, her eyes landing on Cox, who also seemed to be more concerned with Ripper than Kami's violent attempts at getting him to dance with her.

Danny wasn't acting any less obvious either. And Deuce wasn't stupid. Neither was ZZ. If Danny and Ripper weren't careful, someone was going to put together: one, those hateful, needy looks those two were giving each other; and two, Ripper's sudden and unexplained disappearing act, and BOOM, the mess that would follow in the wake of that discovery was going to be worse than if an atomic bomb had gone off. Deuce would know instantly why Danny had fallen apart, and his anger wouldn't just be stemming from the secret affair but Ripper's fault in Danny's superseding emotional demise.

Plus the fact that Deuce had been forced to accept ZZ as a part of his daughter's life. That because of Ripper, Danny wasn't just hanging around the club, she was ZZ's old lady now. It was something Deuce had never wanted for her and had only dealt with because he'd known ZZ was the sole reason he'd gotten some semblance of his daughter back.

There had been so many times Eva had wanted to tell Deuce what she knew, or tell Danny she knew why she was hurting, but the timing never seemed right. The family fights had been unending; neither Cage, nor Danny, nor Deuce could be in the same room and not start in on one another. Telling Deuce would have only added fuel to the already blazing fire, and telling Danny . . .

She had no idea what Danny would have done. She hadn't wanted to push her any further away, and having had no prior experience with brokenhearted teenage girls, she was at a loss.

So she'd said nothing and though it killed her to do so, kept her distance unless her refereeing interference was needed. Eventually things began to settle. Danny would never be the same spunky, covered head to toe in pink and sparkles, sixteen-year-old girl she'd met a few years before, but the girl had recovered enough to start moving forward again and in turn, so had Cage and Deuce.

For Danny's sake, it was a very, *very* good thing Ripper was leaving tomorrow. Although Deuce had convinced him to come back to the club, not that he'd ever been truly out of it, Ripper wasn't returning to his former sergeant-at-arms status. He was going nomad. Dorothy had already replaced the territorial rocker on the back of his cut with a nomad patch, meaning Ripper would be holding no allegiance to any Horsemen chapter anywhere in the country, but would still be accepted as a full member.

It had taken a whole lot of arguing between the two men and a significant raise in equity but Ripper had eventually agreed, more than likely only out of loyalty to Deuce and the club. And despite Deuce wanting Ripper back one hundred percent of the time, this wasn't a complete loss.

Deuce had jobs all over the country that needed "taking

care of," and if there was ever anything that Ripper was good it, it was "taking care" of things.

Just not his own things.

Like Danny.

Feeling Deuce's hands run down her back, stopping on her backside to tightly squeeze, Eva smiled.

"You ready for Belize?" she whispered, holding him tighter.

He grunted. "Babe, I'm ready to take you inside and fuck you 'til you're fat with another kid."

"Okay," she said, grinning. "But after that, aren't you excited?"

He stopped dancing and pulled away from her. "Are you fuckin' serious? You wanna go to Belize?"

Fighting her laughter, she nodded. "Kami booked our tickets months ago. We fly out tonight."

Eyes narrowed, Deuce frowned. "No."

"Yep."

"No."

"Yep."

"What the fuck am I gonna do in Belize?" he shouted.

She shrugged. "No kids, me in one of the thousands of skimpy bikinis Kami made me buy, lots of drinking, lots of fucking—"

"Babe," he interrupted. "You coulda shut the fuck up after 'no kids.'"

She burst out laughing. "Deuce," she breathed out, clutching her stomach. "But you said you wanted more."

"Eva," he growled softly. "I fuckin' do. Just thinkin' 'bout you knocked up, fat with my kid, is makin' me hard as fuck. Don't mean I don't need a break from Ivy whinin' and Danny mopin' and Cage just bein' a motherfuckin' dumbass."

Biting her lip, she stared up at him. How could she have ever thought of leaving him? This, him, them, finally at peace, had been worth waiting for; worth the pain, the tragedy, the seemingly unending heartache. He was worth everything.

Every single thing.

"Babe," he whispered. "Can't look at me like that and expect me to be keepin' it reeled in."

"Baby, don't ever keep it reeled in," she whispered back. "Not with me."

Eva watched his pupils dilate, his nostrils flare, and couldn't contain her body's natural response. His ability to affect her instantaneously and so completely had always been true. From their first meeting, long before the sexual pull between them took root and never let go, she'd always been drawn to him, captivated by him.

She'd always been his.

She always would be his.

CHAPTER 28

"Dude," Hawk whispered, poking Ripper in the arm with his fork. "You need to stop."

Ripper glanced away from Danny and ZZ to glare at Hawk.

"Fuck you, you fuckin' hypocrite," he said. "And fuck off."

He couldn't wait to get the fuck out of here. The only reason he was still here was because Dorothy had begged him to stay for breakfast. Which should have been quick and painless. Only he hadn't counted on having to be seated at the opposite end of the table, directly across from ZZ and Danny, forced to watch the brother manhandle her.

She was a goddamn motherfucking whore. Letting ZZ touch her after he'd fucked her.

Hawk shrugged. "The boys know, brother. They been

talkin' all night about the way you two have been lookin' at each other, guessin' that it's 'cause of Danny you took off. Only reason Z hasn't figured it out is 'cause he's always neck-deep in her."

He didn't give a fuck who knew. He'd be out of here soon enough and if Deuce happened to find out somewhere down the line, fuck it, he'd be more than happy to let the guy put him out of his misery.

"Gotta tell you, Ripper, no one's happy 'bout you disrespectin' Prez like that."

"Oh yeah," he shot back. "You're one to talk, asshole."

Hawk shook his head. "It ain't the same, brother, and you know it."

"Fuck you," he growled. "She killed my motherfuckin' kid and you're spoutin' off about disrespect."

Hawk's eyebrows hit his hairline. "Oh fuck," he breathed.

"Yeah," Ripper spat. "So you can see—"

Hawk stabbed him with his fork. Again. "That 'oh fuck' wasn't for you, you fuckin' asshat. It was for Danny. Shit makes sense now. Her goin' crazy the way she did. Nobody knew what the fuck was wrong."

Ripper's mouth flatlined. "If she woulda told me, I woulda come home."

Hawk's face twisted with doubt. "You sure about that, dude? I mean, if that's true, why did you leave in the first place?"

Yeah, he was fucking sure, what the fuck was Hawk think—

Fuck.

Brother had a point. He'd left so she'd have a better life, one without secrets and bad memories and . . . him.

Would he have come back? For his kid? For her?

Yeah. Yeah, he fucking would have.

As it was, Hawk only knew half the story. He didn't have a clue that Danny had killed Nikki. No one knew except him and Danny.

Oh, fuck.

Cox knew Nikki was dead. And if what Hawk said was true, that the boys had figured his shit out, then . . .

He glanced over to where Cox was sitting, Kami on his lap, trying to eat around her.

He stared at his friend until Cox looked up and caught his gaze.

And yeah, Cox knew. The motherfucker had figured it out. From the looks of it, he wasn't happy with him either.

Feeling sick, Ripper stood up quickly, causing his chair to scrape loudly against the floor. The entire table of brothers, their old ladies, their kids . . . all looked up at him and the room went uncomfortably silent.

He felt his brothers' eyes on him, felt the tension emanating from all around the table, and knew Hawk had been right. With the exception of a few people, the ones who didn't know yet, no one was happy with him.

Maybe he should have cared about that. Cared that his brothers, his only family, men he'd worked side by side with for years, killed for, and nearly died protecting, thought he was a piece of fucking garbage. But he didn't.

He only had eyes for one person.

And she was refusing to look at him.

He never should have left.

But it was done. He couldn't take it back and he couldn't make it right. There was nothing he could do except add it to his long list of mistakes.

He cleared his throat. "I'm out," he said.

Dorothy smiled up at him. "See you soon?"

Everyone else looked away.

"Sure," he muttered.

And left.

Ripper was leaving.

Again.

And I felt like I was dying.

Again.

My stomach started churning and my body grew clammy.

This couldn't happen.

This couldn't happen again.

He couldn't leave.

He couldn't leave me, again.

"I gotta go to the bathroom," I whispered to ZZ and quickly stood up, painfully aware of Hawk's knowing eyes on me.

As soon as I'd cleared the kitchen, I broke into a run, racing down the hallway, through the front room, and slammed through the front door, stumbling out into the sunlight.

Ripper was already on his bike, stopped at the gate, punching in the code.

As if he could sense me there, he paused and turned.

And my heart broke for the millionth time since prom night.

It was all there, everything he was feeling, everything I

needed to know, written all over his face.

He loved me.

And he hated me.

I stood there for a long time, long after the dust his Harley kicked up in his wake had settled.

I lost something that day, a piece of me that's still out there, standing in that parking lot, staring after the man I loved.

CHAPTER 29

In three words I can sum up everything I've learned about life: it goes on.
—Robert Frost

LIFE GOES ON.

If there is nothing else in this world you can count on, you can count on that.

Life will go on.

With or without you.

Before you, after you, all around you, life has always done just that.

Gone on.

After Ripper left, life went on. The world didn't stop turning, the sun didn't forget its nightly duty to set in the west and rise again each morning in the east. The seasons still came and went. Everything, everyone, continued on.

Even me.

When my father and Eva came home from their honeymoon, it was back to business as usual only my father was home a lot more. Things settled.

And life just kept going.

Danny D. got married.

Cage had a girlfriend, a waitress from town, for an entire week.

Kami got pregnant and nine months later gave birth to her and Cox's second son, Diesel. Tegen graduated from high school. Not even twenty-four hours after her graduation ceremony, she was on a plane San Francisco bound where she'd gotten a full scholarship to San Francisco State University and an internship at a small newspaper. She didn't come back for Christmas, or spring break, or the following summer.

Bucket was arrested, carted off to jail out of state on assault charges.

Then Dorothy got pregnant.

Jase didn't leave his wife. Other than Dorothy, no one was surprised.

Hawk left. Went nomad like Ripper, and never came back.

Anger, one of two prospects, eighteen years old, and half Native American, was patched in. From what I knew of him, like Dirty he too had been aptly nicknamed. Mostly, I tried to avoid him and his temper tantrums.

And through it all, Ripper would periodically appear. He'd show up out of the blue, stay for a day or two, and then just as randomly, he'd disappear again.

We never spoke. We barely looked at each other. But there were times when not looking was as unbearable as holding my breath for too long and so I'd give in and I'd look. And every time I did, he was looking back at me.

The pain that followed those brief glances was indescribable. And always took weeks to heal from.

And still . . . life went on.

Eventually two years had passed, during which I continued on with school, and made a concerted effort at spending more time with my family, or alone with ZZ, and less time at the club.

And then, three weeks after I turned twenty-one, during one of the many Horsemen summer barbeques, life came crashing to a stop.

CHAPTER 30

Ripper stared at Danny. Stared at ZZ kneeling on the grass in front of her, asking her to marry him.

He was going to flip his shit.

These assholes all around him didn't realize it, but they were about to get sprayed with blood, bone, and brain when his head decided to explode, which was in about five motherfucking seconds.

Five . . .

Four . . .

Three . . .

Two . . .

One . . .

Fuck him.

Married.

ZZ was asking Danny to marry him.

Ah, fuck. What was happening to him? Everything inside of him suddenly felt all fucked-up and wrong. His heart started beating faster and his skin began to tingle irritably. The air around him grew thick, stuffy, making it hard to breathe. He felt light-headed, his nose stung, and his stomach clenched painfully.

Before he began shredding his own body to pieces, just to make all these damn uncomfortable and unwanted feelings go away, he grabbed Anabeth and yanked her up against him. She responded immediately and curled seductively around his body.

Feeling like ten times an asshole, he kept his gaze on Danny as he groped Anabeth's ass.

Danny's beautiful blue eyes filled with pain and her gaze dropped back to ZZ.

He stopped breathing. She was going to say yes.

Say something, his brain screamed. *STOP HER!*

FUCKING STOP HER!

But he didn't.

He never did.

Because he was a useless pussy, who would never fucking deserve her.

So he just stood there like an asshole, manhandling her friend, and watching in horrified fascination as her lips parted and—

FUCK THIS SHIT.

Fuck the club and the code, and fuck brotherhood.

He would give it all up for her. For his woman. Because she sure as shit was his, and he'd go to hell and back ten times over before he lost her forever.

He shoved Anabeth aside, his right foot moved, and . . .

"DANNY!" he bellowed. "*BABY*!"

But no one heard him. His words had been drowned out by the cracking boom of a bullet being discharged and the horrified screams that followed.

CHAPTER 31

I STARED ACROSS THE LAWN, UNABLE TO MOVE DESPITE the hectic flow of traffic, people arguing, police officers running back and forth, children crying . . .

I just stood there and stared at the spot where not long ago Dorothy had been lying on the grass. Shot.

In the head.

There was so much blood.

And all I could think about was her swollen belly, her innocent baby inside.

What would happen to the baby?

Feeling sick, I placed my hand over my own flat stomach and dug my fingertips into my skin. Was this really happening?

Was Dorothy going to die? Her baby?

The bullet hadn't killed her, at least not yet, and she'd

since been taken to the hospital and her shooter, Jase's wife Chrissy, had been carted off to jail, still screaming incoherently at Jase. I didn't know where Jase was. Either at the hospital or the jail.

I hoped he was at the hospital.

There was so much blood.

"Danny?"

Recognizing Ripper's voice, I didn't bother turning. "Yes?" I whispered.

"Everyone's either leavin' or leavin' for the hospital," he said quietly. "You comin'?"

"Where's ZZ?" I asked.

Out of the corner of my eye, I watched Ripper stiffen. "Hospital," he said tightly. "With Jase. He told you he was goin', yeah?"

I nodded distractedly. Yeah, he had. I think. *God . . . there was so much blood.* And I was freezing.

Glancing up, I noted the sun still shining bright and high in the sky and frowned. Why was I so cold?

"Danny." Ripper stepped in front of me, blocking out both the sun and the blood on the grass.

I glanced up at him. "What do you want?" I whispered. What did he want? Shouldn't he be on his way to the hospital or out of town, whatever . . . ?

"You're shakin'," he gritted out. "I'm tryin' to get you to stop starin' at the motherfuckin' blood and go inside."

I blinked. "I'm no stranger to blood, Ripper," I said softly. "Or bullets," I added.

"Or . . . dead babies."

He visibly flinched and I immediately felt bad. I shouldn't have said it, I don't even know why I had, but I didn't seem to be in control of myself. I was in shock and shaking.

And selfishly thinking about my own tragedies in place of the one that had just occurred right in front of me. During my marriage proposal . . .

Oh my God.

I glanced down at my left hand, at my ring finger. The ring was simple yet elegant, a band made of white gold with what I guessed was a two-carat diamond, princess cut, and circled by a thin line of diamond chips.

It was beautiful.

I hated it.

What was going on?

God, what the fuck was going on?

DANNY! BABY!

Ripper's voice was suddenly echoing through my head, instantly returning my memories. Startled, I glanced up at him. He took one look at me and knew what I was thinking, knew I'd heard him yelling.

Everything about him told me he wanted me to drop it, to let it go, to not do what he already knew I was going to do.

Trembling, I reached out and grabbed his hand. He responded immediately, engulfed my hand inside his much larger, infinitely warmer one.

"What were you going to say?" I whispered.

He shook his head. "Danny, let's get you inside, baby, get you warm."

"No!" I yanked my hand from his. "Tell me what you were going to say!"

His mouth flattened. "Does it matter?" he asked,

nodding briskly at my ring-laden hand.

My insides seized and I fought the urge to scream at him, to beat him senseless. Did it matter? What was wrong with him? He no more wanted me to marry ZZ than I wanted to marry ZZ.

He still loved me.

"Say it," I demanded, refusing to let him leave me again, every bone in my body suddenly protesting the very thought of it.

"Stop it," he hissed.

"You started it!"

"Still so fuckin' immature," he growled. "Thinkin' 'bout yourself when all around you, shit's goin' bad."

"Are you really going to do this?" I cried, no longer caring who heard me, who knew about us. "Especially now? Are you going to keep running from me? From us? Because I can't! Dammit, Ripper, I can't! Not after this!"

I couldn't. Not after I'd just watched Dorothy take a bullet to the head, all because she refused to let go of the man she loved, a man she might have died just to keep. Standing right in front of me was the man I loved and I didn't want to spend one more second aching for him.

"You're gonna fuckin' spew this shit at me!" he yelled. "Right the fuck now? Right after Z puts a motherfuckin' ring on your finger?"

"Stop it!" I shrieked, feeling him in his anger slipping away again. Retreating. Knowing that the second he could, he was going to get on his bike and put Montana and me in his rearview. And I couldn't, *I fucking couldn't*, let that happen.

"Stop ignoring this! Me! Just stop it! Admit it! Fucking

admit you love me!"

"Yeah!" he yelled, grabbing my biceps and shaking me hard. "I fuckin' love you, bitch! I've only ever loved you and I ain't ever stopped!"

Despite his painfully bruising grip on my arms or that he was shaking me so hard I could feel my brain rattle inside my skull, I felt an instant relief flood me. He loved me. And right now, it seemed to be the only thing that mattered to me.

"Don't matter though, does it? 'Cause you didn't give two fucks about me! Proved it when instead of tellin' me about my fuckin' baby, you started fuckin' Z! You coulda told me about the baby, Danny! You shoulda told me about the baby!"

Tears burned in my eyes.

"Don't fuckin' cry!" he yelled, shaking me again. "Don't you dare fuckin' cry!"

"You left me!" I cried. "You just left me here all alone! I needed you and you left me!"

"You're Z's now! You're his fuckin' old lady and I got no right to be lovin' you!"

"I've never been his," I whispered. "Ripper, I've always been yours."

His features tightening, he squeezed his eyes shut, and trembled ever so slightly.

"Dammit, Danielle," he whispered hoarsely. "God fuckin' dammit."

Ripper, I've always been yours.

Ripper stared down at Danny's tear-streaked face, his

body shaking, not from rage, but from need. He wanted her back more than he'd ever wanted anything. He wanted her more than he wanted his fucking eye back; in fact, she could have his other eye if she wanted it.

Fuck him, he loved her. He loved every damn part of her. Every inch of flawless skin, every cell that made her into who and what she was. He loved her eyes and her mouth, he loved her breasts, her legs, all ten of her toes. He loved being inside of her, he loved just being in her presence. He loved the holy fuck out of her and if he'd known then that Deuce would have been not murderous, but instead violently accepting of Danny being with one of his boys, he would have shed light to his feelings long ago. Nikki would have never been blindsided at finding Danny with him, Danny never would have had to shoot Nikki, and he never would have had to leave. He'd be the man taking daily beat-downs and every single one of them would be worth it, worth it because it would have meant he'd be the man going to bed at night with Danny in his arms.

Not ZZ.

Never ZZ.

Something solidified inside of him, the part of him that had been broken and aching to be whole again. The part of him that, for a short time, had experienced what it meant to be truly happy, and he desperately wanted it back.

A quick glance around the lawn reminded him that they weren't alone, and the remaining stragglers were openly gaping at the two of them. Mick and Adriana, Cox and Kami, Dirty, a couple of club whores, and Eva. His gaze caught that of Deuce's old lady, and surprisingly didn't find any disapproval in her eyes. Just tears. For Dorothy or for

Danny or both, he didn't know.

"Please, Ripper," Danny whispered. "Don't leave me again."

He didn't answer her; instead he released her arms and grabbed her waist, heaving her up against him. Carrying her, he strode across the lawn, unapologetically meeting the gazes of everyone who was staring. He didn't care anymore. He was done being a pussy. He was done being angry. He was way past done wishing.

He would deal with ZZ.

He would talk to Deuce.

But first he was going to take back his woman.

Once inside the club, he headed straight to his room where, once inside, the door locked behind him, he set her down on the bed and stood over her.

She said nothing, just stared in disbelief at him, heavy tears streaming down her cheeks, her chest rising and falling with deep, harsh breaths. He fell to his knees in front of her, the longtime pain of missing her, needing her, still radiating inside of him, making him incapable of standing one second longer.

"Danny," he choked out, looking away. "I'm sorry, baby, I'm—"

He jerked, surprised, as she leaned forward to press her lips against his neck, and a shudder tore through him. Unwittingly, his eyes closed.

"No talking," she murmured.

He felt her hands on his biceps, her nails digging in his skin as she gripped him tightly, and then something soft and warm brushed across his lips. Again, he felt her kiss him.

She let out a tear-filled, shuddery breath. "I've missed

you so much," she admitted in a small voice that made his heart swell. "I've never stopped thinking about you, I think about you all the—"

He didn't let her finish. His eyes flew open and he was on her. Shoving her backward, he bore down on her and cupped the side of her face. Tilting her head to the left, preparing to kiss her, he stared down at her perfect sweetheart features. Big blue eyes, a cute little nose, and wide, perfect pink lips, parted slightly as she breathed in and out . . . waiting for him.

The way she always had.

. . . And he kissed her.

And kissed her.

Fucking kissed her.

Kissed the fucking shit out of her.

Kissed her the way he'd been wanting to kiss her since he'd left her.

"Fuck," he muttered in between kisses. Suffocating, nearly violent kisses that were growing harder, even more demanding.

Ah, God, he was touching her now and she felt just as good as he remembered, soft and smooth skin molded tightly over beautifully toned muscles.

"I want you," she breathed out, her words barely audible over the pounding of his heart.

He squeezed his eyes shut. "Yeah, baby," he rasped and slid his tongue back into her mouth.

He kissed her again, harder, his hand fisting tightly in her hair.

Her fingernails bit into his neck. "I love you," she cried softly, breathlessly, but no less demanding. "And . . . I want you now . . . right now."

"Oh God," I breathed. This was actually happening. Ripper was home, I was in his room, on his bed, and he was nearly inside of me.

"Need you, baby," Ripper rasped, pushing my legs further apart. "Need you so fuckin' bad."

"Yes," I whispered, arching my hips for him. "Please . . ."

"Fuckin' love that," he muttered. "Missed that."

"Love . . . what," I panted.

"You beggin' me, baby," he whispered, teasing me with his tip. "You beggin' me for my cock," he continued, pushing inside of me.

Oh God, it was so good, so all-consuming, filling me to the brim.

Which was why, when I burst into tears, I hadn't a clue as to why.

They weren't just any tears; they were an ugly, unstoppable, body-wracking waterfall of hiccupping, breathless sobs.

It was suddenly too much. Me. Him. Dorothy and Jase. ZZ. The club. Everyone and everything. Too much pain and sorrow, years of it, one tragedy after the other, too many bad memories of wasted moments spent yearning, wishing, and aching for something I'd thought I'd lost forever. Too much effort spent trying to fill the hole inside of me, a hole that had grown too big, too deep, and no matter how many new moments and memories I tried to shovel inside of it, it remained forever empty.

Now he was here. I was in his room, in his bed, and he

was inside of me.

How had this happened? ZZ had been down on one knee in front of me, asking me to marry him and now . . .

It didn't make any sense.

Did love make sense?

Oh God, it was all too much.

But like most things involving Ripper and me, they were always impulsive, messy, and confusing, giving new meaning to the term whirlwind romance.

Hasty, impetuous, we were like lightning and tornados in a flurry of both excitement and agitation, making rapid, rash decisions, feeling, only feeling, never thinking, all the while heading face-first into a churning whirlpool of turmoil and not caring who we hurt along the way.

It was too much.

I was aware of Ripper leaving my body, felt the warmth of him disappear, and I cried even harder, the loss of his touch stirring up more unwanted memories.

Then he was back, slipping his hands underneath me, picking me up and cradling me against his chest. I burrowed into him, gripping him as hard as I could, sobbing even harder, unaware of anything but the naked pain that I'd tried for so long to ignore, that had all at once broken through the surface and found it had nowhere to go.

"I can't do this," I cried. "I can't . . . I can't."

"Shhh," he whispered, stroking my tear-soaked hair. "You don't have to do anything, baby, nothin' at all."

CHAPTER 32

SCRUBBING A HAND ACROSS HIS FACE, EXHAUSTED FROM spending the night at the hospital, Deuce, followed by ZZ, stalked inside the clubhouse and found Blue, Mick, Adriana, Cox, and Kami sitting at the bar, sharing a bottle of whiskey.

He walked their way and slipped onto the stool beside Kami as ZZ headed for the hallway, for Danny he guessed. He'd seen her Jeep out front when they'd pulled up.

"How's Dorothy?" Kami asked. "And the baby?"

He sighed. "Baby's fine, healthy little boy. And D just got out of surgery. They got the bullet out and now they're keepin' her in a fuckin' coma, somethin' to do with swellin'."

"Jase?" Cox asked. "He okay?"

No. Jase was a fucking wreck. Between Dorothy getting shot, almost losing his newborn son, Chrissy getting hauled off to jail and the club being questioned by the police, Jase was definitely not okay. Nobody was. Deuce considered Dorothy one of his boys; she'd sure as fuck been around long enough, and Chrissy was Jase's old lady, which meant she too was family.

Nothing about this was okay.

Christ, he was fucking exhausted.

"He'll manage," he said.

The small group fell silent. Nobody needed to speak, everyone already knew what the other was thinking.

"Did anyone call Tegen?" Adriana whispered tearfully. "To tell her . . . that . . . th—" She broke off and covered her mouth with her hands. Mick pulled her barstool closer to him and folded his arms around her.

"Far as I know, Cage called her last night," Deuce said. "Girl's probably on her way here as we speak."

Adriana nodded jerkily.

Speaking of Tegen . . .

"Where are my kids?" he asked no one in particular, feeling a sudden overwhelming need to see each of their faces. "And Eva? Is she home?"

At first it looked like no one was going to answer him.

Finally, Kami said quietly, "Eva's home. With Ivy."

"Cage?" he asked, raising an eyebrow at the odd expressions being exchanged around the bar.

"Sleepin'," Cox said, jerking his thumb over his shoulder. "He got in about an hour before you."

"Okay," Deuce said slowly, carefully studying the somber faces around him. Something wasn't right and it had nothing to do with Dorothy and Jase.

"Yo," ZZ called out, walking from the hallway into the

main room. "Anyone seen Danny? I can't find her anywhere."

Yeah, something sure as fuck wasn't right.

Deuce swiveled around on his stool. "What the fuck you mean 'anyone seen Danny?' Her Jeep's out front, you're her man, so I'm thinkin' that means you should know where the fuck she is."

ZZ put his palms up. "Prez, chill, I just got back too, okay? And she ain't in her room. Or mine."

Feeling what he knew was unnecessary panic stemming from what had just happened to D, but also knowing you can never be too fucking careful when it came to your family, Deuce jumped off his stool and stalked off toward the hallway, yelling Danny's name.

"Wait!" Kami yelled, running after him. She dodged past him and came skidding to a stop a few feet in front of him. "I'll call her," she said breathlessly, holding up her cell phone.

He stared at her. What the fuck?

"What's goin' on?" he demanded, looking back toward the bar at Cox. "Where's my fuckin' daughter?"

Instead of answering him, Cox looked at his wife. "Kam," he said quietly. "Don't."

Kami waved him off. "It's ringing," she said, her cell phone pressed to her ear.

Fuck this shit. Grabbing the cell phone from Kami, he put it up against his ear and continued down the hallway.

Three seconds later he heard Danny's ringtone. A song by Lady Foo-Foo, or some such shit.

He stopped walking and turned to his right, staring in disbelief at the door in front of him.

"Shit," Kami whispered from behind him.

"You're the one who fuckin' called her," Cox muttered.

Deuce glanced over his shoulder and found all of them, Kami, Cox, Mick, Adriana, and ZZ standing there. Even Blue had left the bar to join them in the hallway. Which was pretty much unheard of. Blue didn't leave the bar for much. He wasn't even sure the old asshole even slept.

"What the fuck is goin' on?" ZZ asked, grabbing the phone out of Deuce's hand. The guy shoved the phone in Kami's face. "Dial her again," he demanded.

Looking nervous, Kami took her phone and glanced up at Cox.

Cox shook his head. "Fuckin' do it," he said. "Brother deserves to know."

While the short exchange took place, Deuce had been frozen, in a state of shock. Danny was in Ripper's room? What the motherfuck?

The minute Danny's phone began ringing again, he snapped back to attention and watched as ZZ turned toward Ripper's door, his expression quickly shifting from confused anger to outright shock.

And Deuce felt for him. He really did. As much as he hated Danny being with one of his boys, ZZ was a decent man who loved the fuck out of his daughter.

"What the fuck!" ZZ roared, lunging for Ripper's door.

Deuce caught him, grabbed him by his neck, and slammed him into the opposite wall.

"Prez!" ZZ bellowed, trying to get free. "LET GO OF ME!"

"Why?" he asked calmly, feeling anything but. "What are you gonna do? Storm in there, guns ready? I know she's your girl, but she was my girl way before your sorry ass, and I ain't gonna let you do somethin' stupid that could get her hurt."

He turned to the peanut gallery. "I know you assholes know somethin', so someone better start fuckin' talkin'."

"Sorry, Prez," Mick said, stepping forward when no one else would. Curling his hand into a fist, his VP pounded on Ripper's door.

"We don't know much, just that Ripper and Danny got some deep-rooted shit between 'em."

Deuce's eyebrows shot up. They did?

ZZ, hearing this, struggled harder and he was forced to tighten his grip on his boy's throat. "Reel it in," he growled.

"Fuck you," ZZ spat. "You reel it the fuck in, that ain't your old lady in there with motherfuckin' *Ripper*!"

No shit. But it was his daughter in there with motherfucking Ripper and he wasn't much happier than ZZ was at the moment. The only difference between him and ZZ was Deuce was attempting to stay calm. What had gone down yesterday had done enough damage. The club, his family, didn't need any more tragedy.

"Ripper!" Mick bellowed, pounding harder on the door. "Get your fuckin' ass out here!"

Deuce took a deep breath and tried to ready himself for whatever mess that door was going to reveal, but all he kept seeing was Danny in bed with Ripper and . . .

The door swung open and in the entranceway stood Ripper, wearing only his leathers, in the midst of pulling on a white T-shirt. He took one look at the people standing in the hallway, their expressions varying from pity to disgust, and froze.

"Where is she?" ZZ yelled, struggling harder in Deuce's grip.

"Aw, fuck," Ripper muttered. Crossing his arms over his chest, the guy leaned back against the doorjamb. "Danny," he said, glancing over his shoulder. "Shit just got real, baby."

ZZ visibly shook in Deuce's grip and, fuck, yeah, he felt for his boy, but he was too fucking busy trying to keep his own shit reeled in.

Ripper had broken code. Took another brother's old lady . . . *to bed*. Took his daughter to bed. In an attempt not to toss ZZ aside and beat Ripper into the fucking floor, he gripped ZZ even tighter and held his ground.

It wasn't easy.

Wrapped in only a sheet, Danny appeared beside Ripper, her lips quivering and her eyes filled with tears and, Jesus, his chest went tight.

Fuck him. Ripper . . . Danny . . .

Fuck him.

He didn't know what the fuck to do. His daughter, two of his boys . . .

What the fuck did he do?

"WHAT THE FUCK!" ZZ raged.

Ripper immediately moved forward, positioning himself in front of Danny. It was a protective maneuver. One he often caught himself doing with Eva even when there was no threat.

"YOU'RE FUCKIN' DEAD, ASSHOLE!" ZZ roared. "YOU HEAR ME, RIPPER? YOU'RE FUCKIN' DEAD!"

"I hear you, brother," Ripper said evenly. "The whole damn world hears you."

"Brother?" ZZ yelled. "You don't know what the word means!"

"Mickey," Adriana whispered, tugging on Mick's hand.

"We should go."

His VP's gaze caught his and Deuce gave a slight shake of his head. Things were going to get ugly. He might need help.

Mick stayed but moved his old lady a few feet away and Cox did the same with Kami. Meanwhile, Blue lit up a cigarette.

"You don't understand," Danny whispered as two tears slipped down her cheek. "I love him, Z."

ZZ went rigid. "What?" he asked hoarsely and Deuce could feel the guy's throat working overtime beneath his palm. "Since fuckin' when do you love Ripper?"

Deuce stared at his daughter. He too wanted to know since-fucking-when she loved Ripper. And then he wanted to kill Ripper. Slowly.

"It happened a long time ago," Danny whispered. "Before you, Z. It was—"

"He's the fuckin' reason," ZZ spat. "He's why you were so fuckin' messed up! And you're the reason he left, aren't you!"

Danny's eyes dropped to her bare feet. "Yes," she whispered and Deuce's lungs collapsed. He was such a fucking idiot. How had he not put this shit together? It had been staring him in the face, for how long now?

Ripper leaving.

Danny losing her shit.

Ripper and Danny staring each other down at his wedding.

. . . And fuck, Danny's violent mood swings always coinciding with Ripper's drop-ins.

Ah, Christ. He was such a shit father. A shit president.

A shit everything. He'd been so wrapped up in his own crap, he hadn't even seen what was happening right under his fucking nose. In his club.

Self-disgust switched instantly back to anger. Ripper, his goddamn sergeant at arms, hadn't just disrespected him by doing whatever the fuck he'd been doing with Danny, he'd kept it a secret. That shit didn't fly in his club. His boys knew that.

You patch in, you become family. Brothers.

You don't disrespect your brothers.

"You ain't never been straight with me," ZZ rasped. "I don't even . . . Fuck, I don't even know you!"

Danny's head snapped up. "No," she whispered. "You did, you knew—"

ZZ's upper lip curled into a snarl. "Don't, Danny, you just fucked another guy with my ring on your finger, so *do not* fuckin' patronize me."

"We didn't fuck," Ripper spat angrily. "So you can stop shittin' on her."

ZZ's eyes shot to him and filled with hate. "Oh yeah?" he sneered. "So what, you were just talkin' and decided talkin' would be a whole lot better without clothes on?"

"I think talkin' is better without clothes," Cox called out. "Just sayin'."

Deuce added Cox to the list of hits he would soon be putting out.

"I didn't say that," Ripper gritted out. "I said we didn't fuck, never said I didn't try."

If he wasn't busy holding on to ZZ, Deuce would have smashed Ripper's head through the wall. Then his own. That had been a visual he could have gone five lifetimes without ever getting a glimpse of.

His entire body now trembling with built-up rage, ZZ turned back to Danny. "You are a *fuck-ing* whore," he said quietly, purposely punctuating every syllable with a hard, venomous edge.

Deuce saw red and just reacted. With his hand still wrapped around ZZ's neck, he pulled him forward then slammed him back against the wall. "That's once," he growled. "Next time you call my kid a whore, I will end you, you fuckin' feel me?"

"She ain't a whore, Prez?" ZZ yelled, glaring at him. "So, what the fuck do you call a bitch who agrees to marry a man and a couple hours later is in his brother's bed?"

"She ain't a whore," Ripper growled, his expression one Deuce was very familiar with. It was the same one Ripper had before he took a fucker out, cut him to pieces, and sent him straight to meet his maker. Lethal was the only way to describe it.

His two boys stared at each other, ZZ's chest heaving, ready to throw down the second Deuce let him go, and Ripper, stretching his neck side to side, cracking his knuckles, impatiently waiting for it. Wanting it.

Right. Shit was going to go south real quick if he didn't get these two assholes far, far away from each other. Then he needed Danny to put some fucking clothes on.

Then . . . him and Eva were goin' to have a serious talk about allowing Ivy access to the club. By the time Ivy was Danny's age, he'd be way too old to be holding his boys back from fighting over his daughter. And God knows they would. Ivy looked like a cross between Danny and Eva. As beautiful as both his wife and eldest daughter were, Ivy was going to surpass both of them. Not good.

Jesus. Why couldn't he have had boys? All boys. Little fucking shits like Cage. A whole slew of 'em he could throw condoms at and be done with it.

"Oh Jesus," Mick whispered, and Deuce's eyes shot to him, following his gaze to the end of the hallway. Jase stood there, his white T-shirt and jeans still stained with Dorothy's blood, tears streaming down his cheeks, holding a gun in his hand.

"Jase," Cox breathed. "Broth—"

Jase's arm shot forward and he aimed the gun at Cox. "Don't fuckin' move," he whispered hoarsely. "Don't fuckin' speak."

Nobody moved. Nobody said a word.

And Jase fell to his knees. His hand shaking, he brought the barrel of his gun to his temple.

Deuce dropped his hand from ZZ's throat and stepped away from him.

"Jase," Deuce said quietly, trying to keep his cool. "You got four kids who need you, brother, don't fuckin' do this."

Jase let out a choking sob. "I was gonna leave, Prez, I was gonna leave that bitch a million times, but I felt so guilty 'cause of the kids and I tried to do right by both of 'em and instead I fucked it all up. All I do is fuck everything up.

"I love her," Jase whispered. "She made shit real good, you know? They don't know if she's gonna make it, Prez, and . . . and I don't wanna be here without her."

Using his thumb, Jase pulled back the hammer.

"JASON!" Cox roared, taking off down the hallway. "Don't you dare!"

The echoing boom of a bullet discharging rattled

throughout the hallway as Cox fought Jase for the gun and won. He tossed the piece away and pulled Jase into his arms.

"No, motherfucker," Cox rasped, holding tight to Jase. "You do not fuckin' die. Do you get me? You. Do. Not. Die."

All three women were crying, Danny was wrapped tightly in Ripper's arms, Adriana and Kami were wrapped around each other, and both Blue and Mick were staring down the hallway at Cox and Jase, their expressions a mix between stunned and pained.

He looked around the hallway for ZZ and couldn't find him. He should have cared where ZZ had gone, should have cared that his boy was messed up.

But he was too fucking tired.

Deuce's back hit the wall and he slid slowly down the plaster until his ass met floor.

"Mickey," he whispered. Moving his way, Mick bent down in front of him.

"I got this covered, Prez," Mick said. "Just sit tight."

Right. Like he was going somewhere. Pulling his phone out of his cut, he called his wife.

"Hey, baby," Eva sniffled. "You okay?"

"No," he said softly. "I fuckin' need you."

"Five minutes," she said without hesitation. "And you got me."

CHAPTER 33

"There she is," I said, pointing.

Cage followed my finger to the stream of people flooding the bus station.

"That ain't Tegen," he said, frowning.

I squinted. Yep, that was Tegen . . . sort of. Still of slim build with catlike green eyes and striking cheekbones. But that's where the resemblance ended.

Her long red hair had been dyed a few shades darker and was separated into tens of thick dreadlocks, interwoven with large wooden beads that she'd pulled back in a dark blue kerchief. She was wearing ratty Birkenstocks, low-slung light brown bell-bottom corduroys with a tight black tank top that showed off her pierced belly button and heavily tattooed arms and stomach.

Her neck and wrists were laden with handmade

jewelry, her ears, nose, and lip were all pierced, her ear holes stretched wide enough to fit my pinkie finger through.

"Holy fuck," Cage breathed as she came to a stop in front of us.

"Danny," she said, greeting me icily, refusing to look at Cage.

I reached for her but she took a deliberate step back, dodging my hug. Startled, I dropped my arms and glanced over at Cage, unsure of what to do.

Cage stepped forward. "Te—"

Tegen reared backward. "Don't touch me," she hissed, then tossed me one of her paisley-patterned bags as she shoved past me. "Let's go!" she snapped over her shoulder. "The less I see of this fucking shithole town full of asshole bikers and their pathetic women, the better!"

Cage's mouth fell open.

"Cage," I said slowly. "What exactly happened between you and Tegen?"

He cut his eyes at me. "Nothin'," he mumbled.

"Cage . . ."

He sighed. "I may have . . . you know . . . popped her cherry . . . and she may or may not have told me she loved me."

I closed my eyes.

"And then I may have told her it was just sex . . . and that she wasn't my type . . . although she didn't look like she does no—

"Hey! Don't punch me!" he whined, rubbing his arm.

"You idiot!" I seethed.

"Me?" he yelled. "You should fuckin' talk! Where's ZZ, little sister? Why ain't no one heard from him in two days while you been sittin' pretty on Ripper's fuckin' lap?"

"Shut up," I hissed. "I haven't been sitting on anyone's lap!"

And I hadn't. In fact, during the two days that had passed since ZZ and my father had found me in Ripper's room, Ripper and I hadn't spoken. Actually, no one was doing much speaking these days. Everyone was either at the hospital with Dorothy, or at Jase's house on suicide watch duty. Jase and Chrissy's three kids, all in their teens, had gone to Billings to stay with their grandparents, and no one trusted him to be alone for any length of time.

I also didn't need to be reminded of what I'd done to ZZ. I was doing a good enough job of beating myself up about it all on my own.

Twice now, since Ripper had initially left, we'd come together in a fit of tumultuous emotional overload. The first time it had ended horribly. And this time . . .

This time we'd awoken to chaos.

It seemed to be a running theme for us.

Now I didn't know what was going to happen. I knew what I wanted to happen, but at the same time I felt guilty for wanting it.

But I wasn't going to dwell on it. Something had shifted inside of me since our night together. Yes, I loved him, knew I would always love him, but I was no longer willing to throw my life away for him if he left me again.

If he left, he left. If he stayed . . . well, who knew? I certainly wasn't going to keep throwing myself at him only to lose him.

And never again was I going to deceive another man into thinking I loved him.

Perspective is a bitch when it slaps you in the face, after the fact.

"You got between brothers, Danny," Cage growled. "Dad ain't gonna let that stand."

I glared at him. "What's he gonna do? Shoot me?"

"Not you," Cage shot back. "Ripper."

"He won't," I said.

His brow raised, Cage snorted. "How can you be so sure?"

I just was. Both Cage and my father had already beaten Ripper half to death, and had both stopped themselves before it had gotten that far. Well . . . Ripper had thrown Cage across the room after allowing him a couple of good punches, but that was neither here nor there.

I hadn't been present for his fight with my father, nor did I know the cause of it. But when my father appeared in my room and slammed the door behind him, saying nothing, his long hair flying loose from his ponytail, his nostrils flaring, his clenched fists covered in blood . . .

I knew.

I knew he knew everything.

Several heart-pounding moments passed before he finally spoke.

"You know why I kept you away from the club, Danielle?"

Danielle. *Not good.*

"Because I'm a girl," I whispered.

"No," he growled. "Because you were better than this shit. Too fuckin' good for it. Knew it from day one. Took one look at you and knew you had it in you to get the fuck outta here and make somethin' of yourself."

I didn't say anything. I didn't have anything to say. My father had never said anything like this to me before.

"Knew Cage was gonna be followin' me to hell whether I wanted him to or not. But not you. Not fuckin' you. You were gonna be the one West to make a decent life for herself. The kid I was gonna be proud of, not for followin' me into the life, but for makin' it out."

"Daddy," I whispered, needing to say something, *anything at all*, before I burst into tears. "I'm sorry, I—"

"No," he said gruffly, shaking his head. "I'm sorry. I'm your old man, you were my responsibility and I fucked up. Now you're just like the rest of 'em. Been just like 'em for a while now. My baby girl's got blood on her hands. And that shit's on me."

Then he turned around, pulled open the door, and left.

I slapped my hand over my mouth, muffling a sob as sharp pains shot through my chest, making breathing difficult and painful.

He didn't hate me. He didn't even hate Ripper. He wasn't even mad. He was disappointed. I had *disappointed* him.

It was infinitely worse.

"Danny!" Tegen bellowed. "You do realize I have a mother in the fucking hospital with a hole in her skull!"

I winced as everyone inside the station gaped at Tegen.

"Let's go," I said, slapping Tegen's bag against Cage's chest. "Before Tegen starts airing all the club's dirty laundry in the middle of the bus station."

Cage grimaced. "How about you drive her back to the club. I think I'd rather walk."

"Welcome to my world," I told him, tugging him

forward. "We made our beds, Cage. Now, we both get to lie in them."

Cage frowned at me. "When did you get so fuckin' smart? What happened to my little sister, always talkin' about stupid stuff and wearin' pink shit all the time? I liked her better."

What happened to her?

She had an affair with a man fourteen years older than her and then made the mistake of falling in love with him.

She killed a woman.

She had to abort her child.

She allowed a man she didn't love to fall in love with her. A good and decent man who'd deserved a woman ten times better than she was. Then she'd broken his heart.

Shrugging, I gave my brother a sad smile.

"What happened? Cage . . . life fucking happened."

Blowing out a breath, Cage glanced up at the ceiling and shook his head.

"Fuckin' truth, little sister. Fuckin' truth."

Inside the clubhouse, Ripper glanced up from his channel surfing, watching as Cox slowly approached the couch he'd been calling home for the past two days.

"Yo," he said.

Cox dropped down beside him. "Yo."

Silence.

"Just say it, dude." Ripper sighed. "Whatever the fuck it is."

Clearing his throat, Cox shifted in his seat so he was facing him. "Brother, I've kept my mouth shut a long time now, 'bout Nikki, 'bout Danny, and then Hawk told me about the baby, and still I kept it quiet. But seein' as how all your dirty fuckin' secrets are becomin' public knowledge, now I gotta say this shit."

Great. Where the fuck was Hawk anyway? Knowing how the brother felt about Dorothy, one would have thought he'd have hauled his ass back to Montana by now.

"So spit it the fuck out," he said, glaring at Cox.

"Come clean to Prez," Cox said. "And I don't just mean about you and Danny, I mean, come the fuck clean. Tell him what happened with Nikki, with Danny, tell him you didn't fuckin' know about the baby, tell him all of it."

He wanted to laugh but his split lip was preventing that. "Dude," he said, shaking his head. "How do you think I turned fuckin' purple? You think I beat myself half to death?"

Cox blinked. "I thought Cage and you—"

"Yeah," he interrupted. "Then Prez. Twice."

Unlike his run-in with Danny's punch-happy brother, Ripper hadn't fought back when Deuce had come at him. Actually, he hadn't really fought back when Cage had pounded on him either. He was bigger than Cage, and a fuck of a lot stronger, but he got why the brother needed to beat on him, so he let him get some of that anger out before tossing him across the room.

But Deuce. Ripper knew he deserved worse than a beating from Deuce.

Especially after he'd spilled everything.

He'd begun with Frankie, told Deuce how he'd tried to kill himself trying to escape the crazy fucker, and the miserable years that had followed.

He told him how he'd been blaming Eva for everything bad that happened. Then he told him it was Eva who'd inadvertently saved his life.

He told him about Danny's prom night, what had happened at the lake, and the months following. He told Deuce how much he loved her.

He told him about Nikki's death, that it had been Danny who'd killed her trying to save his life. He told him his reasons for leaving, that it had been all for Danny.

And then he told Deuce about the pregnancy.

He told Deuce everything. And through it all, sitting behind his desk, watching him impassively, Deuce said nothing.

When Ripper finished recounting his fucked-up life, Deuce stood up and slowly crossed the room. Grabbing him by the collar of his T-shirt, Deuce got up in his face.

"What the fuck you want me to say, Ripper? You been fuckin' my daughter behind my back for how long, I don't fuckin' know, and I'm pretty sure I don't want to know."

"She was legal," he said quickly.

"Yeah," Deuce said. "How fuckin' legal?"

"Legal enough," Ripper muttered, looking down at his boots.

"Great. Fuckin' great. Listen, fuckhead, you hurt her again, you do one goddamn thing that makes her even a little bit sad, and I'm gonna beat your fuckin' ass. You do it a third time and I'm puttin' you to ground."

Startled, Ripper looked up. "You're cool with us bein' together?"

"Fuck," Deuce muttered. "Are you fuckin' stupid? No, I'm not cool with it, I fuckin' hate it, straight up, but what am I am gonna do about it? Kick you the fuck out? Took you in when you were nothin' but a cocky-ass teenager who wanted to party more than he wanted to work, always gettin' into trouble 'cause your whorin' ass liked your women dirty and dirty women meant dirty business. And then you were a depressed, drunken, miserable shit after what happened with Frankie . . . but fuck, brother, you been with me for eighteen loyal years now and that means you're family."

Family. Jesus, he was about to break the fuck down in front of his prez.

"I love her," Ripper said quietly.

Under-fucking-statement.

Yeah, he loved Danny, but that wasn't even the half of it. She'd changed him in ways not even he could comprehend.

No longer angry, he'd slowly become a softer version of himself.

The old him, before Frankie, but even more so.

"Christ," Deuce said. "I need a smoke. This shit is worse than gettin' shot. First Z, now you."

Ripper flinched. ZZ.

"I love her," Ripper repeated, this time more forcefully. "And I ain't gonna hurt her."

Deuce's nostrils flared. "You mean you ain't gonna hurt her again. 'Cause you sure as fuck did a number on her already. And I'm thinkin' that an asshole like you isn't gonna be able to make good on that."

"I will. If she'll let me."

Deuce's hold on him tightened. "What the fuck does that mean?"

"Means if she lets me take her back to my bed, and she's on the back of my bike, I ain't never gonna let her outta my sight ever again."

Deuce's eyes narrowed.

Huh. Maybe mentioning Danny being in his bed wasn't the best thing to say to her father.

"You gonna own that shit?"

Ripper's eyes went wide. Was Deuce actually asking him if he'd marry Danny?

Marry? Danny?

Him?

"Yeah," Ripper rasped. "Fuck yeah, I'm gonna own that shit."

"Which means you're patchin' back in, Sergeant."

He nearly choked on his surprise. Not only was Deuce telling him he could marry Danny, but he wanted him back as his right-hand man.

"Yeah," he whispered.

"And ZZ?"

Ripper swallowed. That was going to be a hard one.

"Gonna try and make good on that too."

And he would, he'd do everything he could to fix what he'd fucked up. If the brother ever came back.

"Good," Deuce growled. "Now, you fuckin' ready?"

Yeah. He loved getting his ass kicked. It was a great fucking time.

"Yeah, Prez, I'm ready. You do what you gotta do."

Deuce stared at him.

"Goddamn Preacher," Deuce muttered, breaking the silence, shaking his head. "Goddamn that motherfucker."

Ripper didn't have a clue what Preacher had to do with any of this, but he soon stopped wondering because Deuce had begun beating the ever-loving shit out of him. Twice.

Then left him bleeding on the office floor while he stormed off, yelling for Eva. It had taken Ripper nearly three hours just to drag himself out of the office and onto this very couch. A couch he hadn't left in two days. Aside from several broken fingers and some pretty nasty swelling all over his body, he was fairly certain he had a couple of cracked ribs and a mild concussion, all courtesy of Deuce's steel-toed shit-kickers.

But all that weight he'd been carrying around, especially from the past three years, was gone.

Boom. Fucking gone.

And he wanted Danny back.

Fuck that, he was getting Danny back.

Cox stared at him. "Really? Damn."

Ripper scowled. "Did you really think I'd let Cage beat the fuck outta me?"

Cox grinned. "Little fucker is almost as big as the big fucker."

"Fuck that. Brother is more than ten years younger than me. I gotta rep to hold up."

Laughing, Cox slapped him on the back. "You stayin' this time, right? You gonna go claim that bitch of yours and patch back in?"

He was about to answer when the club's front door banged open and a skinny redhead stormed inside. Cage came in next, looking a mixture of miserable and frightened. Danny was last, scowling as she dragged in two large floral bags.

"Holy shit," Cox breathed. "Either we've been invaded by hippies or that's . . . Tegen."

Since there weren't any other skinny redheads that Cage

and Danny had been sent to collect, it had to be Tegen. But it sure as fuck didn't look like the four-eyed, frizzy-haired, mouthy little shit he remembered her as.

"For the last time, Danny, I am not staying at your fucking house!" Tegen yelled as she disappeared inside the kitchen.

Ripper's brow lifted. Okay. So she was still a mouthy little shit.

Blowing out a breath, Cage glanced their way, his eyes wide and pleading. "Help," he whispered.

Cox snorted. "Fuck that. I got enough crazy bitches to deal with. Between Kami and Mary Catherine hittin' me up for everything under the sun and, fuck me, Anna always askin' for more money . . ."

Ripper stopped listening. Danny had given up on dragging Tegen's luggage through the room and was now standing very still, watching him. Everything she was thinking, feeling, wanting, was showing plain as day on her face.

Are you going to leave?

His gaze never once left those beautiful blue eyes.

No.

Really?

Yeah, baby, really.

Why not?

He glanced down at himself. *Can't exactly get off the couch, can I?*

He watched as she pressed her lips together, fighting a smile.

Fuuuuuck. He wanted to go to her. Touch her, smell her, fucking hold her right here in the middle of the club, in front of her brother, in front of Cox, in front of the whole fucking world. Then he wanted to take her to bed, fuck her half to death, fuck her some more, do some sleeping, fuck her some more.

Fuck, he had to adjust his cock.

Watching him, Danny's cheeks turned a light shade of pink, whether she was flushed from arousal or embarrassed, either way it was a good sign.

Speaking of good signs, the sight of her nipples hardening under her white ribbed tank was ranking pretty high on his list.

Fuck it. He had to do something. He wanted her back in his bed. Tonight. Right now.

I want you, beautiful girl.

She sucked her bottom lip inside her mouth and bit down. *For how long?*

Holding her gaze with his, *For fuckin' ever.*

"Oh my God, seriously?"

Tegen stood just outside the kitchen, a beer in one hand and a sandwich in the other, her narrowed gaze alternating between Danny and him.

She flashed Danny a nasty grin he didn't much appreciate. "You and Ripper, huh? What happened to ZZ? You get sick of him?"

Danny, who'd gone stiff, turned to glare at Tegen. "Don't talk about things you know nothing about."

Tegen kept grinning. "Really? So you two weren't just eye-fucking each other?"

"Tegen," Danny said slowly, her teeth locked. "I know you're hurting but—"

"Oh, shut up," Tegen scoffed. "You know as well as I do these assholes can't keep it in their pants. And he's one of the worst. You know he fucked Kami back in the day, right? Tag-teamed her with Cox. He probably banged Eva too. Hope you plan on getting tested regularly."

"I'm gonna knock her out," Cox said.

Although Ripper resented being accused of fucking Eva, and was pissed the little bitch had brought up Kami, as well as implying that he had diseases, he didn't say anything. Mainly because Tegen was right. He had been one of the worst. But Danny already knew that. And as far as female opinion went when it came to him, the only one he cared about was ready to throw down with Tegen for talking shit. She might not be speaking to him but she sure as shit still cared. That was a good sign. Now he just had to get her talking again.

"Don't you need to go see your mom?" Cage growled.

Tegen's expression turned ice cold. "Fucker," she spat, "I thought I told you that you do not get to speak to me."

Surprised, Ripper glanced over at Cage and, damn, the dude looked half crazed, a little bit confused, a whole lot angry, maybe a touch homicidal, and yeah, there was definitely a unhealthy amount of battle lust raging through him.

What the fuck was going on?

"Stop your bullshit," Cage seethed, his fists clenching.

Tegen let out a loud, humorless laugh. "Why? What are you going to do, Cage?" She shook her head, smirking. "Nothing. You're going to do nothing because you're full of shit. In fact, you are shit. A big fat pile of steaming biker shit."

Ripper and Cox looked at each other. *Damn.*

"Brother's gonna blow," Cox whispered.

Blow a load, maybe. Brother was about to tackle Tegen

caveman-style and fuck her right in front of anyone.

"Naw, dude," he whispered back. "Look at him, he's hard up for that bitch. Who the fuck knew he'd been feelin' Tegen all this time?"

Yeah, who knew? And really, who cared?

Not him.

This fucking club was full of secrets and it was getting straight up exhausting.

"Tegen."

Everyone turned to look at Deuce.

"You're gonna reel this bullshit in right the fuck now and go see your mother. I ain't payin' for that apartment in Cali so you can come home and act like an asshole, shittin' on everyone just 'cause you fuckin' feel like it. You feel me?"

Tegen snorted. "Yeah," she said. "Whoop-dee-fucking-doo. I can't wait to go hang out with my comatose mother. My fucking *idiotic*, comatose mother who got herself shot because she was stupid enough to fall for one of you assholes. Hopefully she'll die, be put out of her misery, and I won't have to keep watching her throw her entire life away for a man who doesn't give two fucks about her."

Everyone was openmouthed staring at Tegen who, even after her rant, was casually taking a bite of her sandwich.

"That's right, fuckers," she said around a mouthful of sandwich. "I said it." Then spinning on her heel, she headed for the hallway.

Deuce started after her but Cage intercepted him. "This is my fault," he said, pushing his father backward. "I'll deal with it."

"Motherfuck," Deuce muttered, staring after him. "Ten bucks says he fucked that mouthy little asshole.

Motherfuckin' little fuck can't keep it in his pants for shit. Cocksucker would fuck a hole in the wall. Probably has."

"Prez," Cox called out, laughing. "You remember his prom, him never comin' home and we went lookin' for him. Found him in the girls' bathroom at the school, pants around his ankles, face in the toilet."

Ripper couldn't help himself, he burst out laughing. That had been some funny shit.

"Fuck me," he said. "That shit was straight up awesome."

"It was disgusting," Danny interjected, her eyes on him. "And embarrassing. You know he had three dates that night, right?" She shook her head. "Disgusting."

"You're all disgusting," Deuce muttered, his accusing stare locked on Ripper.

Ignoring him, Ripper stared at Danny, not knowing what the fuck to say but thrilled she'd spoken to him. She held his gaze, her muddled feelings plain as day. She still thought he was going to leave. She didn't trust him. Not only that, she didn't trust herself. She felt that her love for him was clouding her judgment.

So he tried to convey how determined he was to make it up to her. That he'd wait until she was ready. He didn't want to wait, he wanted to straight up jump her, but he would wait. They could go as slow as she needed and he would fix this shit between them and try his damnedest never, ever to fuck up again.

Swallowing hard, she covered her mouth with the back of her hand and turned away from him. Deuce caught the slight movement, narrowed his eyes in concern, then turned to him and straight up glared.

"Good times," Cox said, looking from Deuce to him

and back to Deuce. "Always good fuckin' times at Horsemen High."

"Yo," Tap called out, walking into the room. "Jase called. D's awake."

"Fuck," Deuce breathed, running his hands through his hair. "Finally, some good fuckin' news."

"Yeah," Tap said. "One problem."

"What?"

"She don't remember jack shit."

"So?" Cox said. "Who'd wanna remember gettin' shot in the head? I wouldn't."

"Idiot," Tap muttered. "She doesn't remember *anything*. Anyone. Nothin'. Not even her fuckin' name."

"She's alive," Deuce said, already heading for the hallway, most likely to grab Tegen. "Let's focus on that."

CHAPTER 34

"IT'S VERY RARE THAT AN INJURY THIS SEVERE doesn't result in some kind of permanent damage. And that's something that can take months or even years to determine the full extent of."

"Danny!" Ivy squealed, bouncing in the waiting room chair beside me, waving my cell phone around in the air. "I beat level thirteen!"

"Shh," I whispered, trying to hear what the doctor was saying to Jase.

"Age is also a factor," he continued. "Individuals in their teens and twenties have a tendency to recover more so than a woman in her thirties."

"Great," Jase growled. "But what the fuck about her memory? She doesn't even know who the fuck I am!"

My father put his hand on Jase's shoulder and on his

other side, Eva slipped her arm through his. Jase shuddered through his next breath, before focusing back on the doctor.

"She's very lucky to be alive, Mr. Brady. Ninety percent of people who suffer gunshot wounds to the brain die almost immediately. In Ms. Kelley's case, the bullet traveled all the way through her brain but luckily did not pass through the brain stem. Right now, as far as we can tell, only her memory has been affected, whereas the majority of survivors of this type of injury not only suffer memory loss, but difficulty reading and problems with hand-eye coordination, some ending up in long-term rehabilitation or nursing care."

Jase was already agitated by Tegen's appearance at the hospital. She'd taken one look at Jase, marched right up to the nurses' station, and very loudly stated that he was not family and under no circumstances was he allowed to see her mother.

And now the doctor was not telling him what he wanted to hear, worsening his mood.

I had to give that doctor credit for facing a room full of emotionally charged bikers and holding his own.

"You mentioned rehabilitation earlier," Eva said, glancing worriedly up at Jase. "Is that something that could help with her memory?"

The doctor nodded. "But I don't want to jump the gun. Her memory loss could be due to swelling from surgery. As she recovers, she might regain what she's lost. We'll have to wait and see."

"Wait and see?" Jase repeated, shoving away from my father and Eva. "Wait and motherfuckin' see?"

My father wrapped his arm around Jase's chest and pulled him backward. Jase pushed away from him and spun around. “Fuck!” he yelled. “Fuck!”

Sighing, my father reached for him again. “Ja—”

“WHERE THE FUCK IS HE?”

My head jerked right. *Now what?*

The occupants of the waiting room went silent as everyone watched Hawk storm through the room. Still wearing his chaps, covered head-to-toe in road dust, his Mohawk significantly grown out, he must have been on the road awhile. He had probably had gone directly to the club, found out about Dorothy, and come straight to the hospital.

The moment Hawk zeroed in on Jase, his entire body tensed. The next thing I knew he was running, quickly closing the twenty feet between Jase and him, and everyone else was backing away.

“Call security!” the doctor shouted in the direction of the nurse’s station.

Hawk bent his head and barreled into Jase, sending them both flying backward into the elevator. Ivy shrieked, jumped into my lap, and buried her face in my chest. I wrapped my arms around her and turned my body away from the fight.

“You fuck!” Hawk roared, sending his fist into Jase’s face. His nose broke on impact, an audible, resounding crack that had me cringing in sympathy. And he just kept going. With every punch Hawk threw, blood from Jase’s broken nose sprayed everything in a ten-foot radius.

Two security guards came rushing from around the corner at the same time my father and Mick were trying to pry Hawk off Jase, without much luck.

It took four men to drag Hawk away and even then, all four of them were struggling to keep a good hold on him.

One hand covering his broken nose, the other grasping for the wall, Jase struggled to stand up.

"What is wrong with you?" he yelled, his voice muffled by his hand.

"What's wrong with me?" Hawk bellowed. "You almost got Dorothy killed. You almost got my fuckin' kid killed! That's what's fuckin' wrong with me!"

Jase's hand fell away from his face. "What did you say?"

"Danny," Eva said frantically, grabbing Ivy's waist and pulling her off my lap. "Let me take her."

Clutching Ivy, Eva headed quickly toward the front doors while Hawk managed to wrench an arm free long enough to elbow one of the security guards in the face. The man went stumbling backward and Hawk used the distraction to break free. My father lunged for him but ended up missing him by a mere thread.

Jase found himself pinned up against the elevator by his throat.

"Do the math, asshole," Hawk hissed. "Nine fuckin' months ago, where the fuck were you?"

I quickly counted the months backward in my head and my mouth fell open. That wasn't Jase's baby. Jase and Bucket had been on a run through Mexico for over a month, if not longer.

"No," Jase whispered. "No, she wouldn't—"

"No? Brother, yes. She's been comin' to me for years, cryin' about you. And if you're still havin' doubts, I know for a fact you were usin' protection with her, and me, I wasn't even tryin' to safeguard my shit. I blew my load inside her every fuckin' time, know why? Because," Hawk growled. "I was tryin' to knock her up. Wanna know why? Because I was tryin' to get her the fuck away from you!"

Spittle flew from Hawk's mouth into Jase's face as he continued laying into him. But Jase couldn't care less. Dumbfounded, unable to speak, he could only stare unblinking at Hawk.

"Just one fuckin' day," my father muttered, grabbing my wrist, startling me as he uprooted me up off the chair. I hurried to keep up as he pulled me toward the hospital entrance.

"Just one motherfuckin' day I would like to not be dealin' with bullshit."

He punched open the door and yanked me outside. Pausing, he scanned the parking lot. Finding Eva and Ivy sitting on the tailgate of his truck, he started toward them.

"Daddy," I said, trying to shake free.

He ignored me.

"Daddy!" I yelled. "Stop!"

He stopped so fast, I crashed into him.

"What?" he demanded.

"I love you!" I shouted. "That's all!"

He blinked. "What? Why you tellin' me this shit?"

I gave him a small smile. "Because it's true. And even though I'm a huge disappointment to you, I thought maybe with all the crap you're dealing with, you needed to hear it."

Blue eyes, identical to my own, surrounded by tiny lines etched finely into suntanned skin, stared back at me.

"You're not a disappointment," he said quietly. "I never said that."

I shrugged halfheartedly. "I can read between the lines."

"Jesus, Danny, I never fuckin' said that, what I meant was . . ."

Trailing off, he let out a frustrated sigh.

"It don't matter what I meant. What's fuckin' done is done and you're my kid and shit fuckin' happens and despite all that shit, I'm still proud of you, darlin'. You met the devil head-on and came out alive. Not many fuckers out there can say that."

He sighed again. "You wanna be part of the club, I ain't gonna stop you. You want to be Ripper's old lady, I ain't gonna stop you. You're twenty-one, a grown-ass woman who's been makin' her own mistakes for some time now and doin' just fine."

"You're okay with me and Ripper?" I whispered, shocked. "I mean . . . even after everything . . . and what I did to ZZ?"

He snorted. "Am I happy that you and Ripper were sneakin' around behind my back? Fuck no. Am I likin' the fact my daughter was forced to kill a bitch? *No.* Is it okay that so far you've run off two of my high-rankin' boys? No. Should you have told me you were fuckin' knocked up? Yeah, baby, you fuckin' should have. But Jesus, Danny, who am I to be judgin' anyone? Made my fair share of mistakes too. I spent too much time wantin' a woman I kept lettin' get away, and I don't want that for you."

My jaw dropped. *Who was this man?*

"Darlin', we live in a fuckin' cesspool of shit and dirty-ass motherfuckers, but if you found somethin' good and true, somethin' that you can bank on bein' there for you when everything else is fallin' apart around you, whoever it is, I'm good with it."

He smiled. A true smile, full of dimples.

"Just don't be tellin' Ripper that. I want that boy shittin' his pants every time I look his way."

My lips split in a smile I couldn't contain any more than I could stop breathing.

"There it is," he said softly, reaching out and running his knuckles down my cheek. "There's my Danny girl."

And just like that, I had my father back.

Life may not always go the way you'd planned, you may not have the perfect family, you may not be the most beautiful, but that doesn't mean you can't make the best of what you do have.

My father wasn't perfect, far from it. He'd made a lot of mistakes and I had no doubt he was going to make a lot more. But he was mine and I wouldn't trade him for the world.

In the club parking lot, I sat inside the truck long after my father, Eva, and Ivy had gone inside. Just thinking.

About me.

About Ripper.

About everything.

I cried a little. Smiled. Closed my eyes and just appreciated the sun on my face.

I knew who I wanted.

I knew he wanted me.

Did I believe he was going to stay? Yeah, I did.

And my father had given me his blessing.

Everything was out in the open now.

No more secrets.

It was time to stop dwelling on the past, time to let go of my painful memories and make new ones, better ones.

With Ripper.

Giggling, I pressed my hand against my mouth.

I was going to be Ripper's old lady.

And maybe . . . someday I would be his wife.

My stomach suddenly full of butterflies, I squeezed my eyes shut and laughed out loud.

Erik and Danielle Jacobs.

Danielle Elizabeth Jacobs.

Perfect.

More than perfect.

It was beautiful.

I jumped out of the truck, suddenly desperate to find Ripper. To start my life, our life, right this very second.

"Well, ain't you adorable."

Startled, I whirled around. A tall, curvy black woman stood mere feet from me, her head cocked to one side, smiling.

There were very few African-Americans living in Miles City, Ellie's family being one of them. In a town where everyone knew everyone, I knew immediately this woman was not from around here.

Which meant one of three things. Either she was a club associate, or she'd met one of the boys on a run and was passing through for a hookup, or . . .

She shifted and her jean jacket opened slightly, revealing a holstered gun on either side of her body.

I backed up a few steps and her smile widened.

"Security's tight," she said. "Wasn't easy gettin' in here."

Or . . . she was here for less than honorable reasons. Yep.

"Um . . . my father," I stammered, my heart in my throat. "Do you want me to get him?"

"Who's your father, boo?" she cooed, her tone sugary sweet.

"Deuce," I whispered. "My father is Deuce."

Her smile turned into a vicious grin and my stomach took a nosedive.

"He's inside?" she asked, nodding at the club.

"Yes," I whispered, fighting the urge to run. This woman might appear calm, but there was something in her eyes . . .

Something that told me running would be a very bad idea.

"I'm gonna need a favor then, Deuce's daughter."

She glanced over my head, at the club. "You go on and get your daddy for me, can you do that?"

I nodded.

"Well, honey," she said, smiling. "You go on then."

Shaking, I turned to go, readying to run . . .

Pain radiated through the back of my skull and my vision went fuzzy.

Then black.

Then I was falling . . . falling . . .

And then, there was nothing at all.

CHAPTER 35

DEUCE STARED AT THE SECURITY FOOTAGE, FEELING nauseous. It was happening all over again. Someone he loved had been taken from right under his fucking nose.

For the fifth time in a row, he watched as Mama Vi smiled at Danny, then Danny, looking scared shitless, turned away, then that fucking black bitch pulled her piece and slammed the butt of her gun into the back of his daughter's skull.

Danny's eyes went wide . . .

His chest went vice-fucking-tight.

And he watched as his daughter crumpled to the ground.

Breathing rapidly through his nose, his heart pounding in his throat, he tightened his grip on the bar top, tighter and tighter until the wood began to creak, splitting beneath his hands.

"That bitch is goin' to ground," he said quietly, trying to breathe through the crushing pain in his chest.

"I'm gonna fuck her with a baseball bat in every motherfuckin' hole she's got, then I'm gonna cut her into pieces, startin' with her feet, workin' my way up, makin' sure she stays alive as long as possible."

Nobody said a word.

"I wanna hear her scream," he continued, still staring at the computer screen, watching as Mama Vi grabbed hold of Danny's arm and dragged her off and out of sight of the cameras.

"I wanna fuckin' record her screamin' and bleedin' so I can jerk the fuck off to it after she's fuckin' dead."

"Baby," Eva said softly, slipping her arm around his waist. "We're gonna get her back."

Yeah, they were. His one saving grace was knowing Danny was, in fact, alive. If Mama Vi had wanted her dead, Danny would have been dead the second contact had been made, if not sooner. The bitch wanted something and she'd lifted his daughter to get it.

But he wasn't stupid. Danny was only leverage, deadweight after Mama Vi got what she wanted. And what she wanted was him. He'd been playing this game long enough to know a revenge vendetta when he saw one. As far as Mama Vi was concerned, it was his fault she'd lost her brother and her business. He'd gone to Preacher; he'd put the wheels in motion.

And she wanted him dead.

And once she had him, Danny was as good as dead.

He turned to his boys; aside from ZZ, every last one of them was here. Even Jase and Hawk. They weren't speaking to each other, but they were here. Because no matter the bullshit, a brother was a brother and you didn't forsake your brother or his family.

"Suit the fuck up and get the fuck out. She's gotta be holed up somewhere in town. You get wind of anything, a fuckin' whisper of somethin' not right, you check in, then check it the fuck out."

While his boys scattered, he turned to the one man that had remained behind. The one who looked as maniacal as he felt.

Turning away from Ripper, he pulled his cell phone and smokes from his cut. He placed the phone on the counter in front of him and lit up a smoke. Inhale. Exhale. Inhale. Exhale.

He sucked that shit down in record time and lit up smoke number two.

By smoke number five, he was ready to jump out of his skin.

"Why the fuck hasn't she called?"

Deuce didn't answer Ripper. They both knew why she hadn't called. She was playing the fear card. Making them crazy waiting, wanting them more focused on getting Danny back than anything else. Then she'd use it against them.

It was working.

Fuck.

He had to keep it together.

He had—

His phone started vibrating.

danny calling flashed on the screen.

"Game on," he growled, hitting answer.

CHAPTER 36

MY BODY HEAVY AND SLUGGISH, MY VISION BLURRED, my head throbbing and ears ringing, I tried to focus on my surroundings. It was dark and I couldn't see much, but I could smell everything. And wherever I was smelled like urine and feces and something else I didn't recognize. Something that smelled like a cross between rotting meat and . . . cat litter . . . and a sweet sort of smell. Sweet in a bad way, like a putrefied, sickly sweetness.

The more I inhaled the sicker I felt, and soon I was gagging and then breathing faster and faster, trying not to throw up. That's when I tried to move, tried to curl in on myself, cover my nose and mouth with my hand.

And found I couldn't.

My wrists were bound together.

Confused, I tried to bring my arms up, my legs jerked

instead. Now panicking, I tried to lift my arms again toward my head, pulling harder this time and again my legs jerked.

I was hog-tied.

Why was I hog-tied?

"Honey, I wouldn't be movin' around too much if I were you. The last man who was in your predicament is still there. What's left of him, anyway. Some dead animals too."

I jerked toward the familiar voice, realizing instantly what had happened. The woman in the parking lot, the fear, the exploding pain in my head . . .

And with my memories came awareness of my surroundings, and suddenly I could feel everything. The slimy surface beneath my cheek, the searing pain in the back of my head, my hair matted, sticking to my neck and . . . oh God, the smell.

The last man who was in your predicament is still there. What's left of him, anyway. Some dead animals too.

Oh my God, oh my God, no, no, oh my God, what was I lying near and that smell, oh my God.

What was that on my leg? Was something crawling on me?

My stomach heaved and more tears burned in my eyes as I fought with my body, knowing that if I threw up, I'd end up lying in it, along with whatever else, whomever else I was lying in.

"Why are you doing this?" I rasped, my mouth dry, my tongue grating painfully against the roof of my mouth.

"Nothin' personal against you, boo, you seem like a nice little girl. Real pretty too. But it's your daddy I'm wantin'."

"He'll give you whatever you want," I choked out. "He has money, he'll—"

"I don't want his money, baby, I want him. Almost three years ago, your daddy killed my big brother. It's time he paid up."

"Are you going to kill me?" I whispered, already knowing the answer.

"Like I said, honey, it's nothin' personal."

It was nothing personal? Was she for real? She'd knocked me out and kidnapped me all so she could get to my father, *to kill him*. Whether she planned on killing me in front of him or after she'd killed him, I didn't know. Either way, it was personal. It was very fucking personal.

And if my father failed at whatever his plan was, because by now I knew he would have one, I was going to die. This was it; I was only going to get twenty-one years.

And all I could think about was out of my twenty-one years of life, I'd only gotten to spend a week of it with Ripper. Secret moments here and there, scattered throughout our summer together, and one single, solitary week.

How was this fair?

He'd just come back to me.

Everything had been falling into place.

And now, I was going to lose everything.

The first sign that something was very wrong was my heart rate. I was already terrified, my pulse racing, but something more was happening. I was suddenly burning up, sweating and shivering, my already aching head began to pound, harder and harder. It felt as if I could feel my heart beating in every limb, beating faster and faster.

I started spinning, the darkness of the room, the inability to see worsening the churning nausea. I needed to turn my body, needed to move, needed something, needed to do something, anything, this couldn't be happening, it couldn't end like this, not before I really had a chance to live.

I couldn't breathe. *I couldn't breathe.* My chest was caving in, my ribs cracking and my heart pounding, exploding, and I couldn't breathe. I was suffocating, gasping for air, choking on the rising bile in my throat.

Desperate, I tried to move, pulling painfully on my wrists and ankles, the binds chafing, burning through my skin, and still it only worsened, the need to get away, to get away, *to get away*, the need to live . . .

I had to live.

I had to see him.

I had to tell him I loved him.

I had to live.

Ripper pulled up to the same grouping of condominiums at the edge of town where he'd last met with Mama Vi. Killing his engine, he toed the kickstand down and looked around. The run-down stretch of building was dark, the lawn still overgrown; nothing had changed since the last time he'd been here. And he saw no sign of Mama Vi or Danny.

Now what?

This was where the bitch had told Deuce to meet her. So where the fuck was she? Their plan wasn't going to work if she'd lied about her location; if it had been her plan from the get-go to fuck with Deuce, take Danny, kill her off-site and then dump her body.

Holy fuck him, he was going to throw up.

That crazy bitch had his girl. That crazy, fucked-in-the-head, sick bitch had his Danny.

And all he could think about was Frankie, what Frankie had done to him, and what Mama Vi was capable of, might be, probably was, doing to . . . *Danny.*

Keep your shit together.

Keep your fucking shit together.

With a shaking hand, he pulled his phone out of his cut and texted Deuce.

Got nothing. Going inside. Wait for my signal.

He put his phone away and got up off his bike.

He was halfway down the walkway when the front door of the first condo swung open and Mama Vi stepped outside and smiled at him. All red lips and white teeth. He wanted to vomit.

"Drop the toys."

Glaring at her, he pulled both his nines from his leathers, his blade from his boot, and tossed them off to the side.

"White boy, you take me for a damn fool? I said drop your toys. Phone too."

Fuck.

"Got nothin' left," he said, after tossing his phone aside.

"Mmm-hmm," she murmured, obviously not believing him. "Wasn't expectin' you, scarface."

"Yeah," he growled. "But me is who you're gettin'."

"Ain't no good, honey. You're just another piece of meat I'm gonna be slicin' up to get to that prez of yours."

"Where's Danny?" he demanded.

She shrugged. "Around. Where's Deuce?"

He gritted his teeth. Where was Deuce? Hopefully, he was ten seconds away from ripping this bitch's heart out through her asshole. But in all probability he was still halfway down the road, waiting for the text message Ripper couldn't send him.

"Where. Is. Danny," he repeated, straining his ears, trying to pick up on any noise that might be coming from behind Mama Vi.

Cocking her head to one side, she gave him a lazy smile. "You're shakin', honey. This personal for you?"

Shit. Fuck. Shit.

Holding up one obscenely long red fingernail, she mmm-hmm'ed him, her finger swinging back and forth like a goddamn metronome.

"I got your girl inside, don't I?"

He was fucked. He'd fucked their entire game plan straight to shit within seconds. He was so damn strung out, he'd lost the only edge he'd had. That he wasn't Deuce and didn't love Danny.

Only he did. And he couldn't hide it. Worry, gut-wrenching fear, a desperate need to see her, touch her, to fucking know that she was still breathing, was radiating out of him in thick, palpable, suffocating waves.

So, now what? More than likely he'd just gotten Danny and himself killed.

So, yeah, now what?

Thinking fast, he said the first thing that came to mind.

"Deuce ain't comin', nobody is," he told her. "He wouldn't risk the club for this bullshit."

Mama Vi lost her smile. "You're lying."

Spreading his arms wide, he shook his head. "Wish I was. He didn't even want me comin'. But you're right, that's my girl you got and she's why I'm here."

It happened fast, too fast. She spun away, disappearing inside the dark condo, leaving him momentarily startled. It took precious seconds for his brain to compute what had happened and then he was lunging for his guns and phone.

But he wasn't fast enough, and Mama Vi was shoving Danny through the doorway just as he was straightening.

"Drop 'em," she spat.

He dropped them.

This was the second time he was witnessing a gun being held to Danny.

It was two times too many.

Ripper scanned Danny quickly, looking for injuries. She was a mess. Covered head-to-toe in filth, shaking and crying.

He zeroed in on her bound wrists and the long stretch of freshly sliced rope that Mama Vi was holding in her hands. She'd hog-tied her. She'd fucking hog-tied Danny and now the bitch was holding his woman on a leash as if she were a fucking dog.

Being tied up like an animal, being demeaned, seeing Danny like this, knowing how it felt, knowing how scared she was, was killing him. It took every last bit of willpower he had not to charge Mama Vi.

If he didn't get to kill her in this life, he'd find her in the next. And she would suffer.

"I lost everything," Mama Vi hissed, shoving Danny forward. "My crew, my brother, everything. And if I can't get to Deuce, the least I can do is make good on my promise to you."

"Bitch," he growled. "You already have."

She laughed. "You think?"

Ripper was quickly losing hope that Danny was going to come out of this alive. Plan A had failed, Plan B hadn't worked, and now all he had left was the hope that his brothers were here, somewhere, waiting to pounce.

Otherwise, they were both fucked.

"You want her?" Mama Vi asked, stroking the barrel of her gun up and down Danny's cheek.

He did. He wanted Danny in more ways than this bitch would ever know, would ever be capable of understanding.

"Yes," he said, his voice breaking.

Grinning, she gestured to the muddy, weed-ridden lawn beneath him. "Beg."

Beg.

He didn't know the first thing about how to beg. What did he say? Please? Fuck that. Danny deserved more than empty pleas.

Especially if this was the last time he had with her.

He fell to his knees.

"I love her," he rasped, his eyes on Danny. "You want me to beg, I'll fuckin' beg. I'll do whatever I gotta do if it means she keeps breathin'."

Danny choked on a hiccupping sob and broke into a fresh wave of tears.

"Let her go," he pleaded. "You're hard up for blood, you want someone to blame, you blame me. I ain't runnin'."

He stared hard at Danny. "I ain't runnin'," he repeated.

Danny's breath left her in shuddering spurts. "No . . ." she whimpered breathlessly. "Ripper, no . . ."

"Ain't that sweet," Mama Vi sneered. "Some real Romeo and Juliet vibes I'm feelin'."

Ripper caught the small movement, Mama Vi's thumb gliding along the hammer of her gun with killer precision. Not even Danny, whose ear was no more than a few inches from the weapon, heard the mostly silent click only a lethally skilled gravedigger could pull off.

He saw it, he knew what was about to go down, knew there was nothing he could do about it.

In the midst of his terror, there was a sudden sense of peace. Danny was going to die, yeah, but there wasn't anywhere in hell or on earth that he'd be living one day without her. Either Mama Vi was going to take him out next or he'd do it himself.

And knowing that—knowing that it was over, knowing they were done here, but also knowing that he'd follow Danny anywhere, that even in death, he knew they'd never truly be done, he found his peace.

What they had was some real forever kind of bullshit.

So he stared at Danny, held her gaze, making sure she knew it all, everything he felt; trying to tell her that none of it, not one fucking second had been a mistake. That he'd do it over again, all of it, even what he'd gone through with Frankie—if it meant he'd end up at her senior prom, she'd end up in his bed, and the two of them would end up forever changed.

He would end up forever changed. A better man.

She'd done that.

I love you, beautiful girl.

Her chin wobbled.

I love you, too.

There it was.

Everything that mattered.

Danny.

Him.

And peace.

He was so consumed by her, ready to die alongside her, that he never saw them coming.

Which, in the end, worked out just fine. Because he was so focused on Danny and Mama Vi was focused on him, she never saw them coming either.

CHAPTER 37

WITH HIS BOOT PRESSED FIRMLY IN THE SMALL OF Mama Vi's back, Deuce watched as Ripper walked off across the lawn, his daughter cradled in the man's arms, her arms wrapped around his neck.

Tap stepped in front of him. "Hold off a minute, Prez," he said, looking down at Mama Vi, his mouth slowly curving into a grin. "Lemme have at her first."

"Fuck you," Deuce muttered. "This bitch needs to be put the fuck down."

"Yeah," Tap said, his eyes never once leaving Mama Vi. "But first I'm gonna show her what the fuck happens when some fuckin' cunt thinks she can mess with my club."

Deuce knew what was about to go down. And normally, he'd put a stop to it. His boys always wanted ass after shit got bloody or just plain crazy, all that adrenaline needing an outlet, but he'd made sure they'd always gone back to the club or a bar for that shit. But when it came to this bitch, he didn't have an ounce of give-a-fuck about what happened to her as long as she had a long and painful journey to being dead. So this time, he was going to let them play.

"You just wanna fuck her," Cox said, lighting up a smoke. "Don't lie."

Tap shrugged. "That too."

"I'm in," Dirty said, appearing beside Tap. He kneeled down beside Mama Vi and grabbed a handful of her hair, yanking her head up. "Don't let the lack of mustache fool ya, baby," he said, grinning. "I'm always down for a gang bang."

"There ain't nothin' you can do to me," she hissed, "that ain't already been done."

Dirty's grin grew wider. "Yeah? You hear that, Tap? Guess we're gonna have to get creative."

"Brother, I am all about creative."

"Have at her," Deuce said. Grabbing hold of her bound hands, he yanked her to her feet and shoved her forward into Dirty's arms. "But it's me who's gonna be puttin' her to ground."

Dirty didn't waste any time ripping Mama Vi's shirt open. Then Dirty was pulling her jeans down and behind her Tap was unbuttoning his leathers.

"You go right ahead and scream, bitch," Tap growled, grabbing her neck, squeezing tightly and forcing her to bend over.

Deuce turned away and Mick stepped in line beside him.

"Prez?"

"Yeah?"

"You okay?"

No. But this shit came with the territory. This life wasn't for the weak.

"Yeah."

Joining them, Cox slung an arm over his shoulders. "He's fine," Cox drawled. "Just pissed that Ripper's gonna be callin' him Daddy soon."

Deuce elbowed Cox in the gut. "Fuck you."

"We all gotta go through it, Prez," Mick said laughing. "My girls are grown, one of them married. It's part of gettin' old."

"None of your girls are in love with Ripper."

Mick gave a mock shudder. "You a better man than I," he joked.

"We could still kick his ass," Cox suggested. "I'm always down to kick Ripper's ass."

Deuce snorted. "He's got plenty of those comin'. Best let him have some time with Danny before I start breaking his shit."

Cox slanted his eyes at him and grinned.

"You're makin' me miss Kami," he said with a dramatic sigh.

"Shut up," Mick growled. "You're a fuckin' pussy-whipped asshole."

"Oh yeah?" Cox threatened. "How about I take your old lady out for a fuckin' ride? You good with that, old man?"

Mick lunged and Cox went running.

"Who's fuckin' pussy-whipped now, asshat?" Cox laughed over his shoulder. "That would be you, bitch!"

"You did not just call me a bitch!" Mick roared, chasing him.

"Bitch! I fuckin' did! Bitch!"

Deuce reached into his cut and pulled out his smokes. Shaking one out, he lit it and took a nice, long, relaxing drag.

Then he pulled out his phone.

"Baby?" Eva answered on the first ring. "Did you find her?"

"It's all good, we got her and she's fine."

"Oh God," she breathed. "Thank God."

"Eva," he said gruffly. "I gotta tell you somethin'."

"Hmm?"

"Your old man, darlin', what he said to me, he was fuckin' right. These assholes would light themselves on fire if I weren't here to dump a bucket of water on 'em."

Eva burst out laughing and he felt his chest loosen and his body warm.

"Fuck, darlin' . . ."

"What?"

"Nothin'." He sighed. "Just . . . darlin'."

For a moment, neither of them spoke, and he found himself holding his breath just so he could hear hers.

"I love you, too," she whispered.

"Babe," he said softly. "Yeah."

EPILOGUE

On my porch, juggling two bags of groceries, my purse, my extraordinarily large belly, and my keys, I tried valiantly to find the one key that would let me inside, allowing me to put down these insanely heavy bags, put on my pajamas, and go straight to bed. I frowned at the bags. What was so heavy anyway? Bread? Milk?

Whatever. Everything was heavy lately and I was always tired.

As are most women in the ninth month of pregnancy.

Although, I was rather lucky. Instead of gaining tens of pounds of weight over the past nine months, all I'd gained was a giant belly, while the majority of my body stayed mostly the same.

The pregnancy had been a planned one. After my kid-napping, Ripper refused to take our relationship at any other speed other than lightning fast.

We were married within a month, a ridiculously small ceremony at the town courthouse, and that night he'd begun trying to get me pregnant. Married at twenty-one and pregnant by twenty-two. It was official. I was a stereotypical small town girl.

But I was Ripper's old lady.

And I loved every second of it.

"Shit!"

Shifting the bags in my arms, I tried to see where my keys had dropped, but all I could see was my belly.

Crying out in frustration, I turned around, ready to heave everything in my arms off the porch, and ran straight into the large, hard wall that was Ripper.

"Yo," he said, laughing as he took the bags from me and set them down on the porch. Scooping up my keys, he stood back up and handed them to me.

Blowing out a frustrated breath, I glared at him. "Why's the door locked? Where were you?"

"Chill, baby," he said, reaching out to brush a sweaty lock of hair off my forehead. "I was out back in the shed."

"Doing what?" I demanded, although I already knew. He was covered in sweat, grass, and wood chips.

"The usual," he said nonchalantly. "Fuckin' whores and killin' puppies."

Rolling my eyes, I turned away from him, and this time successfully managed to unlock the door. Ripper grabbed the groceries and followed me inside.

Throwing my purse on the kitchen table, I dropped into the closest chair and groaned.

"I hurt," I complained dramatically. "Everywhere. And

I'm dying of thirst."

Ripper grinned. "I'm on it, baby."

After setting the bags down on the counter, he headed for the sink, shirtless, sweaty, and dirty, and I couldn't help but smile. He'd changed so much that sometimes I didn't even recognize him. At first I'd thought he was overdoing it because he was terrified of my father, but the more time that passed, I realized that, no, it had nothing to do with my father at all. He'd changed.

And I loved him that much more for it.

"You stop by the club?" he asked, setting a glass of ice water down in front of me, then folding his large body into the chair beside me.

Grabbing the glass, I chugged as much water as I could, gasping for air when I was done.

"Yeah," I breathed.

"You see Jase?"

I nodded. Everyone was worried about Jase. Almost a year had passed since Dorothy had been shot and her memory still hadn't returned. Jase's kids had come home, Chrissy had been tried and convicted of first degree murder and sentenced to life with the possibility of parole, meaning she could end up only serving ten years of a life sentence. I was unsure how I felt about this. As much as I'd liked Chrissy, she'd tried to kill Dorothy.

As for Dorothy's relationship with Jase, it was non-existent. She didn't come to the club anymore and refused to see anyone other than Eva, Kami, or me. Every few months Tegen came home to visit with her and her brother, an adorable little boy Dorothy had named after her own father, Christopher Michael Kelley.

And Hawk . . .

He'd taken Ripper's place. Still nomad, he'd gone back on the road and would return periodically, but never stayed more than a few days at a time. I knew he saw his son on occasion, but just like Jase, Dorothy wanted nothing to do with him.

And ZZ . . . he never came back. I got the feeling my father had spoken to him a few times, may even know where he was, but I didn't ask. ZZ had left because of me and I knew I had no right to any information about him or his whereabouts. But wherever he was, I hoped he was happy.

He deserved to be happy.

"He's . . . okay," I said. "He was drunk, as usual."

Ripper grimaced. "Brother's gonna drink himself to death."

"You didn't," I said softly.

He looked into my eyes. "No," he said, just as softly. "I didn't."

"I hate you," I murmured, smiling at him. "You made me fat."

He snorted. "Hardly. Not sure how you managed it, but I think that baby of mine has made your ass fuckin' hotter. And speaking of ass . . ."

Standing up, Ripper bent over me and slipped one arm around my back and under my armpit. The other he slid under my knees and then he was lifting me up.

"I don't wanna," I whined, looping my arms around his neck. "I'm too tired."

"No, you're not," he growled, nipping at my neck. "How many times I gotta tell you, you don't get to make that decision?"

"Oooh," I teased. "Because you're the big bad biker man who gets to make all the decisions."

"Damn straight."

He laid me gently on the bed and proceeded to peel my yoga pants over my hips and down my legs.

"No underwear," he muttered. "Why the fuck ain't you wearin' underwear?"

"Um, hello," I said. "People are already staring at the giant baby growing inside of me. I don't need the added embarrassment of underwear lines too."

Ripper blinked. "Are you fuckin' serious? You're worried about underwear lines?"

I didn't answer him and he started laughing.

"Fuck, baby," he said, unzipping his jeans. "You are damn crazy."

I tried to think of something mean to say, a witty comeback, but he'd quickly moved onto the bed and was now between my legs and pushing inside of me.

Clear thinking was no longer an option.

"Tits," he groaned, reaching for the hem of my bright pink tank top. "I wanna see your tits, baby."

"No," I breathed, pushing his hand away. "Don't look at my belly."

He stopped moving. "Why the fuck not?"

"Stretch marks," I said, wrinkling up my nose.

He stared at me. "Stretch marks," he repeated. "This shit again?"

"I hate them," I whispered, feeling embarrassed. "They're ugly.

"Uh-uh," he said, slapping my hands away. It took him a few minutes, but eventually he'd maneuvered me out of both my tank top and bra. Immediately crossing my arms over my chest, I looked away from him. Maybe it was ridiculous, but the several jagged red marks that had appeared on my stomach were ugly to me. And I didn't want Ripper to find me lacking in any way.

Grabbing my chin, he forced me to look at him.

"All scars tell a story, beautiful girl," he said, releasing me to trace the marks on my stomach. "Yours are tellin' me how healthy and fuckin' perfect my kid is gonna be."

A tear slid out of the corner of my eye. "Shut up," I whispered.

"And mine," he said softly, grabbing my hand, trailing my palm across his cheek and then his chest. "Tell the story of how I found you."

More tears fell. He would never stop ceasing to amaze me.

"I love you," I whispered.

"Yeah, baby," he breathed, pulling out of me, then pushing back in again. "Me too."

He began moving faster and I closed my eyes, forgetting about stretch marks, forgetting about everything, and just let sensation rule.

I could feel everything . . . the prickly hair on his legs rasping against my smooth skin . . . the muscles in his back tensing, bunching, and releasing with every thrust of his hips . . . his hot breath on my breasts, dampening my skin . . . the scarred flesh on his chest rubbing over my swollen stomach, heightening my sensitivity.

"Ah, fuck baby," he rasped. "So fuckin' good."

"Ripper," I whimpered.

He slammed into me and my eyes rolled back.

"I love you," I breathed, clutching at the sheets. "I love you."

And I felt him, hard and full inside of me, stroking, moving, filling, as his hips continuously met mine, heartbeat after heartbeat, after heartbeat.

THE END

ABOUT THE AUTHOR

Madeline Sheehan is the *USA Today* bestselling author of the Holy Trinity series and Undeniable series. She has also co-authored with Claire C. Riley the Thicker Than Blood series, and *Shut Up and Kiss Me.*

Welcome to her world of fantastical romance, full of unconventional love and unscripted emotions.

www.MadelineSheehan.com

OTHER WORKS BY
MADELINE SHEEHAN

UNDENIABLE SERIES

Undeniable

Unbeautifully

Unattainable

Unbeloved

HOLY TRINITY SERIES

The Soul Mate

My Soul to Take

The Lost Souls: A Novella

Co-Written with Claire C. Riley

THICKER THAN BLOOD SERIES

Thicker Than Blood

Beneath Blood and Bone

Shut Up and Kiss Me